THE PURSUIT OF MURIETA

THE PURSUIT OF MURIETA

A WESTERN NOVEL

THOMAS D. CLAGETT

FIVE STAR
A part of Gale, Cengage Learning

GALE·
CENGAGE Learning·

Detroit • New York • San Francisco • New Haven, Conn • Waterville, Maine • London

LIBRARY OF CONGRESS CATALOGING-IN-PUBLICATION DATA

Clagett, Thomas D., 1956–
    The pursuit of Murieta : a western novel / Thomas D. Clagett.
— First edition.
        pages cm
    Includes bibliographical references.
    ISBN-13: 978-1-4328-2791-5 (hardcover)
    ISBN-10: 1-4328-2791-X (hardcover)
    1. Murieta, Joaquin—1853—Fiction. 2. California—Fiction. 3.
Outlaws—Fiction. I. Title.
PS3603.L337P87 2013
813'.6—dc23   2013021212

First Edition. First Printing: November 2013
Find us on Facebook– https://www.facebook.com/FiveStarCengage
Visit our website– http://www.gale.cengage.com/fivestar/
Contact Five Star™ Publishing at FiveStar@cengage.com

Printed in Mexico
1 2 3 4 5 6 7 17 16 15 14 13

For my wife, Marilyn

"*There was a proverb common in California: It is the unexpected that happens.*"
—Reverend John Steele, 1850

"*We are camped on a hill near Los Angeles, perhaps a mile distant, a pretty place. . . . The clergyman who took us out in his carriage carried along a rifle, he said for game, yet owed that it was 'best to have arms after dark.' The weather is soft and balmy—no winter, but a perpetual spring and summer. Every aspect pleases, and only man is vile.*"
—William H. Brewer
Yale University
Geographical Survey, 1860

CHAPTER ONE:
THE OUTRAGE

CALIFORNIA, MAY 1850

Four men on horseback appeared up ahead on the dusty rutted road. Joaquin Murieta saw them as they came out from the thicket of trees where the road dipped. Their horses stood still, four abreast blocking the way. The riders sat silently, watching, waiting. Murieta, driving an old Schuttler wagon, its red paint weathered off, tried not to look concerned as his wife, Rosita, placed her hand on his arm and squeezed it.

Everything will be all right, Murieta wanted to tell her, but he felt his throat go dry, his mouth draw tight. When he saw the men kick their horses forward, he pulled back on the reins, bringing his horse team and wagon to a stop. He knew outrunning them was out of the question. The horses were tired. They'd been traveling since early morning and it had to be nearly four o'clock now.

He glanced back at the wagon bed at their meager belongings. A carpetbag containing their few clothes, along with an old dresser, a chair, and a pick and shovel inherited from his brother, Jesus. It was all they owned. Nothing anyone else would want, he thought. He and Rosita wanted only to get back home, to Mexico. Another three weeks of travel, hopefully less. They had passed Santa Barbara yesterday. Coming to California had looked so promising months ago. Gold for the taking, Jesus had said. But this *gringo* California was a cursed place.

"Joaquin?" Rosita asked.

The worry in her voice wasn't lost on Murieta. He shook his head easily, so as not to concern her, and resisted the urge to open the battered box that sat beneath the seat. Inside was a heavy Colt revolver. It, too, had belonged to his brother. Jesus said he had taken it from an old prospector he found dead in a creek bed, the sluice pan still clutched in his hands. Jesus had been a pretty fair shot and had let Murieta fire it during a brief visit. It was the first time he had ever fired a gun. Its heft felt so awkward, he'd needed both hands to grip the handle to hold it steady. But holding it level was another matter as he kept allowing the barrel to drop. To his dismay, his first six shots plowed into the ground. Rosita watching him had made it all the more difficult and embarrassing. He had fired ten shots before he managed to hit the empty dry goods can sitting on a stump thirty feet away. Clapping her encouragement, Rosita told him he would get better with practice. He didn't tell her that he felt that his luck with a gun was like his luck with prospecting.

Now he cursed that luck again, seeing the men draw closer. He could see them clearly. All dirty. All armed. All *gringos*. One was heavyset with a large Colt's Dragoon hanging off his hip and a dark beard stained by many meals. Another wore faded blue Army uniform trousers, a green bandana knotted around his neck and a revolver in his belt. He didn't look old enough to shave yet. The third wore an Army blouse that had seen better days. His stiff, light-colored hair stuck out from under a battered soldier's cap. He held a rifle across the pommel of his saddle. The last, dressed in buckskins, carried a sheathed Bowie knife on his left side and a revolver on his right. His hair was close-cropped and his face looked older than the others, deeply lined and hard, mean hard, with cold blue eyes and a drooping fiery orange–colored moustache.

Murieta felt Rosita move closer.

The *gringos* halted before them and the one with the soldier's

10

cap said, "So, what are you pepper bellies doing out here?"

"We are going home," Murieta said, holding in his anger at the insult.

"Home is it?" the soldier's cap asked menacingly.

The *gringo* with the beard and the one with the green bandana rode up to inspect the inside of the wagon bed. Murieta stiffened as the one with the beard grunted like a pig and grinned crudely at Rosita as he looked her up and down, making her clutch her hand to the front of her plain muslin dress.

"We want no trouble," Murieta said, looking from the *gringo* with the soldier's cap and the two pawing through his belongings in the wagon.

"That so?" the soldier's cap asked.

"Well, looky here," the beard said, holding up the pick.

"You doing some gold prospecting there, pepper belly?" the soldier's cap asked.

"No," Murieta said. "It was my brother's. The shovel, too."

He grinned. "Stole it from your brother, did you?"

"He was . . . he died. We only want to go home," Murieta said. He could feel his white shirt and black woolen trousers sticking to him from his sweat. Looking from the cap-wearing *gringo* to the mean-looking one, he knew they did not believe him.

The beard leaned over in his saddle as close as he could to Rosita, sniffed, and said, "Smells like a damn chili bean." The green bandana–wearing *gringo* chuckled. Rosita stiffened and turned her head away. Murieta wanted to reach for that gun in the box.

The *gringo* with the cap scratched his eyebrow and said, "The evidence sure looks like you been prospecting. Don't suppose you got the proper license. That, ah . . . ah . . ."

"Foreign Miner license," the bandana-wearing *gringo* said.

"Thank you, little cousin," he said, then turned back to

Murieta. "So where's your license?"

"When I was looking for gold I had one."

"When you was looking. I see. And, uh, where'd you do this looking?"

"At Murphy's Diggings."

"Oh, up Calaveras County way. Lot of gold found up there, I hear."

Murieta nodded.

"And you didn't find so much as a pinch worth, huh?"

"Some. Gone now. Your tax took almost all of what I found."

"Yeah, well. But you claim you had the license when you was digging. Now, you know you had to renew that license every . . . what was it, little cousin?"

"Thirty days," the *gringo* with the bandana said.

"That's right. And there's a fine for you foreigner bastards digging for gold without a license. Prison time, too."

Rosita jerked her head and Murieta saw that the beard had reached his hand out, like he wanted to touch Rosita's long, thick dark hair.

"I told you, we are going home," Murieta said to the cap, trying to keep his voice calm. "I have done no digging for two months, so I needed no license."

The cap-wearing *gringo*'s eyes turned dark and he said, "And I told you it looks to me like you been digging for gold. I say you broke the law. I say you have to pay."

Murieta felt a sharp blow to his head that knocked him from his seat and onto the ground. He heard Rosita scream. Looking up, he saw the bandana-wearing *gringo* pointing a revolver at him and cocking back the hammer. The *gringo* smiled, showing a missing front tooth. Then he saw the beard grab Rosita by her hair and pull her off the wagon. The *gringo* with the cap took hold of the horse bridle and led the team and the wagon off toward the trees. Rosita ran to Murieta and helped him up. The bandana-wearing *gringo* motioned them to the trees with his revolver. Murieta and Rosita held onto each other as they walked.

"Are you hurt?" she asked.

"No," he said, rubbing his head where he'd been walloped with the gun barrel. Now he wished he'd had that revolver.

Coming through the trees, Murieta saw the other three *gringos* waiting, having ground-tethered their horses. The beard held a rope in his hands. The cap was tearing through the carpetbag, throwing clothes out. The mean-looking *gringo* with the fiery moustache, who had so far said nothing, pulled a bullwhip from his saddlebag.

"Where's your gold, pepper belly?" the cap asked.

"No gold. I told you."

"You sassing me, you Mex son-of-a-bitch?" The cap jumped down from the wagon and hit Murieta in the mouth, splitting his lip and knocking him down.

"Now the fun starts!" the bandana-wearing *gringo* shouted.

Murieta felt hands grab him by the arms and drag him. He heard Rosita scream, "No!" He tried to pull free and a fist punched his face hard. Then a savage kick to the stomach doubled him over. Stunned, he was forced down on his knees, facing a wagon wheel. He felt the business end of a revolver against the back of his head and then his right arm was yanked across to the rim of the wheel and a rope tied his wrist fast to the wooden spoke and then his left.

Rosita cried out, "*¡Madre de Dios! ¡Joaquin!*"

"This little Mex whore's a fighter," Murieta heard the cap say.

"Rosita!" Murieta shouted, still on his knees, fighting against the ropes that bound his wrists. He spit blood from his mouth. A boot kicked him hard in the ribs, nearly knocking the wind out of him. Then his shirt was ripped open, exposing his back.

13

Twisting his head around, he saw the *gringo* with the fiery moustache raise his bullwhip and a moment later felt the lash bite into his back. Murieta cried out. Another lash followed, and the sound of cackling laughter. His back was on fire. Another crack of the whip bit into his flesh. He could feel the blood running down his body.

"Hey, it's my turn on that whore," one of them shouted.

Murieta pulled at the ropes binding his wrists. His flesh ripped and burned. Another lash of the whip seared his back. His eyes squeezed shut and his teeth clenched against the agony. He felt someone grab a fistful of his sweaty black hair and roughly yank it back. He opened his eyes and was looking close into the face of the cap-wearing *gringo*.

"Listen here, Mex," the *gringo* said with a laugh and slapped Murieta's face. "That little hellcat of yours? She ain't no back-sassing coward like you. She knows how to put up a fight."

Murieta tried to speak but the words slurred in his mouth. His head dropped and his jaw went slack when the *gringo* let go of his hair and then he felt the hide of the whip dig across his back, deep and scalding. Every muscle drew tight again. Sweat and dust stung his eyes. He wanted to cry out. Another lash cut into his bleeding back. Everything went black.

The falling rain punished Murieta's flayed and raw back, like needles in his wounds. He was still on his knees, slumped forward, tied to the wagon wheel. Things looked blurry as he tried to open his eyes, and he realized one of his eyes was swollen shut. Twisting his head to look back, he shouted Rosita's name. And he saw it. Something tattered was crawling through the mud to him.

"*¡Por Dios! ¡Rosita!*" he cried.

Then he felt a touch on his leg. Looking down, he saw her bloody, dirty hand. He heard Rosita's weak voice say his name.

Her hand reached up to his. Rosita was trying to untie the rope binding his raw wrist. He looked over and saw the blood caked on her face from a wicked cut on her head. Tears and blood mixed with rain left dirty tracks on her battered face. Her dress was torn.

When she got the rope loose, he freed his other wrist as she collapsed, sobbing against his chest. He held her tight, rocking her back and forth. Looking about, he saw their clothes from the carpetbag, ripped and scattered on the muddy ground. The dresser and chair were broken into pieces. The horses were gone.

Rosita was shaking from her ordeal, the cold, and the rain. He slid through the muck to get underneath the wagon, pulling her after him. His coat lay in a lump within reach. He managed to take hold of a sleeve that had nearly been torn off by the *gringo* when he was ripping through the carpetbag, tossing out their clothes. Pulling the muddied coat toward him, he realized it was snagged on something. Another pull and he saw the box in which he'd placed his brother's Colt revolver. The *gringo* must have tossed the box out without opening it. Murieta could see the box lid laying open on its side, raindrops splashing on it. Yanking the coat free, he saw the Colt still inside.

"They didn't kill us," Rosita cried.

Was it a wail of relief or regret? Murieta wondered as he wrapped the coat around her shoulders, pulled her closer, and gently wiped her wet black hair from her face. Then he saw a clump of her hair in his hand. More were on her dress. Patches of her scalp showed. They'd used a knife to cut off chunks of her hair. The *gringos* had savaged her, humiliated her, and taken her. He fought back his tears.

The rain continued to fall. He wanted it to wash away the shame he felt, the failure for not protecting his woman, and the certainty that the *gringos* didn't kill them because they didn't think they were worth killing. We're less than dirt to them, he thought. They call us pepper bellies. Treat our women like whores.

Hugging Rosita closer, fighting the searing pain of his wounds and his humiliation, Murieta steeled himself to his resolve. They should have killed me, he thought. That was their mistake. I'll make them wish they had. Remember their faces . . . their ugly laughing . . . Rosita crying . . . the outrage . . . the lashes across my back . . . the blows and kicks . . . the screams of my Rosita . . . the blood on her face . . . the ropes tied to my wrists . . . like an animal . . . the taste of blood in my mouth, my blood . . . their faces . . . Rosita crawling through the mud . . . my soul dying . . . the vengeance I'll take . . . every Yankee *gringo* . . .

CHAPTER TWO:
THE CONFESSION

THREE MONTHS LATER

Fray Blas Ordaz was lying prostrate on the red tile floor before the altar in the San Gabriel Mission church, face down, his arms stretched out from his sides, and asking God for forgiveness for his sins committed that day. He had just repented for his sin of pride, loudly admitting, "Lord, I am not your good servant when I righteously and impiously hold that I am in the right and cannot be wrong in my decisions," when the pounding at the church door began. Knowing the hour was well past ten, he guessed that the untimely visitor outside in the night must have seen the glow of the candles he had burning on the altar through the tall glass windows placed high in the walls. Irritated by this interruption and immediately asking God's forgiveness for being irritated, the old Franciscan padre got to his feet, straightened his gray woolen robe, adjusted the carved crucifix hanging off his neck, and retied the rope belt around his bony waist.

He thought it was likely someone had come to get him because one of the Indian parishioners had gotten hurt, or drunk, or had died. Or possibly some American bully cowboy was out raising a ruckus. Ordaz was no stranger to the fact that after they had won their war with Mexico, many of those American bullies and rapscallions, the ones he privately called *Diablos Yanquis,* didn't try to understand and didn't want to

17

understand anything Mexican or Catholic, like this mission. *Diablos Yanquis* had no respect. If such were the case tonight, Ordaz would be ready. He was a man of peace, but after fifty-eight years on God's earth, he'd learned how to deal with unruly sorts. No liquored-up *Diablo Yanqui* with something to prove was going to push him around, like the one about a week ago that tried to "make him do a little dance" when he cornered the padre in the church. That bully cowboy was carried out with a lump the size of a turkey egg on his head after Ordaz hit him with a candlestick. As it had proven dependable before, Ordaz grabbed one of the heavy silver candlesticks from the altar, along with his ring of hammered iron keys.

The glow of the candle was comforting as he made his way down the center aisle of the darkened church, keys jingling, past the comfortable pews in front for the well-to-do parishioners to the heavy rough benches the Indians used in the back. The beating at the door became louder and faster and incessant. Ordaz was starting to get angry. This was enough to make angels blaspheme!

"I'm coming! Be patient!" Ordaz shouted, even though he knew whoever it was on the other side of the door could not hear him over all the racket.

Ordaz set the candlestick down on the bench nearest the door, found the proper key on the ring, and turned it in the lock. The hinges groaned as he pulled the heavy oak door open. In the shadow of the doorway leaned a haggard, sweat-soaked, wild-eyed young Mexican man, one sleeve of his white shirt nearly torn off, and the knees of his black trousers showing holes.

"I need your help, padre," the Mexican said, gulping his breath. "Men are after me."

Before Ordaz could say a word, the Mexican darted inside and hugged his back to the whitewashed plaster wall.

"Close the door!"

Ordaz clearly saw the large revolver shoved in the front of the Mexican's belt, but decided the man had not come here to harm him. He was still annoyed, though, by all the noise and this interruption to his daily prayer time.

"Tell me what this is about," Ordaz demanded, pushing the door closed but not locking it. "Who's after you and why?"

"Water. I need water."

Ordaz huffed and walked away, taking the candlestick with him and leaving the young man in the dark, saying, "You stay right here. *¿Comprende?*"

Returning with a wooden bucket with a hewn cup inside a few minutes later, Ordaz had hoped to find the young man gone. Instead, he saw him sitting on a wooden bench he had pushed up against the door.

"*Por favor,*" the Mexican said, indicating the bench. "It's to keep out the ones chasing me."

Ordaz grunted and set the bucket down. He watched as his visitor yanked the bucket toward him with both hands, scooped water into the cup, and drank greedily, water running down the sides of his mouth and dribbling onto his worn clothes.

"Now, who are you and what is this about?" Ordaz asked, setting the candlestick down on a nearby bench.

After taking another cupful of water, the man thanked Ordaz, closed his eyes, and said, "My name is Joaquin Murieta. A sheriff's posse is after me."

"And why are they chasing you?" Ordaz asked.

When Murieta looked up at him the candle light flickered, and Ordaz noticed something different in his eyes, a dark determination in them. And something else, something unforgiving.

"Because I killed a man," Murieta said evenly and dropped the cup back into the bucket.

Ordaz was about to speak when Murieta pulled a Bowie knife from its leather sheath at his side.

"I used his own knife to kill him," Murieta said.

"You can put that away," Ordaz said quietly. "You don't need it here."

"I'm sorry," Murieta said and slid the knife back in the sheath. "I wasn't . . . thinking."

Ordaz saw no need to be afraid of Murieta. To Ordaz, he looked to be about twenty, the age he was when he had joined the Order of St. Francis. That had been almost forty years ago. He had felt compelled to dedicate his life to God and vowed to abstain from worldly pleasure by devoting himself to attaining solace and salvation by helping others. But this young man, Ordaz thought, has dedicated himself to destruction and death. Without redemption, he'll surely lose his everlasting soul to damnation in the fires of hell.

"Will you hear my confession, padre?" Murieta asked.

"Yes, of course," Ordaz said.

He sat on the bench next to Murieta, closed his eyes, and said a prayer. When he opened his eyes, he saw that Murieta was kneeling beside him, head down, his hands clasped together. Raising his right hand, Ordaz blessed Murieta with the sign of the cross.

"Bless me, padre, for I have sinned," Murieta began. "It has been . . ."

"It's all right," Ordaz said. "Go on."

Murieta was hesitant. "Padre, if I'm not . . ."

"Not what?" Ordaz asked gently.

"I want to confess. I have sinned. But, will God still forgive me if I'm not sorry for my sins?"

Ordaz wondered if he had heard him correctly. "Not sorry for your sins?"

Murieta nodded, but kept his head bowed.

"If you are not repentant, then there is no forgiveness from God."

Murieta raised his head, looking past him. Ordaz thought he might be praying for guidance. Then Murieta stood and said, "I'm sorry I disturbed you. I'll go now."

Ordaz leapt to his feet, saying, "You told me you killed a man. You can't leave here with the stain of that mortal sin on your soul."

Murieta looked back at him. "Then give me the absolution."

"But I can't."

"*Adios,* padre."

Ordaz blocked him from pulling the bench away from the door. "But you will not be allowed to enter the kingdom of Heaven."

Murieta shrugged, cocking his head. "Maybe."

Perplexed, Ordaz wondered what was wrong with this man. He must still try to convince him. It was his obligation as a friar, a devout servant of God. "Tell me why you killed the man."

"I had my reasons."

"Your reasons," Ordaz said, his voice rising. "No. You cannot hide when you confess. You have broken both God's law and man's."

"Man's law is *gringo* law here," Murieta spat. "You're from Mexico, like me. *¿Si?* You know I'm right. *¿Verdad?*"

Yes, Ordaz knew that was true. He knew if the sheriff was after this man it was because he killed an American, a *gringo.* If it had been any foreigner who wasn't white, they wouldn't care. Ordaz knew this sheriff. He knew these Americans. And he knew himself.

"But you still have a chance with God," Ordaz said. "Make your confession."

"Where is my chance if you won't give me absolution?"

"Why do you refuse to repent?"

"I told you."

"*¡Digame!* Give me the reasons."

"I don't have time to argue anymore! That posse, it's coming."

Ordaz's face flushed red with anger. "Listen to me!"

"No!" Murieta shouted. "I will probably get killed if they catch me. I need God's forgiveness before that happens."

Ordaz's head was spinning. He took hold of Murieta's shoulders and pleaded. "Ask God for forgiveness. Tell him you are truly sorry for your sins."

He felt Murieta's cold black eyes bore into him.

"No," Murieta said quietly.

It had the sound of a deadly threat to Ordaz. This unrepentant hardheaded sinner was truly trying his patience. Steeling his determination, he stepped toward Murieta and said, "Committing murder here or in Mexico is a crime and a sacrilege against God and man."

"I'm done arguing!"

"So am I," Ordaz snapped and dragged the bench away from the door, the legs scraping across the tiles. "Go on then. Get out. You will burn in hell." He felt two hands push hard against his chest. The front of his robe was balled up into Murieta's fists. And there was Murieta, inches away, staring him in the face.

"The man I killed today," Murieta said, low and evenly, "he raped my wife."

Ordaz stood there, catching his breath, trying to think of what to say, getting control of his anger. "I understand," he said, and Murieta released his grip and stepped away.

"I . . . I am truly sorry," Ordaz said. "I will pray for her. But, you . . . To you, I say the Lord's own words, 'Vengeance is mine.' Your reason for killing does not excuse—"

"No!" Murieta shouted, cutting him off. "Vengeance belongs to me! Three other men were with him when it happened. They all took their turns. And now, they are all dead."

Stunned, his eyes fixed on Murieta, Ordaz steadied himself. His mouth was dry. Horror swept over him. *"Dios mio,"* he whispered and made the sign of the cross.

"Now will you give me the absolution, padre?"

For the first time, Ordaz felt afraid of this man. He took a deep breath. "I cannot," he said, and then he realized Murieta's hand was closed around the handle of his Bowie knife. Ordaz summoned up what courage he could muster and asked, "Are you going to kill me, too?"

Murieta looked down at his side and quickly let go of the knife, as though the handle had burned his hand.

Ordaz felt air fill his lungs again.

Murieta spun around to the door and grabbed the handle. But before he could get the door open, Ordaz slammed one hand against it and reached out with his other to try to stop Murieta, to help him, still wanting to save his soul. His fingers got a hold of Murieta's frayed shirt collar. When Murieta pulled away, the collar split and the shirt tore easily in Ordaz's grip. In the soft golden glow of the candlelight, Ordaz saw the savage scars crisscrossing Murieta's back.

Murieta turned around, anger etched on his face. Ordaz staggered backward, wanting to stay out of reach. His hand groped for the candlestick. Murieta lunged at him. Ordaz saw the raised fist. His leg caught the edge of the bench. He heard the candlestick teeter. He couldn't move. The fist pulled back to strike.

"You see what they did to me?" Murieta shouted. "They gave me these scars to humiliate me! God didn't stop them! He didn't protect my Rosita! And I must ask God for forgiveness?"

A rush of cool air swept over Ordaz and the candle on the

bench flickered brightly and went out as the wooden door flew open. And just as quickly, Ordaz realized Murieta had vanished into the night.

Ana Benitez knew the man was in trouble when she opened the lop-sided front door of her small adobe house. He looked ragged and disoriented as he crouched by an outcropping of large rocks on the other side of the road. Was he lost? she wondered. Where is his horse? She could tell he'd been startled by the sudden light thrown from her doorway as he scrambled behind the rocks. She took a puff on the half-smoked *cigarillo* hanging from her mouth and rubbed one small hand over the top of the other, the cold night air playing havoc with her fingers that had begun stiffening of late. A moment later, she saw him peek out from the rocks and beckoned to him with a wave of her hand. He stood cautiously, and that's when she caught sight of the glow of torches coming fast from the direction of the mission church a few hundred yards away. With quick jerks of her hand, she motioned to him to hurry. He noticed the glow and moved fast. She knew somebody was after him for certain.

As he got closer, Ana could hear him breathing hard. She pointed to the wooden ladder leaning against the front of the house. When he angled toward it, she realized he was clutching a horse blanket around his shoulders. Then he stopped and she saw the startled expression on his face.

"You're—you're—the angel," he said between breaths.

"*Si, si,*" she said hurriedly. This was not the time, she thought. Seeing the torch glow looming brighter against a stand of oak trees just beyond her house, she waved her hand quickly for him to get moving. She heard the man scramble up the ladder and climb over the low parapet.

Ana pulled her white shawl closer around her shoulders when she saw the ten mounted men come into view on the road.

Each carried a torch.

They rode straight to her. She saw the glow of more torches appear, another ten or twenty maybe, further off in the distance, moving away in a different direction from the mission. A lot of men are searching for this man, she thought.

Ana guessed the big man wearing a silver badge on his blue shirt was the leader of this posse of *Americanos*. He drew his head back and looked at her queerly, something she was used to people doing when they saw her for the first time. The others were gawking at her, too. She heard whispers.

"Old Mex woman's all white. Looks like a damn ghost."

"She's the one got some magic picture or some such thing."

"Mex superstition, you ask me."

"Ah, ma'am," the man with the badge cleared his throat, "you seen ah, ah, a Mes'can man skulking around here, looking like he's wanting to hide? Or maybe he run past and you seen him?"

"Who's looking for him?" Ana asked innocently.

His eyes narrowed at her. "Why don't you just tell me if you've seen anybody."

She blew smoke out of the side of her mouth without removing her *cigarillo*. "I saw no one," she said.

"Well, he's wanted. You best be careful."

"What did he do?"

"Killed a man over in Los Angeles. Used a Bowie knife."

"Yeah," one of the men said. "Carved him up like a damn hog."

"Shut your hole, Gil!" the man with the badge said, shooting a hard glance at the man.

"Want we should search her house?" one of the others said. "See if she's hiding him."

"It's a small house," she said, brushing away ashes that had fallen from her *cigarillo* onto her white muslin dress. "Look if you wish."

She noticed one of the other men eyeing the ladder against the wall and then along the top of her house. He had a scraggly-looking beard.

"Tell you what I think," he said. "That greaser mighta shimmied up that ladder there. Somebody ought to go take a gander."

Several of the men shot a look up at the roof, but Ana kept her eye on the deputy who was watching her, long, hard, and fixed. She felt like he was testing her, waiting for her to twitch or something, anything that would tell him she knew where the man he was looking for was hiding. She blew another stream of smoke from her mouth, eyes on his, determined to win this standoff. It hadn't been more than a few seconds when the deputy broke the contact and glanced up at the roof line.

"No one's there," she said, holding back a little triumphant smile. "I would've heard."

"Go look, Haze," the deputy said to the scraggly-bearded one.

"Me?"

"Your idea. Get going."

Ana resisted the urge to cross herself and instead offered a silent prayer to her saint to protect the young Mexican on the roof. She watched from her doorway as Haze reluctantly got down from his horse, his short height immediately evident to her. He cocked his revolver and began making his way up the ladder, slowly, cautiously. She glanced at the deputy. He was eyeing the roof and quietly drew his pistol from his holster. Looking back at the man climbing the ladder, she saw he was halfway up.

"C'mon, Haze," someone said. "Flush him out. You get shot, we'll know where he is."

Ana saw Haze freeze where he was and look back down at the posse.

"Shut your mouth, Gil!" he hissed and then snapped his head back up in the direction of the roof line.

This Haze reminded Ana of a frightened little boy who'd been dared to go into a dark house.

Several of the other *Americanos* pulled out their revolvers, ready for a fight, and Ana gripped her shawl closer, offering another, stronger prayer to her saint.

She saw Haze had reached the top of the ladder and was inching his head slowly up to peer over the parapet.

"Careful now, Haze," the deputy said. "A Mex'll bushwhack you sure as shit."

A shout in the distance grabbed their attention. "Over here! C'mon boys! He's gone rabbit!"

"Let's go!" the deputy shouted.

Wheeling their horses around the posse galloped away, leaving Haze to leap from the ladder and run to his horse, hollering for them to wait for him.

Taking the last puff of her *cigarillo* and chortling with relief, Ana craned her neck looking up at the parapet and made a short, sharp hissing sound, trying to get her guest's attention. She was startled hearing a voice behind her in the house saying, *"Gracias."* Turning, she found the young man smiling at her. Even with the dirt and grime on his face, she could tell he was very handsome, *muy guapo*.

"What are you doing in here?" she asked.

"It looked like they weren't going to come inside, so I climbed down the back of your house and crawled in through the window," he said, pointing at the small window, its shutters open, on the far wall.

"Very smart," she said.

"Again, *gracias*," he said and started past her to leave.

"Wait. You must eat. You need clothes."

"No," he said, holding the blanket tighter in his fist. "The *gringos* will arrest you if they come back and find me here."

She waved her hand dismissively. "These *Americanos,* they'll be chasing shadows for an hour."

She could tell he was still unconvinced. "You hear your stomach growling. *¿Si?*"

Looking embarrassed, he drew his free arm across his gut.

She patted him on the shoulder, pulled the door closed, and said, "Eat, or all they will have to do is listen to find you."

Ana shuffled slowly across the earthen floor of her two-room home, her tiny body hunched forward. She pointed to the rough-hewn table with two chairs set in the middle of the floor of the main room while she went to the fireplace in the corner where a blackened pot of *frijoles* simmered.

While preparing his plate, she saw he was examining a simple wooden shrine she had in the corner near the front door. The canopy over the altar was festooned with garlands of faded paper flowers and crude drawings of birds and dozens of strips of calico and leather. Tied to ends of the strips were tiny crosses and carvings of wood and stone.

"Anything that suffers is here," she said, seeing him eyeing them more closely. Then his blanket slipped and he pulled it up quickly but not before she saw his shirt was torn and the scars on his back. She looked away quickly.

"Horses, dogs, arms, legs," he said, looking over the carvings. "An ear?"

She nodded. "Hearts and eyes and babies, too. They are offerings of proof from those who have been cured. Some call it the heart of my home."

"The stories about you are true, then?"

"The stories about my saint are true," she said as she set a plate of *frijoles* and a cup of water on the table for him. "Come, eat first."

He pulled one of the chairs around so he was facing the front door and removed the revolver from his belt and put it next to his plate.

She sat down at the side of the table. Lighting a fresh *cigarillo* she watched as he devoured the beans, gulping them down in heaping spoonfuls, careful to keep his blanket over his back. He was feeling better, she could tell, though with every other mouthful he eyed the front door. When he stopped in mid-bite and wiped his mouth on his sleeve, she asked him if anything was wrong.

"Only my manners," he said. "I am Joaquin Murieta. Again, many thanks for saving my life. These beans, they're good. I haven't eaten since yesterday."

"I am Ana Benitez. And there are more beans."

She gave him two more platefuls.

While he was finishing his last helping, she shuffled around to a calico curtain that hung over a sagging rope tied to a couple of nails in the far wall covering a doorway. Pulling the curtain aside, she entered her bedchamber where a small crucifix hung on the wall, and made her way to an old chest at the foot of her bed. Opening it, she pulled out a faded shirt and a brown serape.

Returning to the table, she handed him the clothes, saying they had belonged to her father who was now in heaven and no longer needed them, "but they may do you some good."

"I'm grateful," he said, accepting the clothes.

"Put on the shirt while I pour some coffee. Yours isn't even a good rag now. And that horse blanket, it's seen better days."

Preparing the coffee, she kept her back turned so he could change. A minute later she placed a steaming cup in front of him, sat down, and said, "My father's shirt fits you well."

"Yes, it feels good." Then quietly he said, "I have heard that the Angel of San Gabriel works miracles."

"I wish that was true," she sighed. "Please, I need you to get something for me. From the shrine."

She wasn't surprised when he took his revolver with him. She told him to look beneath the canopy and the garlands and he'd find a small, framed portrait about the size of a slice of bread hanging on the wall. "Bring it to me, *por favor.*"

Taking it from him, she gently ran her fingers over the worn wooden frame, studying the portrait. She glanced at Murieta as he sat down, placing his revolver back on the table. Looking back at the portrait, she hesitated a moment, then said, "Forty years ago a girl woke up on the morning of her thirteenth birthday to discover her hair and her skin had turned white, like pearl," she said. "No one knew what it meant. My parents were poor and this frightened them. Everyone in the village was afraid. My father rode to the mission and brought back the old padre. He came in alone, saw me, and said I was touched by God." She gave Murieta a little smile and shrugged.

Turning the picture for him to see, she asked, "Do you recognize him?"

"St. Francis of Assisi. *¿No?*"

"You know him," she said, pleased. "He is my saint, the protector of the poor."

Looking again at the picture, she continued saying the picture was her birthday gift from her parents. Her father had bought it from a crippled padre at the mission who said he had come on a pilgrimage to California from Santa Fe. "That's a town in what the Yankees now call the Territory of New Mexico." The next day, she said, her father went back to the mission to invite the padre to supper, but was told no crippled padre had been there.

"My father said there was a crippled padre, so there was. And

30

my father had the portrait," she said, running her fingers gently over it.

"What happened after the old padre came to see you?"

"Oh, yes," she said and took a puff on her *cigarillo*. "The padre had gone. I held the portrait in my hands. My father was crying. I remember his hands had become swollen, his fingers bent over the years. Like mine are getting now." She glanced at Murieta, a small smile of acceptance on her face, then back to the picture in her hands. "But that morning, as he held my hands, his fingers brushed the portrait, and at once, his fingers straightened. His pain was gone."

"So the picture works the miracle?" Murieta asked.

"Sometimes prayers are answered," she said. "Sometimes cures come."

He frowned. "What about you?"

"He smiles on some and not on others," she said with a shrug.

"Well, the saint should mend you," he said.

It struck Ana that Murieta sounded offended that her saint had not straightened her back and her fingers.

"He knows best," she said easily, setting the portrait down.

Murieta grunted. Then he picked up the portrait and studied it. His face was hard.

He's daring my saint, Ana thought. She wasn't angry or provoked, and she hoped St. Francis would give her a sign.

Glancing at his revolver on the table, she asked, "Do you want to tell me why they're after you?"

He set the picture down, the anger still set on his face. "It's not the story of a saint," he finally said, his eyes darting once more to the picture and then away.

It seemed to her he was gathering his thoughts. She took one last pull on her *cigarillo* and threw it to the floor.

"*Americanos* came to our village in Sonora," he began, his eyes downcast. "They seemed like good, decent people. Come

31

to America, to California, they said. There is gold for the taking. With gold you will earn respect. I told my Rosita we should go. My brother, Jesus, he was there a year already. I told Rosita we could have a better life."

He closed his eyes and Ana thought he was fighting back tears. Or maybe more anger.

"We had great hopes," he said, looking at Ana. "I loved this country and I had never even seen it."

He picked up his coffee cup, then put it down without taking a drink, his agitation evident to Ana.

"We came and we are treated like dirt," he continued, the bitterness rising in his voice. "Because we are Mexican the Yankees insulted us, stole from us. They called us names. They hanged my brother because they said he stole a cow. Some Yankees, they tied it to his fence. He stole no cow." He rubbed his hand over the back of his neck and let out a deep breath. "I dug gold with my hands and they took it because they said I owed their tax. And when we tried to leave, they . . . they forced . . ."

Ana put her hand on top of his but he pulled it away.

She cried when he told her of being tied to the wagon wheel and whipped and of the brutal degrading of Rosita by the Yankees. And then she heard something different in his voice, something raw and deadly that made her want to cover her ears when he told her how he tracked them down. He said he found two near Santa Barbara one night, drinking whiskey at their campsite, and shot them with his revolver, one in the throat, the other in the chest. "It was easy because they were drunk." He told her about finding the bearded man collecting the foreign miners tax from two men in a livery stable in San Luis Obispo. "I heard one of the men say they were from Bolivia." Murieta said he picked up a pitchfork like he worked there, walked up, drove it into the bearded man's chest, and then gave the money back to the two foreigners.

"The last one," he said, "the one who whipped me, I found in Los Angeles two nights ago. He was coming out of a saloon. I hoped he would have his whip. I wanted to wrap it around his neck and choke him to death."

She held her hands to her mouth, afraid of what was coming.

"I followed him into an alley," he went on. "He was making water and I hit him over the head with my pistol. He fell on the ground. No whip. So I took his Bowie knife. I held it to his neck and asked him if he remembered me. I could see in his eyes that he did. He looked scared, and that was good. I said to him, 'How does it feel to be so scared?' Then I cut his throat and watched him die." He softly blew out a breath. "That *gringo* seed will produce no more. None of them will."

Ana wiped her eyes and rested her forehead against the heel of her hand.

"So much blood," she said softly.

"*Gringo* blood," he said, bitterly. "I hate them all. They hate us."

Ana felt his terrible rage. It filled the room. She hoped for a sign from her saint, but looking at the portrait, she saw none.

"The Yankees took my gold," he said. "I will take theirs. They stole my horses. I steal theirs. They took my honor. I take their lives. They took my wife . . ."

She heard the catch in his voice and laid her hand out across the table to him, but he didn't take it.

"I tried to tell the padre at the mission," he said. "He said I must ask forgiveness if I want to enter heaven." He grunted. "I did not abandon God. God abandoned me. He let them take everything from me. Now I'm taking everything."

A feeling of helplessness overwhelmed her. She realized at that moment that without a true miracle, his vendetta against the *Americanos* would end with blood and death.

He stood up. "I must go. They might still come back."

Ana reached out and touched his hand. "What about your wife? She must need you."

"She is home, back in Mexico. She's safe there."

Yes, Ana thought, at least she is safe.

At the door, she took his hands in hers and told him to be careful.

He thanked her and reached for the door. Then he asked, "Do you have a horse?"

Ana was caught off guard. "You don't have one, tied up somewhere?"

"When I got to the mission, it spooked and ran away," he said, sounding irritated. He shrugged. "It belonged to one of the men I killed."

"You stole it?"

"He didn't need it anymore."

She didn't know whether to laugh or cry. Taking his face in her hands, she said, "I cannot absolve you from your sins, but I will pray for you every day. You are always welcome in my house."

"God did touch you."

She closed the door after he left and hurried awkwardly to the table to look again at the portrait of her saint. The faces of those who had come to her over the years rushed before her like a flood. They were friends and strangers, the afflicted seeking help and hope. They came and touched the portrait. Many times she had seen the face of St. Francis shed tears if no help was coming, or catch a glint of light from his eyes if a prayer was to be answered. Sometimes, days, even months, might pass before St. Francis revealed the answer, but it always came eventually. And whatever the saint's response, only she saw it, and she never told. Some visitors left cured, some did not. "He knows best for us," she'd tell them. And nearly every morning, she'd open her door to find a loaf of bread, tortillas, a tin of jerked beef, a pot of beans, or even a bottle of homemade wine left as tokens of thanks.

Taking the portrait in her hands, Ana looked and saw nothing. Her saint remained still. She got slowly down on her knees, clasped her aching hands together, and asked her saint to protect Joaquin Murieta.

Chapter Three:
The Reward

THREE YEARS LATER

After signing his name on the document, Governor John Bigler set down his ink pen, closed his eyes, rested his elbows on top of his desk, and rubbed his temples with his pudgy fingers. His head was pounding like a smithy's anvil on horseshoeing day.

"This better take care of that little son-of-a-bitch," Bigler said.

He heard the sound of paper crinkling and knew his efficient secretary, Ben Ryland, was rolling a blotter over his signature.

"Governor, can I get you or Mr. Covarrubias anything?" Ryland asked.

Bigler opened his eyes and sat back in his chair, his elbow brushing a short stack of newspapers on his left as he did so.

"Not for me," he said, and looked at the nattily dressed House Assemblyman from Santa Barbara County sitting across from him. "Jose?"

"I'm fine," Covarrubias said.

Ryland rolled the document up in his freckle-covered hands, nodded sharply, and left Bigler's office.

Bigler pushed his chair away from his desk and went to the upright cabinet standing between the high open windows. It was a spring day and the afternoon breeze felt refreshing, but Bigler preferred distilled spirits as a cure-all. He also had something important to discuss with the Assemblyman and figured a little whiskey might help things along.

Opening the cabinet, he took down a couple of glasses and a bottle. Returning to his desk he poured two fingers into each glass. He pushed one toward Covarrubias. Bigler had raised his glass in a silent toast when Covarrubias interrupted.

"To the new California Rangers," he said, lifting his glass.

Bigler grunted in agreement and swallowed his whiskey. He tipped the bottle toward Covarrubias who nodded and Bigler poured him another two fingers.

"All right," he said, pouring another drink for himself. "Now tell me about these two you found to command this outfit. Love and, who's the other one?"

"Alexander Hope. A good man, even though he hails from Texas," Covarrubias said and ran his finger over his finely trimmed moustache. "Distinguished himself at Churubusco during the war with Mexico. A bloody thing, he told me. He vouched for Harry Love, who fought with him in the war. That's good enough for me."

"Well, they better be good enough to hunt down this little bastard," Bigler said.

"Captain Hope and Captain Love understand that they're charged to apprehend this Joaquin and his cohorts," Covarrubias said. "But Joaquin is the key."

Bigler guessed that neither Covarrubias nor anyone on his committee knew the difference between a bloodthirsty bandit and horseshit. Why else would they say "apprehend" Joaquin? Hiding his disgust, he gulped down his drink.

"My committee was quite specific about the mission of the rangers," Covarrubias continued. "We made it clear that certainty of identification is paramount in order to bring this bandit to justice. The problem has been compounded, as you know, by the wild stories and erroneous accounts of this Joaquin robbing and murdering in different places in the state seemingly at the same time."

"So how many of these Joaquins are there now?"

"Five. Maybe six."

Bigler sighed. He wondered why in the hell he had ever left a fine law practice in Pennsylvania. Of course he knew the answer: the siren song of gold. But panning for the shiny stuff had been a bust for him. And a successful term as governor was looking somewhat less than favorable now, as well.

"Just this morning," Covarrubias went on, "I received a report that a bunch of prospectors on the Yuba River near Long Bar organized themselves to protect their diggings and half of them got shot up and were robbed of over ten thousand dollars' worth of gold. Joaquin was blamed, but not identified as one of the bandits. And on that same day a thousand miles away near San Diego, a man claiming to be Joaquin robbed three men of their purses and their boots."

"Took their boots? Little bastard," Bigler said.

"My own district saw atrocious violence only two days before these incidents. Two robbers, both wearing bandanas over their faces, waylaid a visitor from England on his way to Sunday services. They demanded money but all the man had on him was ten dollars. They made him turn out his pockets to make certain, then shot him and left him for dead. He was found barely alive and said one of the robbers told him he was being robbed by Joaquin."

"This Englishman live?"

"Thankfully, yes. But you see it's not possible the same Joaquin committed each of these crimes."

"Yes, I see," Bigler said.

"Also, this particular incident with the English visitor provoked such outrage that prominent citizens in my district have told me, in plain words, to hunt these rattlesnakes down. I can now tell them we have the rangers." Covarrubias smiled confidently.

Bigler grunted. "I can't help wonder how long it'll take before every bandit in the state starts calling himself Joaquin."

"Obviously others are calling themselves Joaquin," Covarrubias said, "but the real Joaquin is the one we want, of course."

"And how will we know if we have the real one?" Bigler asked, spreading his hands. "We don't know what the hell he looks like."

"Captains Hope and Love know what they're doing. Between them, God, and a little luck, the rangers are our best course of action."

Bigler blew out a long breath and rubbed his eyes. In his experience, he'd concluded God was fine but tended to take his time, and usually too long. If there were such a thing as luck it had never smiled on him, otherwise he'd be a wealthy man of leisure. As for Hope and Love, they were untested as far as he was concerned, regardless of Covarrubias's feelings. And they would require a special breed of man to fill their ranks, namely man hunters. Ridding the state of Joaquin and his band would be no easy task. He didn't want to take any chances. He had something extra in mind, something special to sharpen these new rangers, to turn them into fanatics. The question was how to get it.

"Damn it, my head hurts," Bigler said, then looked at Covarrubias. "Fifty men for each company would have been better."

"My committee did its best to get fifty," Covarrubias said, "but with the state budget already strained, it wasn't feasible. At one hundred and fifty dollars per month per man, twenty men per company were all the legislature would authorize. And even that was a battle."

"Yes, yes, I'm aware of all you did," Bigler said.

"As I said, Hope and Love are very capable. I believe Love

and his company will be here in the northern districts and Hope and his men will scour the southern part of the state."

"And they're aware of the time limitation to accomplish this task?"

Covarrubias nodded.

"Three months only gives them to the end of August," Bigler said.

"The legislature will decide then if another three months is feasible, based on how things have progressed."

Bigler sat back in his chair and made a steeple of his fingers, his thumbs pointed down, the tips touching. "Tell me then, in your opinion, will these rangers have enough incentive to . . . progress?"

"What do you mean?"

Bigler sensed Covarrubias knew something was coming.

"Is that the best we can do?" Bigler asked. "One hundred and fifty a month."

"It sounds like you have something in mind."

"I do," Bigler said, flexing his steepled fingers twice. "A substantial reward."

He watched Covarrubias sit up straighter in his chair.

"Governor," Covarrubias said, setting his glass on Bigler's desk, "you no doubt recall the legislature debated that issue and decided to table the discussion."

"Maybe it's time to sit at that table again," Bigler said. He picked up a newspaper from the stack of several on his desk. "Let me read you something, 'How much longer must we wait before something is done? When will the red hand of murder be stayed?' That's the *Los Angeles Star.*" Tossing it aside, he took another from the stack. "And here, from the *Daily Alta California,* 'When will a bold, unflinching voice speak in thunderous tones against the abuses and daring outrages being perpetrated nightly throughout our state and upon our citizens by this

40

unchecked banditry?' These newspapers are addressing us, the elected officials of this state, me in particular. They are telling me these god damn Joaquins need to be brought in, dead or alive."

"It is my opinion," Covarrubias said, "and one shared by others in the legislature, that the state of California cannot offer a reward on the head of any individual who has not been convicted by due process of law."

Bigler didn't like the haughty tone of the Assemblyman's voice, but he didn't let on. He picked up another newspaper and read from it. " 'Will the depredations of the notorious bandit under the name of Joaquin ever be quelled?' "

"The opinions of newspapers are not conclusive evidence of a crime or proof of guilt."

" 'Hunt down these rattlesnakes.' Those are the words of your constituents, are they not?"

"What you propose isn't a reward. It's a bounty."

"I see it as an incentive. Necessary and vital."

"No."

"These are extraordinary times."

"The offer of such a reward is dangerous. Some unscrupulous type could simply bring in a body claiming it to be Joaquin. It might be mistaken identity, or worse, a case of outright deception."

"I say the people of this state are fed up. They want to be rid of this Joaquin. Hell, all these Joaquins!"

"You can't do this."

"Anyone who's lost a family member or a fortune to this Joaquin might disagree."

"We must uphold the laws of this state."

"And we must keep the citizenry safe."

"On that we agree."

"In principle, yes. In practicality, no."

"The state cannot condone murder!"

Bigler's head felt like two smithys were pounding on it now. This stubborn man sitting across from him refused to listen to reason or good sense. Those laws he kept harping about were fine, meanwhile things were spinning out of control because of this damn Joaquin. As a lawyer Bigler knew the law needed to be strictly followed without favor. Being a politician, he was aware that the law could be interpreted with a bit of bending, finessing. That was what he needed, finessing without favor. Then he recalled the words of his former law partner, Ellis J. Nott, who said that litigation and politics share a distinct and inviolate rule: win at any cost.

"What are your ambitions, Jose?" Bigler asked.

"Ambitions?"

Bigler nodded. "Politically speaking." He enjoyed watching the frown deepen on Covarrubias's face.

When the Assemblyman didn't respond, Bigler asked him if he entertained aspirations of becoming governor.

"I . . . It has . . . crossed my mind, yes."

"Good. Now put yourself in my place. You've been governor for seventeen months. Joaquin and his band have been ravaging the state for three years. The governor before you, that idiot McDougall, didn't catch these outlaws, but you're the one being crucified daily." He pointed at the newspapers. "What do you do?"

Bigler watched as Covarrubias nervously put a finger to his lips and recrossed his legs. He bet the Assemblyman's stomach was churning.

"I will not sacrifice our laws as a remedy," Covarrubias finally said.

"I didn't ask you what you wouldn't do."

"All right . . . I put my faith in the rangers. And remember," he said, wagging his index finger, "their stated mission is to *ap-*

prehend Joaquin, not kill him."

"Do you honestly believe this Joaquin, or any of these other Joaquins for that matter, will allow himself to be apprehended?"

"Well, that's not my concern."

Spoken like a true politician, Bigler thought, then he said, "But you agree this situation is dire."

"The state is strapped. The legislature will not authorize money for a reward."

At that moment, the answer came to Bigler. It was clear, necessary, and obvious, and it didn't require permission from the legislature. Those smithys up in his head had just been trying to hammer it out.

"Then, it's simple," Bigler said. "Action is called for. As the governor, I'm willing to take it. As governor, I can take it."

"What action?" Covarrubias asked.

Bigler savored the moment. Litigation and politics. Ellis J. Nott had been right. That cool May breeze wafting through the window felt intoxicatingly serene.

"Governor?"

Bigler smiled. The citizens would love him. The newspapers would praise him. His head had stopped hurting.

Chapter Four:
The Mexican

The way the heat was clinging to Murieta on this hot August night, he knew tomorrow would be a scorcher. He'd taken off his faded *serape* and rolled it up behind his saddle. His loose white shirt and open black vest were damp with sweat. His long dark hair under the yellow broad-brimmed hat felt sticky. Even the brass buttons up the sides of his *calzoneros*, his Mexican buckskin pants, seemed to be sweating. Soon enough, though, he'd be gone from this damn *gringo* California. Enough was enough. But he had to see the Angel once more.

Murieta figured he'd been through the village of San Gabriel more than a dozen times since that first night three years ago when the sheriff's posse was chasing him, the same night he gave up on God and then met the Angel. The last time had been nine months back when he avenged the honor of a chaste Mexican woman. On that chilly November evening he had ventilated Joshua Bean's chest with five rounds from his Colt revolver. He also recalled San Gabriel, built among the oaks at the base of a mountain, as a handful of squat adobe and planed wood buildings along the dusty rutted path called El Camino Real. There was a cobbler's shop, a harness maker and Singer's Trading Post. There were also saloons, like Ybarra's Cantina and the Monte. And sitting across from those two saloons on a southwest corner a good stone's throw from the old mission was the Headquarters, the first saloon in the little village. All the other shops and businesses radiated out from the Headquarters in a kind of haphazard circle, like spokes on a busted wagon wheel.

But this night, under the pale sliver of an early August moon, as Murieta and his large friend Feliz Contreras, the one the *gringos* called the Animal and who Contreras's wife called El Bruto, rode quietly into the village, they saw a new general store and a blacksmith. Then Contreras pointed out another recent enterprise, Mosely's Undertaking Parlor.

"I bet that opened after you killed that *pendejo* Bean," Contreras said. His voice, like his face, was rough as tree bark.

Murieta grunted in agreement at his grinning *amigo.* He knew, though, that the true growth of the place was evidenced by many more whitewashed flat-topped adobe homes that had sprung up. It was still a small village, though, and he liked that because it reminded him of his village in Mexico, not like the town of Los Angeles nine miles west. It was sprawling with two thousand people.

Catching sight of a gallows frame, Murieta stiffened, feeling the hairs on the back of his neck bristle, but quickly relaxed when he realized it was not a gallows at all but the wooden frame of a partially completed building standing bare and stark in the pale moonlight. Probably for another *gringo* saloon, he thought bitterly.

Seeing San Gabriel's three saloons already rowdy with customers, light from their open doorways and windows spilling out in golden shafts, raised Murieta's bile and further steeled his desire to leave this country. To him, these saloons were just one more way the Yankees took advantage of Mexicans and other foreigners, as well as the poor Indians living near the old mission who had the coin. All Yankees wanted was more money.

"Must we see the woman tonight, *jefe?*" Contreras asked.

"*Si*," Murieta said.

Out of the corner of his eye, Murieta saw his heavy friend, who was twice his age and almost twice his size, slouch in his saddle and then heard his loud sigh as they approached Ybarra's Cantina.

"Well then," Contreras said, "if we must see the woman, it would be better if I had a drink. *¿No?* Besides, it is Saturday night. I always drink Saturday nights."

Murieta shook his head. "She wouldn't approve smelling whiskey on your breath. And you drink every night."

His friend growled long and low, but it made no difference. Murieta knew that if Contreras got to drinking, someone would get killed. It always happened that way with him. It was hard enough keeping Contreras from killing Yankees and Chinese when he was sober. Drunk, Contreras would kill anyone, even Mexicans and Indians.

They didn't keep to the shadows in the village. Murieta believed that might arouse suspicion. Besides, this was the way he had always entered the village. There was no skulking around, no hiding, but no grandly announcing himself either. Just like the night he killed Joshua Bean, the Yankee who called himself a general, and who thought nothing of taking advantage of young Mexican women. Murieta had waited patiently on the road until they came face to face. Without saying a word, he'd quietly drawn his revolver and emptied it into Bean. That piece of *gringo* trash would never harm another woman.

At Singer's Trading Post they stopped and dismounted, spurs jingling. Enough light from the doorway of the Headquarters Saloon shone across to Singer's that they could see the notices posted on the board by the door. They stepped up on the veranda to examine them. Murieta took off his hat and wiped the sweat from his forehead on his sleeve. The announcement of a temperance meeting at Our Lady of Angels Church in Los

Angeles was of no consequence to him. Neither was the advertisement of a sorrel mare for sale, "termes: cash or kabbige tayken."

"Here!" Contreras said, tearing off other flyers to reveal a faded yellow notice. "See what they want for you."

At that moment, light from the Headquarters across the way dimmed as the figure of a man filled the doorway.

"I said nobody out-drinks Pete Bonner!" the figure shouted into the night, and with a mighty belch, he fell backwards into the saloon. A raucous cheer from inside the one-story adobe grog shop greeted the thud of his body hitting the floor and a voice rose above the din, proclaiming, "*Nobody* can out-drink Roy Bean!" More cheers followed and the raucous laughter of women.

Murieta knew they were whores, the *putas* of Screaming Addie's. Lots of whores worked out of saloons.

He looked from the Headquarters to his friend. In this light he could see only half of Contreras's face.

"Roy Bean," Contreras whispered and then licked his lips. "Why not rub out the rest of that seed?"

Murieta could tell Contreras was getting restless, hoping for an excuse to kill someone, anyone. It had been better than a week since Contreras robbed, stabbed, and hung two Yankees near San Diego.

"No killing tonight, Feliz," Murieta said, keeping his voice relaxed on purpose. "We're nearly done with their California."

Murieta heard him sniff and grunt. He knew those sounds well. They were the ones Contreras made when he was disappointed or didn't get his way.

Contreras tapped the yellowed notice on the board. "*Jefe*, you have to look at this one."

A Reward
is hereby offered on the head of the notorious bandit
JOAQUIN!
The sum of
$1,000
is personally offered by the Governor of the State of
California
for this outlaw
captured or killed

Murieta chuckled. "I would like to meet this *gringo* governor," he said.

Contreras snorted. "What for? He's nothing."

"He has the courage, you know?" He pointed at the bottom line of the flyer. "Captured or killed, he says. Dead or alive. *¿No?* He wants to show he is a serious man. But he also shows he is a fool."

"*¿Que?*"

"Which Joaquin does he want?" Murieta shrugged. "Is it our *amigo* Joaquin Valenzuela who takes his men and steals so silently horses and cattle from the Yankees here in this county? Or is it Joaquin Carrillo who relieves the *gringo* miners of their gold? Maybe Joaquin Botillares, or Ocomorena and their men, eh? They have put an end to the lives of many *gringos* who say we had no right to look for gold, had no right to even be in this country. Those *gringos* have paid dearly. *¿No?*"

Contreras made a low happy sound in his throat.

"But is it possible," Murieta said with exaggerated wonder, "it is the Joaquin they say gives the gold he has stolen to his less fortunate countrymen here? Do you think he is the Joaquin the *gringo* governor wants, the one who calls himself Murieta?"

Contreras grinned. "What do you say, *jefe?*"

Turning his face away from the light, Murieta took a pencil

from his vest pocket and, humming cheerfully, wrote across the bottom of the flyer, "I will give $10,000!" Then he signed it, "Joaquin." With a flourish of his hand, Murieta invited his friend to see what he had written.

Contreras heaved a heavy sigh. "I do not think the *gringo* governor will find this so funny." His solemn face widened with a wicked grin. Both men laughed.

"Or his rangers, either. *¿No?*" Murieta asked.

"*Vámonos muchacho*," Contreras said, clapping his friend on the back.

"*Si*," Murieta said. "After I have seen her."

Contreras scowled.

"You know I see her whenever I am down this way," Murieta said.

"*Si, si*," Contreras said. "But this woman, she . . . makes me uneasy."

"But, you fear no man," Murieta said with a chuckle.

Contreras hesitated. "Her skin is white. Her hair is white. Everything is white, except she has green eyes, like the emeralds," Contreras said. "It's . . ."

"What?"

Contreras shivered. "She's . . . different. And, I . . . I don't want to catch it."

"That's what you thought, all this time?" Murieta decided to have a little fun. "Listen to me, you will not catch it."

"How do you know?"

"Because your eyes are brown."

"*Por favor, jefe*," Contreras pleaded. "No jokes, eh? If you must see her, let us see her on the return."

"We won't come back this way."

"What is this power this woman has over you?"

"She's my friend."

Contreras looked defeated.

Murieta put his foot in his stirrup and a gust of wind blew a torn section of newspaper against his red-topped boot. He pulled it off and held it to the light from the Headquarters. The *Los Angeles Star.* He had not seen one in months. He folded it and put it inside his vest figuring to read it on the trail tomorrow.

The wide brims of their hats kept their faces in shadow as they rode through the village. Murieta counted a dozen bodies already lying in the road. Drunken Indians from the mission mostly. He knew that in the morning, the sheriff of the county would investigate anyone who had not moved. Anybody still alive would be taken to jail. Except the Indians. They would be sold off to the Yankee landowners as slaves for a week as their punishment. That was the Yankee way, ever since they took California from Mexico. Damn *gringos*! He was glad he was almost done with them.

Murieta paid no mind to a couple of men who staggered out of the Monte, arms around each other for support, singing drunkenly. Inside, someone strummed a frantic rhythm on a guitar while the patrons clapped to the beat, howling like coyotes.

Near the edge of town, away from the glow of the lights of the saloons, Murieta thought he saw a short *gringo* wearing a vicuna hat walking backwards dragging a body by its arms across the road. He could hear the *gringo*'s heavy breathing. Murieta and Contreras looked at each other and realized they were both seeing and hearing the same thing. They were about fifteen feet away when they saw the short *gringo* slip and fall on his ass, the jolt knocking his tall hat off and exposing his fiery orange-colored hair. Murieta held the reins tighter as his black horse Diablo snorted and bobbed his head, which startled the *gringo* who snatched up his hat and mumbled something but didn't look up. It sounded like, "Watch out, you damn greasers."

Murieta's hand flew to his Colt revolver, but he stopped himself from pulling it. He saw Contreras sliding his Bowie knife from the sheath at his side and took hold of his arm. "Not now," he whispered to him. "Not this one, *hombre*."

Murieta saw the sanguinary rage ebb in Contreras's eyes. He felt his own blood slowly cool, too. The fiery-haired *gringo* passed, but kept his head down, still muttering as he dragged the body away.

"Eight days is too long to go without washing my hands in *gringo* blood," Contreras said, sheathing his blade.

"Soon," Murieta said. "You'll have your fill." He knew there were plenty of farmers, gold hunters, the *gringo* governor's rangers, and county sheriffs for Contreras's pleasure. But not now. He had other business this night.

Off in the darkness in the direction the fiery-haired *gringo* had gone, the sound of a loud crash followed by an "Aw, shit!" drew Murieta's and Contreras's attention. They looked at each other and laughed.

"Clumsy *gringo pendejo*," Murieta said.

As they prodded their horses on, it occurred to Murieta that there was something familiar about that little *gringo*. Like he'd seen him before maybe, a long time ago. Then he got the feeling he'd be seeing him again. It was a strange feeling, one that made him wonder if he shouldn't have let Contreras cut the little *gringo*'s throat after all.

CHAPTER FIVE:
THE RANGER

Ambrose Quick was sitting in the sparse front parlor of Lucy Barton's house, a flat-roofed adobe on Macy Street in Los Angeles. His shock of blond hair was slicked down with oil that turned it darker and shiny in the lamplight. A sweeping blond moustache that curled up at the ends was the most pronounced feature of his slender sunburned face that was hot, not because of the warm evening, but with embarrassment. He could feel the rings of sweat that had formed in the underarms of his best white shirt, and he fought the urge to loosen his tie. Besides, Lucy still held both his clammy hands in hers.

"It would be my fondest wish to marry you, Ambrose," he heard Lucy say. "I love you, and I love you for asking me. I thought I was doomed to spinsterhood at nineteen, but—oh Ambrose, look at me!"

Quick jerked his head, startled. "I'm sorry, Lucy."

She was the most beautiful woman he had ever seen. He fell for her the moment he saw her walking out of Downey's Pharmacy four months ago, the day he arrived in town. She smiled at him, blue eyes twinkling, her flaxen hair a bouquet of ringlets—like now, but those ringlets framed a sad face. "You look like you're about to cry," he said.

"Well, I am! It's like a big ball of fret's inside me."

What Quick had anticipated being the most fulfilling moment of his twenty-six years, aside from last May when he was sworn in as a lieutenant in the rangers, had turned to disaster, like gold dust blown away in the wind.

"You know I want to marry you," Lucy said, "It's . . . I just wish daddy felt differently about you is all."

"He will, come next election."

"And I have all the faith in the world in you, Ambrose, but—"

"But what?"

"Well, did you have to tell people you'd make a better mayor than Don Antonio? I mean, most people around here love that man."

Quick detested Mayor Antonio Coronel, affectionately known by the populace as Don Antonio. The man had made a fortune in the gold fields up north a few years back and flaunted his wealth. He bought fancy clothes and owned a big house on the other side of town. He was adding more rooms to make it even bigger. The man also owned three thousand acres of grape vineyards and fruit orchards east of town. And there was a rumor that he'd gone in on a herd of beef cattle. Quick, who had been raised on a tiny patch of farmland in Ohio and came to California to find his pappy's grave, had been dirt poor all his life.

"Why couldn't you of said you'd be a councilman?" Lucy continued. "Get started there. You might've been one of them by now, probably. Mayor's not till next year."

"Lucy, you know my reasons. My mama and pappy always said public office is a public trust. And 'Don Antonio,' " he stretched the name out sarcastically, "is just using it to grab up more for himself, seems to me."

"But I'm thinking of us, of our future," she said and stood, wringing her hands. "You just need to show daddy you're not the full-time nobody he says—"

Shocked, her hand shot up and covered her mouth as Quick leapt to his feet, his face stern and hard.

"Oh, Ambrose, I didn't mean to say that," she said breathlessly. "It just slipped out. I'm so confused."

The front door opened, revealing Lucy's father, Sheriff James Barton, a rangy, pot-bellied fellow with a bushy goatee that ended abruptly in a straight across cut. Two heavy Colts, butts forward, hung about his waist. He also wore a leather vest with a shiny badge pinned to the pocket. When he spoke, his slow drawl betrayed his Missouri roots. "One thing I'll say for you, Ambrose, you ain't hard to find. Mayor's waitin' for us. You, me, an' the marshal got a job tonight."

Quick didn't move. He felt his own ball of emotion churning up his insides. And that ball was growing spikes.

"Go on, then," Barton said. "Kiss her g'night. We got important business."

"What kind of business?" Lucy asked, looking worried.

"All night business, I 'spect. Go to bed now, young lady. I'll be home when we're done."

Quick gave Lucy a peck on the cheek. She looked sickly.

Outside, Quick and Barton headed up Macy Street toward Alameda and the Bella Union Hotel. At two stories, it was the tallest building in town.

"What's so all important tonight the mayor's got to see us?" Quick asked stiffly.

Barton cocked his head. "All I know is he come racing back early from that Don del Valle's *fandango* sayin' Father Anacleto told him something urgent an' for us to get to his office pronto."

Quick hoped whatever it was wouldn't take long. Here he was, holding a position of authority and respect as a lieutenant in the California Rangers, and he just wanted to crawl into bed. This whole marriage proposal fiasco with Lucy had left him feeling deflated and bamboozled. At least it was quiet and Barton wasn't asking him a lot of questions. Then he noticed Barton looking at him out of the corner of his eye.

"I know it ain't none of my business," Barton said, "but I got the feelin' when I come into my house, you an' my Lucy was talkin' kind of serious."

Quick didn't answer. His jaw was set. Those spikes were digging into his craw now. He breathed loudly, forcing the air out of his nostrils.

"That's fine," Barton said. "Nothin' wrong with a man keeping his own counsel."

Quick's mind was a jumble. He didn't want to say anything for fear of what he might say and regret, but damn it, this was too much! He blurted it out. "You don't much approve of me. Why is that?"

"That's a good question, Ambrose," Barton said. "I've been kinda hopin' you'd get around to askin' me. It ain't I flat don't approve of you. It's just you ain't proved nothin' to me by way of bein' worthy of my daughter."

"Not worthy? I'm a lieutenant of the rangers."

"Yeah. Your Cap'n Hope told me when he mustered up your ranger company he made you a lieutenant cause he figured you had the makin's, like your pap. Said he served with him in the Mex war an' that your pap had a will of iron. It was too bad he got kilt at San Pascual. Brave man."

"If you want me dead, sheriff, just say so."

"Smart aleck remarks ain't goin' to help you none," Barton said, a little edge creeping into his voice. "Let me put it this way, Ambrose: You shot your mouth off about wantin' to be mayor. But all we heard you do is complain about how rich Don Antonio is. Fine. He's got money. That ain't no crime. And in case you didn't notice, the man's a dang hero to most folks hereabouts. Durin' the election he spoke to us Americans and *Californios* in town about how he was a loyal and true citizen of the United States, but—"

"Yeah, I know all that," Quick broke in. "I heard him stumping, mostly in Spanish—"

"Well, his English is like my Spanish. I don't know a lot of it."

"And I also heard he was on the Mexican side in that war we had with them."

"He never said he wasn't. But he's accepted we're all Americans now. Said we got to look forward. No goin' back. Folks put a lot of store in that kind of gumption. And most figure he ain't been doin' such a bad job mayorin'. But nobody's heard a peep out of you about what *you'd* do as mayor. Sure you talk fine, but you ain't proved nothin'.

"And let me tell you somethin' else. Before he went off searchin' for Joaquins, Cap'n Hope give you six good men and his trust to safeguard the citizens here, 'specially since we're kinda low on deputies right now. But what Cap'n Hope give you was a sacred responsibility. You know how important that is?"

"Now hold on," Quick said, the two men stopping in the middle of the street facing each other. "It's not my fault the captain took Quincy Masefield as his lieutenant on the hunt instead of me. Maybe it was luck of the draw that the rich mama's boy got to go, but I assure you, I was itching to go. I didn't ask to be left here."

"That's what I'm talkin' about, Ambrose. To you, bein' here is bein' left behind."

Quick was stumped. He didn't know what to say.

Barton grunted and headed toward the Bella Union where a banner over the entrance boasted "The Best Hotel South of San Francisco." Quick followed, his pride wounded and his feet dragging.

Quick sat on a hard chair in a corner in Don Antonio's first-floor office. Barton and Marshal A. S. Beard had taken the two comfortable-looking leather chairs in front of the big desk. He heard Beard saying something about the mayor having been at some *fandango* party thrown in his honor at *Señor* del Valle's home this evening and he'd be right in. Aside from Beard's pock-marked face, thinning hair, and the black coat he wore no matter how hot it got, Quick didn't know much about him as he had taken the job of marshal only two months earlier, about the same time Quick had joined the rangers. But Quick did know that the walls of the mayor's office were yellow and it smelled of fresh paint. He thought the color was ugly and the smell awful. He hated being there.

Mayor Don Antonio Coronel burst in through the door and went right to his large chair behind his desk. It made Quick sick to look at him all decked out in a gold-embroidered red outfit that Quick guessed he had made special just for del Valle's *fandango.* He didn't care what Barton said about the mayor. To him, Don Antonio was nothing but a rich, fancy-dressed blowhard who had no doubt bought his election.

As Don Antonio spoke little English and Quick had picked up enough Spanish to get by, he was just as glad Marshal Beard, who spoke Spanish fluently, was there to translate since Quick had no desire to say anything to the mayor. However, Don Antonio got Quick's immediate attention when Beard said the mayor said that he learned from an unimpeachable source that Joaquin Murieta is in Los Angeles this very night.

Quick saw Barton sit up and glance over at the marshal.

Beard said the mayor wants to move fast and act decisively.

Quick spoke up. "Joaquin's a job for the rangers."

"Mayor says he's decided differently," Beard translated.

"The rangers have the authority," Quick said.

"He says you can take it up with Captain Hope when he returns. Right now, he wants every available man on this."

Quick sniffed. First Lucy had turned down his proposal of marriage, then her father told him he wasn't good enough for his daughter as well as being a sad excuse for a ranger, and now this uppity mayor was dictating how he should do his job. Things just weren't working out tonight.

"Your honor," Barton said, "we've had reports in the past about Joaquins bein' in town, even this Murieta fella. Sometimes it don't amount to nothin' but hearsay. Just a couple weeks ago a woman down in San Pedro claimed he tried to rape her."

Beard translated and Don Antonio responded.

"He says he knows the woman and her family," Beard translated. "If she said he tried to do that, then he did."

"All right," Barton said. "There's also folks thought it was him they saw kill that deputy down from San Luis Obispo last year right on our plaza."

"I heard about that," Beard said, addressing the sheriff. "Witnesses claimed the murderer rode off on a black horse shouting 'I'm Joaquin' and 'Catch me if you can.' " Then he translated what they'd said for the mayor.

Quick smiled. He could tell from Don Antonio's expression that the mayor had been annoyed at being left out of Barton and Beard's little conversation. Then from his tone in response to what Beard had told him, it seemed clear to Quick that Don Antonio was losing his patience.

Beard apologized to the mayor and then translated his response. "He says he doesn't care about what happened last year. He says Joaquin is a menace and he was seen in town this night by Father Anacleto. He says the padre swore it to him, and he's never known him to lie."

The words shot out of Quick's mouth before he had time to think.

"That may be," he said, "but I'm not so sure about his being right."

It pleased Quick considerably when Don Antonio gave him an irritated look after Beard translated.

"Thing is," Quick continued, "the good father is part Mexican, and every Mexican in the state's considered a confederate of these Joaquins."

Beard gave Quick a sharp look then translated. Furious, Don Antonio slammed his hands on his desk and spoke.

"Careful now you," Beard warned Quick. "Mayor tells me to remind you that he is of Mexican heritage but holds no sympathy whatever for these bandits." He cleared his throat. "And speaking from my postion as marshal, I'd suggest you apologize to his honor for your remark about Mexicans." He shifted in his chair. "The mayor also says how dare you imply Father Anacleto is a liar."

Quick wasn't about to apologize. "Tell him I'm not saying the priest is lying. All I am saying is, if we're hearing about this, chances are whichever Joaquin may be around here likely realizes we know by now."

"The boy's got a point," Beard said to Barton. "Word in these parts got more legs than a horse. He could've lit out by now." Then he translated it all for Don Antonio.

Quick took a dim view of being called a "boy" but decided to let it pass since he could tell Don Antonio was getting more riled up. Maybe he'll bust a vein or something and keel over and die right here.

"He says his orders will be carried out," Beard said. "He wants this so-called Robin Hood of El Dorado captured. He says he's suspected of trying to rape women. He is suspected of murder. All of it right here in our own jurisdiction. Mayor says the law applies to all."

Quick saw Barton turn and give him a look.

Then Don Antonio spoke again.

"Jim," the marshall said to Barton, "he wants to know how many killings there've been in the county so far this year."

"About thirty, I'd say."

Beard translated and the mayor asked him a question.

"About as many in town, your honor," Beard replied. "Maybe a few more."

Don Antonio stood up and Quick and the others followed. The sternness in his voice was not lost on Quick.

Beard translated. "He's dead serious, so listen tight. He says Los Angeles will not be a Bowie knife society and our citizens will not live under revolver rule. He says this damn bandit has declared war, and we will respond to it in kind. Joaquin Murieta is said to be right here this very night. Mayor says sweep the town. Find him!"

Quick was excited by the prospect of finding a Joaquin, but disappointed Don Antonio had not exploded like a Roman candle.

Outside on the front steps of the Bella Union, Quick was digging a coin out of his pocket. He wanted to tell Sheriff Barton and Marshal Beard, who were standing there with him, what he believed to be the real reason Don Antonio wanted the town swept for Murieta, namely, to protect that herd of cattle Quick was certain the mayor had invested in. Just last month four hundred head of Johnny Blinn's cattle had been rustled and two of his prize bulls were killed, their ears and gonads cut off. Word had been a Joaquin had done it. The plain truth was Quick didn't like Don Antonio and didn't trust him. But he was also certain that the sheriff and the marshal didn't want to hear it and more than likely didn't care what he thought.

Holding the silver piece in his hand, Quick said, "How do you want to do this?"

"Winner's choice," Barton said and then looked at the marshal. "All right by you?"

"Fine," Beard said.

"Call it in the air," Quick said and flipped the coin up with his thumb.

"Heads," Barton said.

The coin landed on the stair and Quick peered down at it. Things just weren't working out for him tonight.

Chapter Six:
The Angel

Ana Benitez was eating her supper when she saw Murieta standing in her doorway. Her eyes filled with tears of happiness. She shuffled over to him, pulled his face down to hers with shaking hands and kissed his cheeks, first the right, then the left.

"My Joaquin, you have come, just as you said you would," she said, her voice light and filled with comfort. "Look at you. You have grown the little goat's beard on your chin."

Then she saw Contreras standing in the shadows behind him and added with a hint of sarcasm, "And I see you have brought El Bruto with you."

Contreras, his head down and holding his hat with both hands in front of him, gave a low grunt.

"Come in, come in, *por favor*. Sit down. I have beef stew in the kettle." Lighting a *cigarillo*, Ana moved toward the fireplace with halting, aching steps, her feet bare and puffy. She knew she had gotten worse since Murieta had seen her last. Casting a glance back toward him, she saw the concern on his face.

"It's no use, Joaquin," she said. "The saint does not smile or cry for me."

"Yes, I know," he said.

She heard the disappointment in his voice.

After ladling stew into two bowls, she took them over to her guests at the table, noticing that Murieta and Contreras sat angled so that each faced the doorway. After putting the bowls down, she sat and moved a burning candle sitting in a holder in the middle of the table closer to her, out of the way of the two hungry men.

"Oh, I forgot, there is bread." She started to get up.

"I can get it," Murieta said, motioning for her to stay.

"It's on the shelf, wrapped in the cloth," she said, pointing to the spot near the fireplace.

As Murieta sat back down, tearing off a hunk of bread and then offering the round loaf to Contreras, Ana pushed herself up off her chair, ashes falling from the *cigarrillo* in her mouth onto her white dress.

"I have something to show you."

She shuffled over to her shrine and picked up a red clay vase holding a few cut yellow marigolds. Taking the marigolds out, she placed them on the altar. She stole a glance at the portrait of the saint hanging on the wall of her shrine. There was no change on the face of St. Francis. Smiling, she gently touched the edge of the portrait with her white fingers and prayed he would smile on her friend this time.

"Do you remember this vase?" she asked as she sat back down.

Murieta set down his spoon and took the vase from her quivering hand. "I gave this to you the last time I was here," he said.

"I was so grateful, you know. Look at it closely." Ana pushed the candle toward him, revealing the thin irregular lines running all over the brown clay.

"It looks like it was broken," Murieta said, "but I can't feel any breaks."

He handed it to Contreras who scratched at it with his thumbnail and frowned.

"You're right," Ana said. "It slipped out of my hands a few days ago when I was changing the flowers. I was very upset. I picked up all the pieces and laid them on the altar. I got down on my knees and prayed to my saint. I told him it was a gift from you and I would miss putting flowers in it very much." She smiled. "The next morning, it was mended as you see it."

Contreras nearly dropped the vase, putting it down quickly, like it had burned his fingers.

"Be careful with that, you," Ana scolded him.

She tossed the end of her *cigarrillo* onto the floor, placed another between her lips, and leaned toward the candle to light it. She noticed Murieta and Contreras shoot each other perplexed looks.

"If the saint will mend a vase, he should mend you," Murieta said.

"He knows best," she said with a short wave of her hand. "This flesh is my cross that will take me to heaven."

Ana saw Contreras look over toward the pot simmering on the fireplace.

"Help yourself, El Bruto," she said. "If you must do murder, do it on a full belly."

Contreras grunted his thanks, went to the pot, and scooped stew into his bowl.

"You too, Joaquin," she said.

While they ate, she returned the vase and marigolds to the shrine. The face of her saint remained unchanged when she looked at it. She reminded herself that for some the saint took a long while to respond. Infirmed or healthy made no difference. But for her Joaquin and those he brought with him to her house, the saint had never offered her a sign. She thought it odd, but her Joaquin always returned, always safe. Unharmed. Her Joaquin.

As she turned to go back to the table, she felt a tight pang in her chest, like something clutched and squeezed her heart. It struck, faded, and then was gone. Her *cigarrillo* fell from her mouth. She leaned against the shrine, catching her breath, her eyes closed tight. At once, Murieta was at her side.

She took a shallow breath. "I'm . . . Just let me sit down."

She felt his arm around her, helping her back to the table where she saw Contreras steadying her chair. Once she sat, she heard Murieta tell Contreras to get some water.

After a few minutes and several sips from the cup, she nodded she was all right. She looked at Murieta. "This is the last time I will see you. Yes?"

"Don't worry about that now."

She waved away his concern. "I'm going to be fine. But I must know. *Digame, por favor.*"

"It's not important," Murieta said.

"But it's true?"

"Si. Es verdad."

"Because you are going away. Back to Mexico?"

Murieta nodded. "Very soon."

"What do you mean, soon?" she asked. "You're not going now?"

"We're going north, to Arroyo Cantoova first."

"Where's that? What for?"

"It's near Salinas. It's where I have all my money hidden."

"Why didn't you bring it with you?" she asked crossly. "Mexico is just a few days' ride from here."

He smiled and she calmed down.

"I only decided to go home a few days ago," he said.

She sighed. "Of course. Forgive my anger. I'm glad you're going home. It's time." She made a little sideways jerk with her head toward Contreras. "You will take this one, too?"

"If he'll come."

"I will go," Contreras said and slurped another spoonful of stew into his mouth. "I follow my *jefe.*"

"But I know you," she said to Contreras. "When you get the urge, you'll cross the border and come after *gringos*. Don't look

65

at me like that, so surprised. It's the truth. *¿No?*"

Contreras sniffed, shrugged, and said, "*Sí.* It's the truth."

"But you will stay in Mexico?" she said, looking back at Murieta.

"I've had enough of the Yankee *gringos*. I have their money. Some of it I gave to our people here. You know they had no chance, like me. I gave them a little of what the Yankees refuse to give them."

"So the Yankees have paid enough to suit you?" Ana asked.

"They won't forget me. I taught them about loss."

"And for what they did to Rosita?"

After a moment, Murieta said, "It's time for me to go to her."

She was pleased and relieved to hear him say it. This vengeance of his had taken its toll. It was in his eyes when she looked at them. She knew a deadly shadow had clutched his soul for a long time. Maybe now he would find his way home.

"We better go," Murieta said.

"The *gringo* eyes are everywhere," Contreras said.

"Don't worry," she said. "When you sent word you would be here tonight, I told my friend, Father Anacleto. He's the priest in Los Angeles. He promised to keep the *Angeleno* sheriff away. He told me he would have to tell a lie, but he was sure God would understand."

Her eye caught the portrait. Tears were on the face of the saint! Only a few, but they were there. She fought to keep her hands from flying to her mouth. They have to leave, she thought. Go right away. Flee, my Joaquin. Sadness welled up inside her. Something was coming for them. She could feel it, dark, foul, and bloody.

"But maybe you're right," she said, trying to still the tremor in her voice. "You should go."

At the door, she put her arms around Murieta and kissed his

cheek. Then she hugged Contreras. She knew he had always felt uncomfortable around her so she wasn't surprised when he tried to pull away.

"I will ask my saint to watch over both of you on your journey," she said, her voice almost cracking

"Thank you, my friend. For everything," Murieta said.

"Wait, wait," she cried, flustered like a schoolgirl. She went to her bedchamber and got her Bible from her bedside. Pressing it into Murieta's hand, she said, "Please take it. Tomorrow is Sunday. You should read from it."

"Adios, mi Angel," he said.

She kissed his cheek again. "St. Francis will keep you well. I will see to it." The lie nearly caught in her throat. She hoped Murieta and Contreras hadn't seen the fear in her eyes. Hiding the sad truth—that it was too late for them—tore at her heart.

After watching them ride into the darkness, she tottered to the altar and looked at the portrait again. Her eyes grew wide in horror. A moan, sad and desperate, escaped her white lips. Tears flowed down the portrait and dripped onto the altar forming small puddles. Her saint was weeping.

Murieta and Contreras followed a thin glistening stream that ran down the mountain above San Gabriel. The night had started cooling, but Murieta hardly noticed. He was thinking about Ana. Something about her good-bye felt wrong. She seemed afraid, fearful somehow. Like the way she trembled when she kissed him, saying she'd ask her saint to keep them safe. An uneasy feeling swept over him. A long shiver shot through his body, making him jump in the saddle.

"Ah, the cold, she comes," Contreras said. "But the whiskey will keep her away from you, *jefe.*"

"No whiskey, Feliz," Murieta said distractedly.

"Just one," Contreras said. *"Por favor."*

"We have a long way to go," Murieta said, annoyed. He was still concerned about Ana, and all that there was yet to do. Besides, he knew Contreras was never satisfied with one drink and that meant more drinks and he would get meaner and then kill someone and there was just no time for it.

They rode on and Murieta knew Contreras was sulking. His head was down and he was talking to himself.

"When the *jefe* refuses to stop for the whiskey, it is to punish me," Contreras grumbled.

As they neared the mission church, Murieta breathed in the sweet aroma of orange buds wafting though the night air. Ana had told him about the large orange grove planted by the early Franciscan friars. He was thinking that the *gringos* didn't deserve to breathe this same honeyed scent when he caught sight of the old Mexican with long gray hair and a thin beard sitting cross-legged on a broken section of wall near the entrance to the mission cemetery. The old man had on the loose white shirt and pants so many Mexican peasants wore, the same kind Murieta remembered he wore in his village in Mexico.

Murieta glanced back at Contreras to make sure he wasn't pulling his revolver to shoot the man. But Contreras appeared to still be pouting. He didn't even look up.

Murieta nodded at the old Mexican as he passed.

"*Vaya con Dios,* Joaquin," the old man said.

Reining in his horse, Diablo, Murieta turned. How does he know my name? Who is he?

The old man was looking right at him, rocking back and forth on his perch, grinning, toothless.

Suddenly, Murieta felt cold, the bitter kind that went through his bones, yet there was no wind. He took his red serape from behind his saddle and put it on, sticking his head through the opening. Then he realized that the old man was gone, his perch empty. Glancing about, he didn't see him anywhere. He was about to ask Contreras if he'd seen the man, but he had already passed him, head down, still in his sulk.

Murieta turned to follow and saw the mission church, ghostly in the partial moonlight. He stared at its long palisade wall, the six bells hanging in three rows of open arches sloping upward and crowned at the peak with a wooden cross. He had not stepped inside it or any church since the night he had asked the padre to hear his confession. Though raised to revere every church as the house of God, a holy place, he saw only a silent thing. Dead. Desolate.

Murieta and Contreras crossed the stream. Not far ahead was a lone, tall sycamore tree. A pool formed nearby and they stopped to water the horses. Murieta knew that soon Contreras would get tired or hungry again, and thankfully forget about whiskey and stop sulking.

"Did you see the old man back there?" Murieta asked, trying to sound unconcerned as he filled his water bag, the bubbles breaking softly on the surface of the stream.

"What old man?" Contreras asked, standing at the edge of the stream, water bag in hand, and pointing toward the sycamore tree. "All I see is a body over there."

Murieta saw it, lying facedown only a few feet away near the black shadows of the sycamore. Going over to it, Murieta gave it a nudge with his boot. There was a low moan. Murieta bent down and rolled the body over. The face was bruised and bloodied. The man was unconscious.

"This *gringo*'s been in a fight," Murieta said. "His head's going to hurt when he wakes up."

Contreras grinned and pulled out his Bowie.

"No. Put it away."

"Check his pockets then."

Turning out the man's pockets, Murieta found nothing.

"Beat up and no money. He's had enough tonight."

Contreras grunted.

It occurred to Murieta that this unconscious man's clothes looked familiar, even though they were plain enough. And maybe his size, too. Looking back along the stream, he saw what looked like drag marks in the grass and dirt, but they didn't go very far. That *gringo* with the fiery orange hair was the only man he had seen dragging a body this night. This was probably it. He must've hauled him all the way from town. Why do that? Murieta wondered. Better yet, why waste the time?

"Let's go," he said, heading back to his horse.

"What old man did you see?"

Murieta knew he'd seen and heard that old shirtless man. Maybe the man was *loco*. But just thinking about him brought back that cold feeling in his bones. Only colder now. Suddenly he didn't feel like explaining it. *"Nada,"* he said, shaking his head.

They mounted their horses and rode away, following the stream.

CHAPTER SEVEN:
THE RAID

Quick knew when he lost the coin toss that Barton and Beard would choose to search the quieter, safer north side of Los Angeles where most families lived, as well as the vineyards, orchards, and outlying homes. That left him with *Calle de los Negros,* the most raucous precinct in town. Shrewd gamblers, besotted drunkards, and would-be assassins from around the state congregated on that dusty track of an alley comprised solely of saloons and gambling parlors. With any luck, he'd capture this Joaquin Murieta. That would sure turn this night around.

Pacing in front of the Ranger Barracks on Requena, Quick snapped his gold pocket watch shut, the only remembrance he had from his father. It was ten past midnight. The sweep of the town was to begin at 12:30. Looking down Los Angeles Street he saw a crowd gathering between the Coronel Building and the plaza at the entrance to *Calle de los Negros.* It looked like they were watching him, waiting for him. Did they already know about the raid?

Irritating as that possibility was, Quick's real concern at the moment was that only five of his rangers had reported in. Ezra Doyle, Sam Prizer, and Horace Wheat were already at the barracks when he went looking. He'd seen Charley Biggs earlier and sent him off to the El Dorado Saloon to bring back Uriah Clegg. That's where Clegg could usually be found. Charley had found him and brought him to the barracks where a pot of cof-

71

fee was waiting to help sober him up. Then Quick had sent Charley back out to see if he could locate Ned Needle. That had been nearly half an hour ago.

Ned Needle could make out the faint lights of Los Angeles less than a quarter mile off and gave his horse a kick. Once he got to town he might get a seat in a poker game in one of the parlors on Nigger Alley. He couldn't figure out why they still called it *Calle de los Negroes* since California didn't belong to the greasers any more.

Or maybe he'd have a few drinks at the El Dorado Saloon. He could use a couple of shots of good whiskey seeing he had whipped the tar out of Abel Tyner earlier. It was bad enough that greaser-loving sheriff's deputy Tyner was married to a Mex over in San Gabriel, but he'd also had the gall to try getting sweet on Ned's girl Clarissa. Even if Clarissa was one of Screaming Addie's whores, she was the one Ned wanted and he sure as shit wasn't going to allow anybody that was rutting around regular with a Mex to go poking his girl.

Yes sir, he'd given Abel just what he deserved all right. Took his money to boot. Three dollars was three dollars. And Abel never saw it coming. Mother Needle taught her boy well. It's a hard world and fighting fair is bullshit, she used to tell him.

Needle wished things had gone a little differently earlier over in San Gabriel. If he'd been a hair faster dragging Abel's body through town and over to the stream near the mission, then those two greaser bastards on horseback wouldn't've been able to sneak up on him. That's right, they nearly ran him down. That's how he remembered it. And they made him trip and fall is what they did. Falling in the street on his ass in front of greasers wasn't right and it wasn't proper. Any other time he'd've gutted them like fish. Next time that's just what he'd do all right.

Since it was Saturday night, he wondered if the rangers might be called out to break up a fight somewhere. Playing poker, drinking, or fighting. Any one of those sounded good to him after the night he'd had over in San Gabriel.

Quick pushed open the door to the barracks and reminded his men to check their guns. "We don't want any misfires tonight."

"Right, Lieutenant," Ezra Doyle answered. "Gunfire on *Calle de los Negros* on a Saturday night's as sure as fleas on my sister's cats."

Sometimes Quick wasn't sure if Doyle was just having a little fun or pushing it a little further. He had that cocky streak about him. But that aside, Quick had witnessed more than once that Doyle knew how to handle horses and a rope better than most of the hired hands hereabouts, and that made him an asset to the rangers.

Turning back toward the street, Quick saw Charley coming up Requena, alone.

"I looked everywhere I could think of but couldn't find any sign of Ned Needle," Charley said.

"Go on inside and get ready," Quick said.

"We after a bandit tonight, Lieutenant?" Charley asked.

"Going to do our best."

Quick liked Charley. At seventeen, Charley had been sworn in as the youngest ranger. Charley had worked in his uncle's barbershop, and they were the first two Negroes living in Los Angeles. Quick remembered Charley saying he didn't care for barbering, that he had ambitions and the desire to make something better of himself. Quick appreciated that. It sounded just like him.

Through the open barracks door, Quick listened to the men talk.

"Hey Charley," Doyle said, "no luck finding Needle?"

"Nope," Charley answered.

"Well, with any luck some gambler's shot him dead," Horace Wheat said. "I swear I know he tries cheating at cards."

"I've told him he better watch that," Doyle said. "But he told me to shut it and mind my own business. Don't think he likes me."

"He doesn't like anybody much," Wheat said.

"I heard there's a whore over in San Gabriel he likes," Sam Prizer said.

"Her name's Clarissa," Wheat said, "and I hear tell she's fond of little chicken-brained men."

Quick heard the others laugh. Wheat's comment made him chuckle, too. Wheat was a good man, but there was something about him that Quick couldn't pin down. He had a full beard and a bald head, round as a billiard. While it struck some as queer that a man would shave his head, it was Wheat's haziness about his past line of work that had struck Quick as odd.

"Hurry up in there!" Quick hollered through the door. "We got ten minutes. Uriah Clegg! You sober yet?"

The gruff ornery voice of Clegg roared, "I'm getting there, damn it! Give me some more of that coffee somebody."

Quick thought highly of the famous Uriah Clegg. At age forty-eight, he was the oldest and most experienced of the rangers. He was also something of a giant, being over six and a half feet tall and barrel thick. Quick knew Clegg was the best tracker in the state, and before that, probably the best tracker in the U.S. Army. His fame was the result of having amputated his own leg below the knee after being hit by a musket ball while chasing renegade Cherokees deep in the hills of north Georgia. The problem with Clegg wasn't the loss of the leg, though, but keeping him sober.

Checking his watch again, Quick glanced at the growing crowd and cursed Mayor Don Antonio, the day he was born, and everything he owned. Then he saw Orrin Appleyard come out of the crowd and lope toward him. Orrin was thin as a reed and seemed taller than he was because of the cocked top hat he wore. Bespectacled and carrying a pencil behind his ear, Orrin was the reporter for the *Los Angeles Star*.

Having an ally on a newspaper would be a good thing for a man thinking of running for public office. Cultivate alliances, Quick thought. Make good impressions. He adjusted his black hat, brushed the gold embroidery on the sleeves of his blue uniform coat, and straightened the red Mexican sash around his middle.

"Hello, Ambrose," Orrin called as he got closer.

"Orrin," Quick said. "Big crowd down there."

Orrin nodded his head. "They're waiting for you."

"Now why would they be doing that?" Quick asked, trying to make light of it.

"Because the word's out," Orrin said. "His honor, the mayor, told me that you, the sheriff, and the marshal are after a bad bandit."

That son-of-a-bitch Don Antonio, Quick thought.

"When did he tell you that?" he asked.

"Little while ago." Orrin said. "He's sipping juleps in the back room over at the Bear Flag Club with my boss."

"Alone, was he?"

Orrin snorted. "He's drinking with my boss. There's a reason he knows everything that goes on in this town. He's got friends everywhere."

"So what did 'Don Antonio' tell you?"

Orrin opened his notepad. "I quote his honor: 'It affords little amusement to me and our citizens that more than sixty murders have already been committed in our district this year, each perpetrated with impunity. And every murder and every other criminal outrage has been attributed to the nefarious

Joaquin. Always Joaquin! This will be put to a stop tonight.' "

Quick was livid, but held it in check. "Then it's no surprise what we're doing here."

"Looks like," Orrin said.

"Well let me tell you something, off the record," Quick said. "That backstabbing, double-talking bastard mayor ordered Barton and Beard and me not to leak a word about who we're after and then he runs his mouth. What the hell is he thinking?"

"Look at it this way," Orrin suggested, "if you don't catch Joaquin, what the mayor said is just another speech on crime, and this is just another Saturday night raid in *los Negros.*"

Disgusted, Quick shook his head. "Guess we'll have to watch for suspicious characters then."

"Uh-huh." Orrin flipped to a blank page in his notepad and took the pencil from behind his ear. "Now let's say you do catch him, your stock will go up considerably. Gratitude, fame, the governor's reward. You'll be known as the man who got Joaquin."

"What are you driving at, Orrin?"

"Whig or Democrat?"

"What?"

"Your run for mayor. Whig ticket or Democrat? Election's less than a year off."

Sounds like somebody's taking me seriously anyway, Quick thought. Things were starting to look up some. Maybe this night wouldn't be a complete bust.

At that moment the rangers stepped outside in their plain short blue coats, revolvers, and Bowie knives stuck inside the red sashes they wore around their middles. Quick was dismayed to notice that Clegg—the now sober, white-whiskered, red-eyed giant—could not button his coat due to his thick girth. Three missing brass buttons were torn testimony to an earlier attempt.

"Gentlemen," Quick said, "you know Orrin Appleyard of the *Star*."

Short, chunky Sam Prizer, with ears that stuck out like handles on a cup, surprised Quick and the others by speaking up, something he hardly ever did, being kind of mousy. He pulled off his battered hat and asked, "You putting our names in the paper there, Mr. Appleyard?"

"All depends," Orrin said.

"I'd, I'd sure like that," Prizer said. "Seeing my name in the paper. My wife, she'd be right proud. She'd make sure everybody who came in her millinery shop saw it."

"Tonight we might all be famous, Sam," Quick said. "Men, Joaquin Murieta is said to be somewhere in town this night."

His men looked from one to the other, some excited and some scared, Quick could tell.

"If he's in *Calle de los Negros*, we will find him," Quick continued. "If he's captured, the citizens of Los Angeles and the rest of the state will breathe easier and thank us dearly for it."

"Hey!" Ned Needle said as he came around the corner of the barracks. "What's everybody dressed up for? Nobody told me about nothing."

Quick didn't care much for Needle, not because he looked ridiculous with that wild orange hair sticking out from under his tall vicuna hat, but because he was a nasty, whiny little shit. However, he was a ranger and Quick needed all six of his men this night.

"Glad you showed up," Quick said. "You got no time to get into uniform. That revolver of yours loaded?"

"Always." Needle patted the Colt he carried stuck in his belt.

"You may need it," Quick said and finished his address. "The rangers are the remedy, the remedy for freebooters, brigands, and assassins." He liked the sound of that. Orrin was grinning, and writing fast.

"Who we going after? A greaser?" Needle asked cheerfully.

"Joaquin Murieta," Quick said.

"The Joaquin!" Needle shouted.

"Damn it, Needle!" Quick said.

"Shut your trap," Wheat said to Needle at the same instant.

"Yes, Lieutenant," Needle said and then shot a look at Wheat. "I don't like you, Wheat. Never have."

"So what," Wheat said.

"That's enough!" Quick said. "We got a job to do and a man to find."

He found more encouragement when he saw, out the corner of his eye, Orrin nodding his head.

"We have word that Joaquin Murieta was seen in town tonight," Quick said. "Our orders are to find him."

"Sorry, Lieutenant, but how're we supposed to know it's him?" Doyle asked. "I mean, if it's some Mex breaking the law it might be him, but what if he ain't doing nothing?"

"You know what looks suspicious," Quick said. "Somebody acting guilty, like they're hiding something, you question them. They get surly or try to run, arrest them and take them to the jail. It's a Mexican we're after. I expect you all know who the regulars are in the saloons and gambling houses. I'm talking about the *Californios*. You know who they are, so leave them be. It's the ones you don't know you want to talk to."

"Ah, Lieutenant," Clegg said, "I think maybe we got a problem."

"What's that?"

"Well, look," Clegg said and pointed at the crowd. "They know we're coming. If a Joaquin was here, he's more than likely skedaddled by now."

Quick looked at each of his men and could see a similar conclusion on each of their faces, much like his, he guessed, when he proposed that same concern to Don Antonio earlier.

But he had his orders, even if they came from a dumb bastard like the mayor. However, Quick was determined to make the best of this. He would not be accused of shirking his duty, and maybe, just maybe, he'd even get lucky.

"It might be that Joaquin has already gone," Quick said, "but there's always that chance he hasn't and he wants to see what we're made of."

"We'll show him, then," Charley said.

"Exactly," Quick said. "Vigilance. Keep your heads. And your eyes peeled and ears open."

Quick told Clegg and Charley to check rooftops. "Charley'll get on the roof and Clegg, you keep an eye out for anybody climbing down. Prizer, you and Needle start with Gibson's Gambling House. Wheat and Doyle, you'll come with me to Taos' Bar. We'll work our way down *los Negros.*"

As they formed a phalanx, Needle chortled, "Nigger Alley, here we come."

"I don't care for that name," Quick said.

"Hell, Lieutenant, that's what everybody calls it," Needle said.

"I don't, and I don't want to hear it again," Quick said, taking the point of the phalanx.

"Well, ain't you the one," Needle muttered.

Quick ignored the taunt in Needle's tone. He had more pressing matters to attend to now. He checked the Colt .44 Navy revolver he carried. Orrin hurried to his side.

"What's your answer, Ambrose?"

"About what?"

"Running for mayor."

"I'll tell you after I catch Joaquin."

"I'm coming with you."

"I expected you would."

Quick led the rangers down the street with Orrin following,

careful to skirt and step over the *zanjas,* the water ditches used for drinking and various household purposes. The crowd appeared to be quieting down to Quick, like they were impressed he was coming. As he got closer, it looked like the crowd was parting for him. He was nearly to Taos' Bar when he slipped and fell on his ass into a *zanja* with a loud splash. The waiting spectators bellowed and applauded. Getting to his feet, embarrassed and angry with himself, Quick saw Orrin jotting in his notepad.

Bad as this humiliation was and as wet as he was, Quick refused to turn tail.

Entering Taos' Bar, Quick was greeted with jeers and a few shouts of "Welcome to Nigger Alley, boys!"

Quick had Wheat and Doyle peer under monte tables and check behind the bar counter. Every back room, alcove, and storage bin was investigated.

"Free drinks if you find a Joaquin!" the barkeep shouted.

A loud cheer of approval and shouts of raucous encouragement from the patrons in the bar followed, but Quick did his best to ignore it. And he wasn't surprised when nobody offered anything free if a Joaquin wasn't found.

Quick only found one Mexican, a boy really, no older than Charley, slumped over a table. And Quick knew that the Mexican was no more a Joaquin than he was, but the boy was so liquored up he couldn't stand on his own feet, so Quick had Doyle take him to jail for drunk and disorderly.

Clegg and Charley reported to Quick they were finding nothing suspicious on the rooftops, and Prizer and Needle weren't fairing any better.

By the time Quick got to the Sonoran at the other end of *los Negros,* he was greeted with choruses of "The Star Spangled Banner" drunkenly blared when he appeared in the doorway. But he carried on with the sweep, "Oh, say can you see" echoing in his ears, and Orrin close by taking notes.

Nothing's going right for me, Quick thought.

A few hours later, Orrin sat at his desk at the newspaper office and wrote his story for the following Saturday's issue. His lead stated that while the rangers' search resulted in no sign of Joaquin Murieta, "the iron fiber of Lieutenant Ambrose Quick of the California Rangers was tested in the fiery caldron of humiliation, resulting, in our opinion, in a pernicious scalding." The search, Orrin wrote, "opened with an unrehearsed pratfall soon followed by patriotic singing." He concluded his story, stating, "To call the night's festivities disappointing and farcical would be neither unkind nor unfair. Indeed, they were a far cry from the appearance last Christmas at the Merced Theater of the traveling prestidigitator, the Great McKinney."

In his bare room in the barracks, Quick laid on his bed, his uniform coat tossed over a chair, his arm across his eyes. He didn't know where the other rangers were and didn't care. It was after four o'clock in the morning. And somewhere outside in the dark a jackass was braying.

"That's just perfect," Quick said.

He knew he'd done his duty. He'd stuck with it through the night. And he was absolutely certain he was now the town laughingstock. From the moment he fell in the *zanja* he knew he had looked like a damn fool. He was pretty certain nobody was laughing at Sheriff Barton and Marshal Beard when they took their men through the north part of town. And he had no doubt Don Antonio was praising the sheriff and the marshal for jobs well done, and calling him a sapheaded snot-nosed kid.

A few more weeks and the rangers would be disbanded. Then what would he do? Would they make him give back his horse? If he had to give the horse back, he wouldn't even have a pot to piss in. And where would that leave him with Lucy? She'd have nothing more to do with him then. Her daddy would be right. He really would be a full-time nobody!

"Oh, God," he whispered and rubbed his eyes.

Before leaving Los Angeles, Captain Hope had told him to safeguard the citizens. He'd done that by helping the sheriff and marshal bring in a few card cheats and disorderly drunks in the last week, but there was no big prize, no Joaquin Murieta. And there was no prestige or glory or future vote-getting in ordinary arrests.

Quick opened his eyes. The room was still dark. He felt numb and tired. Lucy, fame, being mayor, his whole future was all slipping away. He was going to be nothing, and have nothing. His pappy was remembered all right, a man of iron will, a brave man, killed at the battle of San Pascual. But he, Ambrose Quick, would always be known as the fool who fell in the *zanja*. How could it get any worse?

CHAPTER EIGHT:
THE BODY

Addie Moody heard the woman yelling and crying. She heard words like *muerta* and *dios* and let out a groan. She opened one eye and looked through the crack in the window shutter. The sun had barely come up.

It was bad enough Addie had to contend with the cramps of the female curse that had left her curled up on Roy Bean's bed in the back room of the Headquarters saloon on a Saturday night—a busy business night for the Headquarters and Addie's girls—but to be jarred awake at the crack of dawn Sunday morning by some hysterical Mexican woman was clawing at her nerves and by damn she was going to put a stop to it right now!

Pulling on a dark skirt and grabbing a dirty white blouse, Addie charged out of the back room and into the saloon. Buttoning up her blouse, she saw Roy Bean flinging open the double wooden front doors.

"Shut the hell up!" Bean shouted.

Reaching behind the bar counter, Addie grabbed the heavy Colt's Dragoon Bean kept there in case a customer got out of hand. She heard the woman outside scream.

"¡Mi esposo es muerto!"

"I'm putting her out of my misery," Addie said. Getting to the open doors she raised the Dragoon. A second later Bean snatched it out of her hand.

"Give me that back," Addie snapped at him.

"Hell I will," Bean said as he shoved the revolver inside his

83

belt. "I don't like Mexicans either, but I ain't lettin' you plug no woman. Damn, my head hurts."

"*¡Madre de Dios! ¡Ayúdame!*" the woman cried.

"Well do something to stop that God-awful screaming!" Addie said.

"Dry up and let a body get some rest!"

Addie turned and saw Phoebe, one of her girls, lying on top of the bar, naked to the waist, her arms and legs drooping over the sides. Phoebe turned her head away.

Going out on the veranda, Addie's vexations slowed as she halted like she'd walked into a wall. She could feel the heat was already heavy and wiped sweaty hair off her forehead. Bean stopped next to her, a disgusted look on his face.

Putting her hand up to shade her eyes, Addie recognized Guadalupe Tyner, round and moon-faced, flailing her arms with strands of long black hair clinging to her tear-streaked cheeks. Her worn white nightgown showed fresh grass and dirt stains at the knees. One end of her black shawl had slipped from her shoulder, trailing behind her as she stood barefoot in the street, sobbing.

"Thank God, she shut up," Bean said. "What the hell was she hollerin'?"

"*Mi esposo,*" Addie said, rubbing her eyes, adjusting to the brightness. She knew enough Spanish to know that meant my husband. Glancing up and down the road, she hoped to see Guadalupe's husband, Abel, coming along to take her away.

Guadalupe let out another screeching wail.

"Go shut her up!" Addie shouted at Bean as Joe Singer came out of his trading post across from the Headquarters. Dressed in his shirtsleeves with half his face covered in shaving soap, his graying hair wet, he was yelling something in Spanish and waving his hands at Guadalupe.

Addie watched as Singer started toward Guadalupe, who fell

down in a heap, crying in the dusty road.

Singer tried to help Guadalupe to her feet but was having trouble. Next thing Addie knew he was motioning to her and Bean to help him.

"Damn it," Addie whispered, wishing now she hadn't come outside. Turning to Bean, she said, "Don't stand there gawking. Come on."

When Addie and Bean reached Singer, he had a hold of Guadalupe's arm and was trying to get her out of the street. She started screaming again about her *esposo* and pointing frantically toward the mission.

"Take her other arm and let's get her over to my place," Singer said.

Bean tried to grab Guadalupe's arm but she was flailing it around so much she accidentally smacked him in the face and he stepped back.

Addie managed to get a hold on her and she and Singer got the sobbing woman over to the shade of his store veranda. Singer pulled a chair over for Guadalupe to sit while Addie got one for him.

"Get her some water," Singer said as he sat down. "There's a pitcher sitting on the counter inside."

Addie went into the trading post and when she came out with a cup and the pitcher, she saw that more people had gathered around, including several Mexican men and their wives. The wives were crying and Addie wished they'd all go away.

Filling the cup with water, Addie handed it to Singer. "What's she saying?"

"She says her husband's dead," Singer said, giving the cup to Guadalupe. "Says he was murdered."

"Murdered . . ." What the hell was going on here? Addie wondered.

85

Addie and the others listened as Guadalupe tearfully told Singer in Spanish what happened and he translated into English. Guadalupe had expected Abel home last night. She had fallen asleep waiting for him. When she awoke this morning just before dawn, she found herself in bed alone.

"She says she went outside and her husband's horse was nowhere to be found. She got scared, started calling his name, checking behind the house, running, looking everywhere."

Addie was surprised when Guadalupe pointed at her and Bean.

"She says Abel liked going to the Headquarters for a few drinks," Singer said. "She wants to know did he come in last night."

"Beats the hell outta me," Bean said. "I was having a drinkin' contest with that blowhard Pete Bonner."

"I don't remember seeing him," Addie said. "But I'll ask around." She had an idea her other girl, Clarissa, might know something. Addie had seen Abel talking to her a few times but wasn't sure if Clarissa had ever given him a ride. Glancing over at the Headquarters, Addie didn't see any sign of Clarissa, but Phoebe was still asleep on the bar.

Singer continued translating Guadalupe's story. She saw Abel near the mission lying in the grass under a sycamore tree. Relieved to find her husband, she ran to him calling his name, crying and laughing. She would gladly forgive his drunk and foolish ways. He was lying on his stomach. She knelt down next to him and saw blood on the grass around his head. She said his name, shook him. He didn't move and when she rolled him over, she saw his throat was cut.

Addie winced when Guadalupe let out a wail and covered her face with her hands.

"You know the rest, I guess," Singer said to the crowd and stood up.

When several of the Mexican women came up to take Guadalupe home, Addie moved away and caught sight of Clarissa standing back at the edge of the crowd, nervously biting her thumb nail. She had sandy-colored hair, sleep in her eyes, and was wearing a plain dress. Barely nineteen, she was thin as a bodkin. Addie had been in the whoring business for nearly three years and knew most men weren't particular when overcome with the urge for a ride, but some had a preference for the young thin kind. She knew Ned Needle sure did and wondered now if Abel Tyner might have developed a taste for it.

Addie went over to Clarissa and whispered, "Wait for me over in the saloon."

From the sudden worried look on Clarissa's face combined with that nail biting, Addie felt certain Clarissa knew something about all this. Addie had cautioned her girls about dealing with men, telling them, "You make your money with your ass, but let your eyes show you the way."

Going back over to where Bean was talking with Singer and a few other men in the street, Addie heard Singer saying something about getting there as soon as he finished shaving, then he hurried inside his trading post.

"Something else now," Addie said.

"We're goin' over and take a gander at Abel," Bean said. "You comin'?"

"I'll be along," Addie said. "Got some things to take care of first."

As she walked to the Headquarters, Addie could feel the day and the ground getting hotter. She saw Clarissa peeking out from behind the doorway.

Taking hold of Clarissa's arm, Addie pulled the girl outside and around the corner of the saloon to the covered wagon in the back the girls used for business purposes.

"What was all that fidgeting out there this morning?" Addie

demanded, still holding on to Clarissa's arm.

"What do you mean?"

"If you know so much as a fanny hair's worth of how Abel got killed, you better speak it now."

Addie held fast when Clarissa tried to pull her arm away.

"Let go of me," Clarissa said.

"Answer me first and don't lie. I can tell."

"I don't know."

Addie released her arm. "Well, what were you acting so nervous and guilty about?"

"I just don't like those Mex women is all."

"They don't like us either. What about Abel? He come by to see you?"

"No. And if he had, he would've seen I was with Ned and left."

It struck Addie that maybe Clarissa had become picky about how she parceled out her attentions.

"How long was Ned Needle with you?" Addie asked.

"Long enough for a ride."

Addie knew Needle's rides were the easiest and fastest ways Clarissa could make that dollar she made her girls charge because Clarissa had admitted that Needle had never lasted more than a nickel's worth.

"When did he leave?" Addie asked.

"I don't remember."

"Try! He leave right away or stick around?"

"I don't know. It was dark. We came back inside, he bought me a drink, and sweet-talked me awhile."

"In all that sweet-talking, did he mention Abel?"

"Just what he always said." Clarissa shrugged and looked away.

"And?" Addie asked, exasperated. "Answer me!" She grabbed Clarissa's arms.

"He said Abel was less than a dog for marrying a greaser Mex," Clarissa said, "and the thought of him rolling on top of her made him want to puke."

Addie let go of Clarissa and looked at her hard. "You ever give Abel a ride?"

"He never asked," Clarissa said flatly.

"All right," Addie said, then looked into the wagon. The old, torn feather mattress was jammed up to the front, and petticoats and stockings and other clothes were strewn around and hanging from the cover struts.

"Get a bucket and scrub the inside of the wagon real good," she said. "It smells worse the longer I stand here. And air out the mattress, too."

Pulling rapidly on the front of her blouse to fan herself, Addie turned and headed back to the front of the Headquarters. She was thirsty and wanted a drink of water before she went to find Bean and take a look at Abel's body.

Something about her talk with Clarissa bothered Addie. It had always been her feeling that if a man wanted to court a girl, he took her on a buggy ride. But, if he wanted something a little less permanent, he could pay for a ride, like in Addie's wagon. And right now, Addie thought Clarissa was pining for that proper buggy ride. And maybe Clarissa thought Ned Needle was going to offer to drive that buggy. Addie knew there was more to life than sweet-talk and giving a man a ride. But what could Ned Needle possibly say to her that would be sweet? Then it hit her. It wasn't Needle doing the sweet-talking. Maybe Clarissa was sweet-talking *him*.

Approaching the front of the Headquarters, Addie noticed Bean across the way at Singer's Trading Post.

"You been to see Abel's body already?" Addie asked as she stepped up on the veranda where Bean was looking over the notice board and scratching his beard.

Bean nodded. "He's croaked all right. Throat's cut slick as you please. Deep, too."

She caught sight of her reflection in Singer's window. The white scar across the bridge of her nose, the result of a catfight in a tent city miner's saloon up north, appeared more pronounced. Looking back at Bean, she noticed him squinting at the flyers.

"You could read those better if you were wearing your specs," Addie said.

"Yeah, I know. I also know that what with a murder, folks might be comin' to have a looksee. Might be a good idea to roll Phoebe off the bar and open for business early."

"Then what're you doing over here at Singer's?"

"Gettin' some new cigars and a couple other things."

Addie was about to ask Bean if he'd noticed Ned Needle in the Headquarters last night when Singer came out his door carrying a basket under his arm and handed it to Bean.

"I just thought of something." Addie said. "Has anybody gone to get the sheriff?"

"Don't think so," Singer said. "Suppose I could go. I could sure tell him what happened."

"Good idea," Bean said. "You better bring those ranger boys, too."

"What for?" Addie asked, noticing a big grin on Bean's face.

Bean pointed, and Addie and Singer followed the line of his finger to the governor's wanted poster for Joaquin.

"I will give ten thousand dollars," Singer said, reading the flyer. "Signed Joaquin."

"Hell, he probably came into the Headquarters last night," Bean said, sounding excited. "I could put up a sign sayin' so."

"The son-of-a-bitch was here," Addie whispered grimly.

CHAPTER NINE:
THE ANIMAL

Murieta woke in the still quiet just before dawn. He heard Contreras snoring lightly. Checking on their horses, he fed Diablo fresh grass from his hand. He and Contreras had tethered the horses to a particularly strange-looking oak the night before. It had always struck him how many of the oaks on the hillsides in some places didn't grow upright, but curved, following the slope of the hill. If he'd wanted to, he could have easily touched the top bough of one that looked like a letter S lying on its side.

He sat down with his back propped against his Mexican saddle and, using a stone, sharpened the blade of his Bowie knife. Tilting his head up, he saw the twilight fading against the rising white glow in the east. He felt satisfied and peaceful, and the last words Rosita had said to him came into his head. "The scars the Yankees left on my body are not on my soul. Come back to me, and we'll be happy again." He made a vow to be in the arms of his Rosita before Christmas.

Sheathing the Bowie, Murieta stood and gave Contreras a nudge with his boot. "We don't have time to sleep all day. Get up."

Grumbling, Contreras rubbed his eyes, got to his feet, and cursed as the sun broke over the eastern edge of the hillside.

"She is going to be hot today," he said and began rolling up his bedroll.

Murieta knew that was true enough. Diamond-backed snakes, toads, and lizards would be slithering and scurrying for cover under a pile of rocks or in a cactus patch or even down a hole. They knew when it was time to get.

He was putting the saddle blanket on his horse when Contreras took a couple of cold biscuits out of his saddlebags and tossed them to him.

"Eat, *jefe*," Contreras said. "We have far to go today."

Murieta weighed the biscuits in his hands. Adobe bricks felt lighter. Bacon drippings might soften them up, but as they had no bacon, Murieta gnawed on one.

"You sleep good, eh?" Contreras asked.

Murieta nodded. "I woke up early. I was thinking of Rosita," he said and decided to stop fighting the biscuit.

Contreras grunted. "Like the rocks, I know. But keep them. You'll eat later. I know you, *jefe*. You dream of your woman and your stomach shrivels up, like mine when I have not killed someone." He patted his ample stomach and grinned. "Today I better kill something and take away this ache in my belly."

"Hello the camp!" someone called out.

Drawing their revolvers, Murieta and Contreras spun toward the voice.

Two bearded men wearing floppy hats and buckskins were coming through the trees. One was supporting the other who was hopping on one foot and had his arm around his friend's shoulder. The one hopping had no boot on the foot he appeared to have injured, and he helped steady himself using his musket like a staff. He was holding on to the barrel and putting the butt to the ground. His friend carried a Hawkin .50 caliber. They also had Colt revolvers at their sides.

"Need some help," the one who could walk said. "Got a hurt man."

Murieta shot a look at Contreras that said to be careful. He saw Contreras quickly scan the trees for other *gringos*. They both kept their revolvers in hand and ready.

"Stop right there," Murieta said. "What happened?"

"We was hunting game," the first man said, coming to a halt. "My friend here slipped and got kinda tangled up in some rocks. I think his foot's broken. Had to cut his boot off."

The injured man groaned. "Please, I need some help."

"Don't blame you for being wary of strangers," the other one said.

Murieta heard Contreras's low, sharp, short whistle and looked over at him. He was pointing his revolver back and forth from one *gringo* to the other along with a hopeful nod of his head. Murieta knew he wanted a sign from him to shoot. As much as Murieta hated *gringos,* these two seemed to be in real distress. Maybe seeing Ana last night had left him feeling generous. He shook his head. He could tell Contreras wasn't happy.

"Let me down, Gil!" the injured man said. "I think I'm going to be sick."

Gil eased him down fast so he could sit. The injured man leaned forward and started coughing.

Murieta glanced at Contreras, saw him grimace and take a step away.

When Murieta looked back, Gil had his Hawkin leveled at him. "Go easy, you," Gil said.

Contreras jerked his head toward him, his revolver moving in the same direction.

"Stop right there, big *hombre*," the injured man said, grinning, his musket pointing at Contreras.

"Drop them guns," Gil ordered.

They hesitated. Murieta could hear Contreras's low growl.

"Right now!" Gil shouted.

Murieta glanced over at Contreras and gave him a nod. They dropped their revolvers.

"Smart, ain't they, Haze?" Gil asked.

Haze grinned and stood up. "Right accommodating," he said.

"This fake busted foot works every time."

"One of my better ideas, if I do say so," Gil said, his eyes moving from Murieta to Contreras. "Now, before we get to taking your valuables, how about something to eat."

"Nada," Murieta shrugged and shook his head.

"Oh, now don't start fooling like you don't understand," Gil said. "We're hungry and we're taking your valuables. *¿Comprende?"*

Murieta didn't move.

"Let's just shoot them and be done," Haze said.

"Hold off now," Gil said. "Maybe they don't know who they're being robbed by. You know who we are?"

Murieta didn't move, but he heard Contreras sniff.

"You're going to have quite a story to tell your kin and friends," Gil said. "You can tell them you was robbed by a Joaquin."

Murieta and Contreras exchanged glances and Murieta started laughing. Contreras joined him, his laugh starting low and becoming louder.

"What the hell . . ." Haze wondered.

"We don't have to let you live, pepper belly," Gil said, taking a step toward Murieta.

Murieta stopped laughing and put his hands up, acting serious. "No, let us live. We have food." He looked over at Contreras. "In the saddlebag, *amigo.* The biscuits."

"Ah, *si,"* Contreras said.

"Keep a watch on him, Haze," Gil said. "I'm not liking these two."

Murieta locked eyes with Gil, bracing for his chance.

"Just you be real careful now," Haze said to Contreras. "And whatever gold you got, get that out, too. Don't try hiding it. We'll check."

Contreras scratched under his nose and reached carefully

into his saddlebag. Pulling his hand out, he held up three biscuits.

"Give 'em here," Haze said.

Contreras threw them at Haze, hitting him in the face. Haze flinched, jerking his hands and the musket up.

Gil turned. Murieta pulled his Bowie and threw it. The heavy handle struck the side of Gil's face. He screamed, "Ah, shit!", his reflex causing him to pull the Hawkin up to his chest.

Murieta lunged and drove into Gil's gut, knocking him off his feet. They hit the ground hard. Murieta stayed on top, the heavy gun caught between them. Gil bucked trying to let loose of the Hawkin. It fired, the roar almost deafening Murieta. One of the *gringo*'s hands got free, covering Murieta's face. Gil grabbed a fistful of Murieta's hair and yanked. His head snapped back. He jammed his forearm against Gil's neck, grabbing for the revolver at his side. Gil struggled, trying to reach the gun first. Murieta yelled as the *gringo* pulled on his hair, yanking his head to one side. He caught two of Gil's fingers and forced them back fast, breaking both. Gil screamed and Murieta grabbed the revolver. Shoving it under the *gringo*'s chin, he cocked it. His hair was free, his head his own again. The *gringo*'s hands sagged in surrender.

Murieta took a deep breath. "Move and I blow your head off."

A few feet away, he saw Contreras had Haze jammed against a tree, his beefy hand squeezing Haze's neck and his Bowie up under his crotch, ready to start cutting.

"Not yet!" Murieta said.

With his grip still tight around Haze's throat, Contreras jerked him away from the tree and threw him to the ground. On his back, Haze, his face red like raw meat, sucked in air between coughs, while Contreras reached down and relieved the *gringo* of the Colt at his side.

"Don't kill us!" Gil cried. "Please!"

Murieta pushed the revolver harder under his chin, forcing his head back into the dirt.

"Do you know who we are?" Murieta asked.

Gil shook his head, his eyes squeezed shut.

"I am Joaquin Murieta."

Gil's eyes snapped open.

"And that one," Murieta said, nodding his head toward Contreras, "is the one you *gringos* call the Animal."

Murieta watched as Gil's eyes went wide with terror and his mouth opened but no sound came out as he looked over at Contreras.

"Oh, my God!" Haze cried out.

"Don't move," Murieta told the two frightened robbers. Then he and Contreras snatched up their revolvers, and Murieta picked up his Bowie. He stuck Gil's revolver inside his belt and kept his pointed at the *gringo* while Contreras kicked Haze in the ribs.

Murieta told the two *gringos* to get up.

"Please let us go," Gil said in a shaky voice, cupping his broken fingers.

"Get your hands up," Murieta said. "Who are you?"

"Miners on hard luck," Gil said, almost crying.

"You know," Contreras said, taking a coil of rope from his saddle, "you don't look too good. You look like the weasel, only more scared," he said to Gil, then turned to Haze who was stooped over, his arm holding his ribs. "And you, *muy mal*. Very bad."

"W—we're real sorry," Gil said. "Let us go and we'll git. Promise."

"How many times?" Murieta asked.

Gil frowned. "What?"

"The people you rob, how many times you tell them you're Joaquin?"

"Just a few. When it's Mexes, ah, I mean Mexicans."

"Why Mexicans?"

Gil didn't answer.

Murieta looked at Haze and saw he had peed down his pant leg. Murieta grunted. He glanced at Contreras who chuckled.

"Puta madre," Contreras said.

Murieta stepped closer to Gil. "Tell me, why Mexicans?"

When Gil didn't answer, Murieta pulled out his Bowie and put the point of the blade right below his eye.

"We thought it was funny," Gil blurted out.

Murieta waited a moment before stepping back. "It's not so funny now. *¿No?*"

Gil shook his head and tears ran down his cheeks.

"I didn't think it was funny," Haze said. "I got nothing against Mexicans."

"Liar!" Gil shouted at him, then looked back at Murieta and pointed at Haze. "Calling ourselves Joaquin was his idea."

"Hell it was!" Haze shouted back.

Contreras laughed. "They sound like women, these two."

"Listen," Haze said, glancing from Murieta to Contreras, "I ain't going to rob no more so you can let me go."

"Oh," Murieta said. "Feliz, what do you think?"

"I think something special for these two," Contreras said, holding up his rope, looking from one to the other. "First, tie you to a tree. Maybe I start with your toes." He waved his knife back and forth at Haze. "And then your knees. And then your balls."

"Please, no," Gil wailed and jerked his head toward Haze. "I hate you! This is all your fault!"

"Go to hell!" Haze shouted back.

Gil moved toward him. "No, you go to hell, you stupid bastard!"

"Don't you call me a bastard. I knew both my parents' names!"

"Enough, *gringos*," Murieta said, and before he realized what was happening, Gil shoved Haze hard then ran for the nearest tree.

Murieta aimed and fired, hitting Gil in the back. He dropped face first to the ground. Murieta heard Contreras curse as his revolver misfired. He turned, saw his friend cock his revolver, aim at the fleeing Haze, and fire. The slug splintered a tree branch near his head.

"*¡Su madre es puta!*" Contreras shouted at the running *gringo*.

Murieta fired at Haze who yelped, grabbing his bloodied ear.

Contreras fired again. Haze spun around and fell.

"Better make sure the *gringo*'s dead," Murieta said.

While Contreras went to check, Murieta walked over to Gil and rolled him over with the toe of his boot. His eyes were open. Murieta had seen the stare of the dead many times. Going through his pockets, Murieta found a letter addressed to Mrs. Gilbert Opdyke. He was about to throw it away, but something told him to put it in his vest pocket. As he did, he realized he still had the piece of newspaper he'd picked up last night in San Gabriel inside his vest.

Looking up, Murieta saw Contreras standing over Haze. He held a revolver in each hand and aimed them at the man. The *gringo* raised his arm, covering his face. Contreras cocked the revolvers and fired. The body jumped. Contreras wiped his nose on his shirtsleeve.

"Check his pockets," Murieta called to him and then walked toward the horses.

Murieta was already mounted on Diablo when Contreras came back.

"Did that one have anything on him?" Murieta asked.

"A pocket watch, but my slug went right through it," Contreras said, sounding disappointed. "These two, they didn't deserve to die so easy."

Murieta kicked Diablo and they started down toward the valley. He wanted only to get back up north, collect the gold he had hidden at Arroyo Cantoova, leave this *gringo* hellhole, and return to Mexico to his Rosita. He had the feeling he shouldn't waste any more time.

CHAPTER TEN:
THE WHORE

Addie was pouring drinks behind the bar inside the crowded Headquarters when she saw Sheriff Barton, Lieutenant Quick, and his rangers ride up to Singer's place. The rangers were in their uniforms, or at least wearing the short blue coats like Horace Wheat and Ned Needle. She saw Singer come out and hand the governor's wanted poster to Barton. That Quick fellow was anxious to see it, too, she noticed. It looked to her like Quick and Barton were having words and then Quick and two of his rangers rode off with him and the sheriff while the others tied their horses to the hitching rail at Singer's and split up. Sam Prizer headed into the Monte and Ezra Doyle went into Ybarra's. She was glad to see Wheat and Needle coming toward the Headquarters.

She heard Bean coming in from the back. He carried three bottles of whiskey in his arms.

"What'd I tell you," Bean said, setting the bottles on the bar. "There ain't been this many citizens together in one place since the last hangin'." Then he hollered out to the thirty or so men in the place, "Plenty of everything here, boys!"

Addie kept her eye on the door as the two rangers walked in. She was glad Wheat made a straight line to the bar when he saw her, and she wasn't surprised when she saw Needle stop inside the door, looking, she was certain, for Clarissa.

Addie smiled as Wheat approached and Bean was right next to her hollering over the din of the crowd.

"Hey Horace!" Bean shouted. "I knew you boys'd be coming. What'll you have?"

"Nothing for me," Wheat said, blowing out a long breath.

"Well, let me tell you," Bean said, "some are sayin' that wanted poster is somebody's idea of a joke, and it was some malcontent Abel once arrested come back for revenge. And others claim maybe he was playin' around and a jealous husband put a permanent stop to it. But I say it was Joaquin did Abel. Feller over there at the window, he come up with a new name for Joaquin: the Sonoran Ghost. How you like that?"

"Real catchy," Wheat said and unbuttoned his uniform coat.

Bean saw three cowboys at the other end of the bar. "Got customers," he said to Wheat and hurried over to the men, saying, "What'll it be, boys?"

Wheat smiled at Addie. "Been awhile, Addie. How are you?"

Addie smiled back sweetly. "About the same." She liked Wheat as much as she could like any man. She liked that she and Wheat were not romantically inclined toward each other, just friendly and respectful. And she liked that Wheat never asked for credit.

"I could sure use some coffee if you've got it," Wheat said.

"You do look tired," Addie said and put the cup on the counter and got the pot Bean kept behind the bar.

"Bone tired, and hot, too, but I still need this coffee," he said and nodded his thanks as she finished filling his cup.

"What've you been doing?"

He sipped his coffee and told her about the search through *Calle de los Negros* last night and then being rousted up this morning by Quick who told them to get up and get their horses saddled because they were riding to San Gabriel immediately.

"I only had a couple hours sleep," he said. "Can't vouch for the others."

"So does your Lieutenant Quick think Joaquin was here last

101

night?" Addie asked. "He might've been, you think?"

"I don't know. But the lieutenant was riding like a demon to get here. And that was giving Barton fits. I don't think those two get along."

"So it sounds like he thinks it really was Joaquin here last night," Addie said as she poured him another cup of coffee.

"Thinks and hopes I'm sure, particularly after last night's fiasco."

"You'll be going after him then, more than likely?"

"He's got Uriah and Charley looking for tracks over to where Abel's body was found. They find anything, you can bet we'll pursue it. That reminds me, the lieutenant sent us in here to ask what you and Bean and maybe your girls know."

"I just saw the poster and heard Abel's wife screaming is all," Addie said. "Didn't see anybody new in here last night. The girls said they didn't either." She decided to hold off telling him about Clarissa and Abel until she had a chance to talk to Ned Needle who was coming toward them through the crowd, still craning his neck and casting his eye for Clarissa.

"Roy!" Wheat called out and Bean came back and stood next to Addie.

"All right, so what's Quick doin'?" Bean asked, and pulled a large jar of jerked beef from under the bar and offered it to Wheat.

"He's over to Abel's wife's place with the sheriff," he said and waved off the jerky. "They're asking her a bunch of questions about Abel. What happened, when she saw him last."

"What do you think?"

"I'm supposed to be asking you the questions, Roy."

"I don't know nothin'."

"You can say that again," Addie said and watched as Needle got to the other end of the bar and leaned against it like he was waiting while she listened to Bean and Wheat talk.

"One thing I'd like to know, Roy, is why's it always smell like old piss in here?"

"That's stale beer and sweat you smell in here," Bean said matter-of-factly. "Old piss is along the side of the buildin'. I'm thinkin' of findin' a mean ugly dog and stakin' him out there to keep the damn drunks from pissin' on my place. I complained about it to Barton but he claims there's nothin' he can do. And judges around here ain't worth a damn, neither. If I was a judge, I'd make pissin' on a buildin' a hangin' offense."

Addie moved down to where Needle was. "No use eyeballing for her, Ned. She's doing chores."

"Chores?" he said, frowning.

"Yeah," she said. "They need doing so you just stay right here and don't bother her. She's got no time for you now and I want to talk to you anyway."

"About what?"

Addie hated that arrogant tone of his. She saw the two men sitting at the table in the corner leave and motioned for him to sit down.

"First off," Addie said, "did you see Abel Tyner last night?"

Between his hesitation and his face flushing red, Addie believed she knew the answer.

"I didn't see nobody 'cept Clarissa last night," he blurted out. "And who do you think you are? We come in here to ask the questions. We're investigating a killing in case you don't know."

"Don't you sass me, Ned Needle." Addie felt her cheeks getting hot. She saw him draw his lips in and then heard Wheat call his name.

"I got ranger business to tend to," Needle said and stomped over to Wheat and Bean.

She almost laughed when he turned and gave her a dirty

look. As he joined the other two, she watched him sneak a handful of jerky out of the jar and stuff it in his pocket.

Quick was helping Sheriff Barton and a couple of Guadalupe Tyner's neighbors put Abel's body into a wagon.

"Watch you don't drop his head now, Ambrose," Barton said as Quick helped lift the body into the wagon bed.

Quick was coming to the conclusion he didn't like Barton, who invariably seemed to talk down to him.

"All right, Miguel," Barton said to the wagon driver, "take him on over to Mosely's Parlor."

Jumping down from the wagon as it rolled away, Quick dusted off his uniform coat. He watched the men who'd helped with Abel's body head off to Guadalupe's house down the way, then went over to see Barton who was headed for the sycamore tree where they had tied their horses. Quick stepped around the dark crimson spot in the grass where they'd found Abel's body.

"Joaquin was here," Quick said to Barton, "if you'd open your eyes and see it."

"Somebody writin' the name 'Joaquin' on a flyer don't prove it was him," Barton said as he untied his horse to let it drink.

"The hell it doesn't," Quick said. "Guadalupe Tyner told us both she heard voices and horses passing her place sometime after midnight. And those voices were speaking Spanish, she said."

"She *thought* that's what she heard."

"And they were heading north, which means they passed the mission and the tree here and rode on past her place," Quick said, pointing out each spot as he spoke.

"That poor woman ain't sure of nothin' 'cept her husband's dead."

"That's right," Quick said. "Somebody beat the hell out of your deputy and then killed him, but, you know, sheriff, I'm beginning to wonder if you really give a damn."

Quick saw the fire in Barton's eyes as he turned to him, but just then, Uriah Clegg and Charley Biggs rode up fast on their horses.

"Ambrose," Clegg said, "Charley found a trail leading north. You tell him, Charley."

Quick noticed Charley seemed surprised. He guessed Charley figured Clegg would give the report, Clegg being senior man.

"It's two, ah, men on horseback," Charley said, his voice sounding nervous. "One pretty heavy, my guess. The prints are deeper than the other set. We followed the trail about a mile or so. It goes right on past the Tyner place there and on up to—"

Barton interrupted. "Them prints tell you who murdered Abel, did they?"

"Well, no. Can't decipher that exactly," Charley said, looking over at Clegg who nodded, and then took a pull from one of the three canteens he had hanging on his saddle. "A lot of people been tramping over the grass hereabouts before we got here. But the trail is pretty clean on past the lady's house and toward the mountains. Probably on through the pass there." He pointed off to the northwest.

"It's reasonable they came this way," Clegg said. "Trail's maybe five to ten hours cold, I'd say. My guess, they've made for the San Fernando."

"That's good enough for me so we'll get to it," Quick said to Barton.

"Damn it, Quick," Barton said, "don't go off half-cocked. All right, there's a trail. Miz Tyner don't know for sure it was Mexes she heard or what direction they was goin'. Condition she's in, she dreamed it, more'n likely."

"Sheriff," Quick said, "we're standing here talking, and murderers are getting away."

"He's got a point there, sheriff," Clegg said.

"Well my point is you don't know who killed Abel, but you're talking like vigilantes!" Barton said. "You're rangers. Act accordin'ly!"

Quick stepped up close to Barton, nearly nose to nose.

"Last night you said I was a full-time nobody, that I wasn't holding my responsibilities sacred." Quick said quietly. "Well, I say this might very likely be the work of Joaquin Murieta. And he's a wanted desperado."

"You're makin' a big mistake here, boy." Barton said. "You're also makin' the wrong kinda name for yourself, and I won't have you attachin' it to my Lucy."

"Abel here is dead," Quick said. "And that deputy from San Luis Obispo. And—

"You hold on—"

"No, you hold on!" Quick said, cutting him off. "The mayor said he wants something done. The governor wants something done. The newspapers and the people want it. I'm a ranger. I *am* acting accordingly."

Barton gritted his teeth. "You listen here, you little—"

A woman's screams caught their attention.

Quick and the others looked toward the Tyner place and saw Guadalupe stumbling toward them. Several of the Mexican women came out of the house after her, trying to help her, or maybe stop her. Quick couldn't tell for sure. She was shrieking something in Spanish.

Quick's Spanish may have been fair, but this bawling he couldn't untangle. "What's she saying? Somebody tell me," Quick said.

Clegg rode over to where the women were and, after removing his shabby sombrero, spoke with one. Quick saw his grim expression as he returned.

"She's saying find him," Clegg said. "Find who killed my husband. She asks, are you men or cowards?"

Quick met Barton's stare and watched him reach into his vest pocket, pull out the folded wanted flyer, and throw it on the ground.

"Don't forget your evidence," Barton said.

Quick smiled, picked up the flyer, and put it inside his coat. Then he mounted his horse and doffed his black hat at Guadalupe and the other women.

"*Señoras,* tell her the California Rangers will find her husband's murderers!" He turned to Clegg and Charley. "Let's get the others. We got to move."

Addie was going around to the back of the Headquarters to check on Clarissa's progress and to make sure Needle wasn't with her back at the wagon when she saw Quick and the others ride up to Singer's place in a flurry of commotion. She couldn't make out what Quick was saying. Prizer and Doyle, on the veranda filling their canteens from pitchers of water Singer had brought out to them, scrambled for their horses. Quick shouted for Wheat and Needle.

Addie ran to the street. Wheat and Needle came running out of the Headquarters.

"Everybody make sure you got water!" Quick shouted.

Addie cupped her hands over her eyes to shield them from the bright sun. She saw Wheat and Needle mounting their horses and gathered up her skirt and hurried to them.

"What is it?" she asked Wheat.

"We're going after Joaquin," he said.

Addie ran into the Headquarters.

Quick was leading his rangers past the mission when he saw an old Mexican with long gray hair and a thin beard, wearing the white shirt and pants he'd seen many Mexican peasants wear, sitting cross-legged on a broken section of the wall gently rocking back and forth. Quick didn't know why he needed to stop and talk to the old man. Something just told him he should. He halted his men.

"*Señor*," Quick said, "last night, did you see anyone pass this way? *Digame, por favor.*"

"I see only the dead, *señor*," he said and nodded once.

Quick tried again. "Two men, Mexicans on horseback. One very heavy, riding north. *¿Si, o no?*"

The old Mexican grinned at him.

Quick heard Needle behind him.

"He's just a crazy old greaser," Needle said and then called out to the Mexican, "Hey, how come all you greasers use bed sheets to make your clothes, anyway?"

Quick snapped his head around at him. "Quiet!"

He saw Needle drop his head and could tell he was mumbling something under his breath. He looked back at the old Mexican who had stopped his rocking.

"*Señor*," the old Mexican said, "hundreds of Indians are buried in this place, put here by the Spanish. And those Spanish in my cemetery, they were put here by the *Mexicanos*. And many *Mexicanos* rest here because of you *Yanquis*. It is very full, my cemetery." He grinned at Quick. "Where will they put you, *señor*?"

He's loco, Quick thought. He kicked his horse. "Let's go!"

They galloped past the mission grounds and scattered a flock of sheep drinking from the stream. Quick saw a lone rider up ahead at the sycamore tree, sitting atop his horse, waiting. He thought it must be Sheriff Barton and was glad of it. Now the sheriff could eat his ugly insinuation about this being a vigilante action. Yes, sir, an apology would be in order, too.

As he got closer, Quick realized it wasn't Barton after all. Whoever it was wore a floppy hat, and a checkered shirt with brown striped pants that appeared to swallow up the body inside them.

Quick put up his hand to halt the rangers and their dust trail swirled up behind them, settling on their uniform coats.

The lone rider was Addie Moody.

"What are you doing here, Miss?" Quick asked, noticing the butt of the big Army Dragoon revolver stuck into her belt. She would need both hands to hold that, he thought.

"Thank you, Lieutenant Quick," she said. "I don't hear 'Miss' too often. You should come around once in a while."

Quick was about to speak when Wheat beat him to it.

"Addie, what do you think you're doing?"

"I've been waiting for you boys."

"Looks like you're swimming inside them pants, too," Needle said. "Where'd you find that getup?"

"Kind of borrowed them from Bean."

"Quiet down, everybody!" Quick snapped. He turned back to Addie. "Miss, we'll be going. We have a murderer to apprehend."

"I know," she said. "I'm coming with you."

"The hell—" Needle stopped himself, seeing Quick's glare.

"I cannot allow that," Quick said to Addie.

"I don't see why not. I'm dressed for it. And I'm pretty fair with this," she said, patting the big Dragoon. "Just ask Roy Bean, or that thieving son-of-a-bitch I shot."

Wheat laughed. "I was there that night. This fella stole the money he'd just paid her and he's running down the street and Addie's near naked but she grabs Bean's Dragoon and shoots that thief right in the ass."

"If he'd turned around, I'd've got him where I wanted," Addie said.

"All right, all right," Quick said, quieting down the laughter of the rangers. Then he looked at Addie. "I don't care how good you are with a gun. This is no place for a female. We're riding hard and fast."

"Hard and fast I've done before, Ambrose. It's my business."

Quick heard Wheat and Clegg clearing their throats. Clegg sounded like a horse whinnying.

"You might be on the trail of a Joaquin, maybe even Murieta," Addie said. "If it is a Joaquin, it could be the man who butchered my little sister."

A woman with a vendetta was the last thing Quick needed. "Miss . . . Addie—"

"I intend to find out!" Addie said.

Quick saw the hard determination in her eyes under the sagging brim of her hat.

"Can't cross her there, Lieutenant," Wheat said. "We catch this ol' boy, she's got a right to face him. And him her, particularly if she takes it to mind to accuse him."

Sometimes Wheat sounded just like a lawyer. He wondered if maybe that's what Wheat had been before. Quick noticed Needle looking sourly at Wheat. He knew Needle didn't like him and he suspected that if Wheat had been a lawyer, Needle probably would like him even less.

Quick looked back at Addie. "Is there *any way* to keep you here?"

"As some of your men know, for the right amount of money, I'll do damn near anything," she said. "But enough money hasn't been made to keep me out of this."

"I say no, it's not right," Needle said. "Sorry, Lieutenant, but I don't like it and I had to say my piece."

Addie jumped in before Quick could speak.

"Well, Ned," Addie said, "some would say it's not right you don't last more than two pullbacks with Clarissa, but that won't stop me from taking your whole dollar."

The rangers laughed, even quiet Sam Prizer, Quick noticed. But Needle didn't say a word, though he looked like he wanted to kill Addie.

"Careful now, boys," Addie said. "All men got their peculiari-ties."

"Enough!" Quick said. "Let's ride before the rest of the town decides to hitch on, too!"

Chapter Eleven:
The Valley

Murieta had crossed the San Fernando Valley many times, in every season. Someone, he couldn't remember who, had called it "Everyman's Eden" because it lay "rich in pasture and promise" nestled between the mountains of the Sierra Santa Monica on the south and the rocky, scrub oak–covered Santa Susanas to the north.

This morning, riding toward the Susanas with Contreras, who was chewing on a hard biscuit, Murieta noticed, maybe for the first time, that here on this rolling plain, the oaks stood straight, forty to fifty feet tall, not curved like on the hillsides. And that wasn't all. Wild mustard grass and buckwheat burned golden brown by the hot summer sun stretched out before him like a blanket of gold. Though it wasn't the fabled gold the Conquistadors sought, it was a part of what he had hoped to have with Rosita—life in a golden land, and bags of gold to live on.

He reached down and snapped off the top of a mustard stalk and gently rubbed the petals. They left a fine yellow dust, like gold, on his fingers.

"Everyman's Eden," he said to himself and then thought that the *gringos* had ruined it.

Murieta and Contreras rode easily, neither feeling much like talking. They had watered their horses several miles back and shucked their *serapes*. The heat was already sweltering and it wasn't even ten o'clock yet. Murieta knew plenty of water and grass for the horses awaited them in another seven or eight miles at the home of his friend Andres Pico, a *ranchero,* one of the wealthy landowners from before the *gringos* came, who sometimes stayed on the old San Fernando Mission lands. He remembered Pico telling him about the priests having to leave the mission when they could no longer maintain it. Things had changed when the *gringos* took over, Pico had said.

But Murieta was certain his friend hadn't changed, a friend he often thought of more like a father, a *patrón.* Pico would see to his and Contreras's comfort. Neither Pico nor the other *rancheros* had forgotten the ways of hospitality to visitors—be they friend or stranger. Pico would feed them, allow them rest, and gladly give them fresh horses if they desired. Those were the old ways, Murieta thought, the ways of decent people, before the *gringos* came. If only he had been here then. That was the true Eden.

"*Jefe,*" Contreras said.

Murieta looked over to see him offering one of his biscuits. Hard as they were, Murieta was hungry enough and willing enough to try working on one.

"Tell me again about your *amigo,*" Contreras said. "He lives here but he doesn't own the land?"

"*Señor* Pico owns a hundred thousand acres and a house south of Los Angeles," Murieta said. "But he runs his cattle here on land he leases from his friend. Over a hundred and twenty thousand acres, he told me. And when *Señor* Pico is here, he stays in the house the priests had at the mission."

"If he has so much land of his own, why does he need this land to graze?"

"I don't know," Murieta said. "Maybe the cows were already here."

"And who is his friend?"

"*Señor* Eulogio de Celis," Murieta said. "He and *Señor* Pico were here long before the Yankee *gringos* came. You know *Señor* Pico was a General in the war."

"He fought the *gringos?*"

Murieta nodded and grinned. "Crushed them at the battle of San Pascual."

Contreras looked puzzled. "But now he's friends with them?"

"His home is here," Murieta said. "He's made his peace with the *gringos,* but he's not one of them. Never."

Contreras snorted. Then he asked, "What was it like?"

"What?"

"Here. Before the *gringos* came. Did he tell you?"

Murieta said Pico had told him stories about those early days in California, when a man and his family were always welcomed in the home of a *ranchero,* whatever the occasion. They would have tables piled with food. No one would be turned away, not strangers, not anyone. To do such a thing would be considered not only inhospitable, but also dishonorable.

"Tell me more about the food," Contreras said, looking hungry.

"They would roast a steer on a spit," Murieta said. "And there would be chicken and tamales and tortillas." He managed to bite off a chunk of the biscuit and hoped it would soften up in his mouth. "And after the meal, dancing and singing."

"And drinking. *¿No?*"

"*Si,*" Murieta said, "but mostly dancing. Mexicans love to dance."

Contreras grunted. "In Chile, we like to dance, too."

Murieta finally managed to get the piece of biscuit soft enough to chew. It wasn't too bad, but he was also very hungry. He wiped the sweat from his face with his bandana yet somehow the heat wasn't bothering him much. Soon he would see his friend, refresh himself, and he and Contreras would hopefully reach the next valley by nightfall.

Remembering the piece of newspaper he picked up in San Gabriel the night before, Murieta pulled it from inside his vest. The *Los Angeles Star* was written in both English and Spanish. His English was fair but his Spanish was better. Unfortunately, much of the newsprint had rubbed off on his shirt from his sweat. But maybe he could find something. He noticed Contreras was looking behind him, like he was studying the way they had come.

"What is it?" Murieta asked, glancing back over his shoulder.

Contreras sniffed. "Something."

Murieta saw he had his hand ready to draw his pistol. *"¿Gringos?"*

Contreras inhaled deeply.

Murieta thought he was trying to catch the scent of whatever it was.

"Maybe *gringos*," Contreras said. "Or maybe I'm hoping."

Murieta had seen his friend edgy like this before. Maybe he smelled *gringos*, if it was *gringos*. He remembered Contreras telling that once he had killed a Chinese man he had smelled a good mile off.

Murieta looked over the piece of newspaper, trying to find something to distract his friend.

"Listen to this," Murieta said. " 'How to quiet a baby. As soon as the squaller awakes, set the child up, propped by pillows, and smear its fingers with thick molasses. Then put half a dozen feathers into its hands, and the young one will pick the feathers from one hand to the other until it drops to sleep. As soon—' That's all. It's torn off. But what do you think about that? About babies?"

"I don't like babies."

"Why not?"

"Because to have the babies you have to have the woman, and I cannot stand the woman, and the woman can't stand me." Contreras took a biscuit from his saddlebag and started chewing on it.

"Ah, I forgot you were married once."

"*Sí*. In Chile. And my wife, she tried to kill me pouring lead in my ear while I'm sleeping. I told you before."

Murieta shook his head, even though he did know the story. He liked hearing Contreras tell it.

"My wife," Contreras said, "she said I smelled bad after we were married. I tell her it was the scent of a man. She said no it's the smell like ox piss. I thought it over and I said ox piss smelled different. She called me El Bruto. Soon she was calling me El Bruto everywhere we went, in front of everyone. I liked it. I even told people to call me that. And they did! And my wife, she just got madder. Then she poured the lead in my ear."

Murieta laughed. "And then what happened?"

"It hurt. I still can't hear in this ear so good." He pointed at his right ear. "I told her don't do it again. One day I woke up, she was gone." He shrugged.

"How long ago was that?"

Contreras thought a moment. "Four years, *mas o menos*. You know, some said I killed her, cut her into pieces." He bit off a chunk of his biscuit. "I didn't. But I still like it people call me El Bruto."

"Maybe you'll find a good woman soon, eh?"

"No," he said, spitting out the hunk of biscuit and throwing the rest away. "She was the best woman, my wife."

"But she tried to kill you!"

"*Sí*, but if it wasn't for her, I would be cold and poor back in my village in Chile today."

Murieta laughed and turned the page over. His blood ran cold.

"*¡Pendejos!*" he said.

"*¿Que?*"

"Filthy *gringos*," Murieta said, staring at the paper. "They say that I tried to rape a woman."

"Rape?"

"It says right here Mary Miller says she was attacked by a Joaquin."

Contreras sighed and shook his head.

Murieta looked at him. "*No molestar.* Never! You know that. *¿Si?*"

"*Es verdad.*"

"Why would they say this?" Murieta shook the paper at Contreras. "I did no such thing."

"No, you didn't."

"I don't know this woman. I would kill any man who did such a thing."

"I know you would."

"These lies. *Gringo* lies," Murieta said. "Robberies, killings, *si,* those I do. But this. Joaquin is blamed for everything, but not this. I want to tell this newspaper I would never do this."

"You can tell them, *jefe.* It won't change what the *gringos* say. But you can tell them."

Murieta knew his friend was right but he was still angry. He was about to throw the paper away when he noticed Contreras had stopped again, and he reined in his own horse.

"Do you see anyone behind us?" Contreras asked.

Murieta looked back. He saw no movement, no dust clouds, just that gold blanket extending for miles.

"I see land the *gringos* don't deserve," Murieta said.

Contreras grunted, took off his hat, and fanned himself with it. "Maybe it's the heat playing tricks on me."

Moving again, Murieta decided he would show this newspaper to his *compadres* at Arroyo Contoova. He'd have words with them about it. And if he found out one of his men had done what the paper said, he would shoot that man himself.

Opening the small saddlebag below the horn, he stuck the piece of newspaper inside and felt the Bible Ana Benitez had given him. He remembered it was Sunday and the promise he made to Ana to read from it. But he was still too angry with the damn *gringos* and their lies. He closed the saddlebag flap. He'd open the Bible later.

Contreras was starting to get worried. His *amigo* hadn't let him kill the fiery-haired *gringo* who insulted them in San Gabriel, and he didn't let him skin the two robbers this morning. That wasn't like him. He was reading about babies in the newspaper, so maybe the *jefe* wants to have a baby. But he also wants to tell *gringos* to stop writing lies about him.

The more Contreras thought about it, the more worried he got. Then he thought maybe it was best Murieta really was going to leave California and go back to Mexico after he got his gold at Arroyo Cantoova. He would never say it out loud, but he was beginning to think maybe Murieta no longer had the stomach for this kind of life.

But now that he thought it, Contreras didn't want to admit it might be true. He had ridden too many miles at his *amigo*'s side. He could still remember that first day they met two years ago when he was ready to cut Murieta's throat because Murieta had killed and robbed two prospectors on the same road he used to ambush and rob and kill prospectors on. And what had Murieta said to him facing the point of his knife? Let's work together for a week and if you aren't happy, you can kill me. That had made Contreras laugh, but they had much gold at the end of that week, and they rode many miles together after that. He felt obliged to his young *amigo,* the *jefe,* for all the gold he collected.

Contreras felt the side of his head beginning to throb. There was a knot there, a lump that had never gone away. He rubbed it and remembered the Dutch prospector who gave it to him. Contreras had surprised him at his campsite when a couple of the Dutchman's friends came along, drawing Contreras's attention. He didn't see the skinny Dutchman grab a spade but he felt it when he whopped him over the head with it. Contreras didn't take it well. He shot the Dutchman's two friends, and the Dutchman he cut into pieces. Contreras later heard that one of the men he had shot lived long enough to tell what happened. After that, the *gringos* called Contreras the Animal. He liked that. It made him smile.

But right now that knot hurt worse and that got him thinking about all the scars he'd gotten from raids and shootouts with sheriffs and vigilantes and *gringos* who wouldn't hand over their gold. He had half a dozen knife wounds and thirteen bullet holes for his trouble.

And then it occurred to him that all his wounds and holes and knots had come from raids and robberies he did without Murieta. When he was with Murieta, no matter how many bullets flew or how many *gringo* lawmen swarmed around them, neither of them had gotten so much as a scratch. And the *jefe* was never scared, almost like he knew nothing was going to touch him. Or could touch him.

But now Contreras was having doubts about Murieta. This was very bad. He thought maybe the ghost woman, Ana Benitez, had something to do with it. Strange forces were at work in her house. Broken pots went back together by themselves. A saint painted on a piece of wood talked to her. Maybe she did something to the *jefe*, a spell maybe. All this started after he saw her last night, didn't it? Contreras always thought she had some kind of power over Murieta.

He shuddered. His thoughts disturbed him. Things were changing too fast. Murieta was different, not the same man. He was giving up being a bandit and going back to his wife in

Mexico. He didn't let him kill the *gringos* the way he wanted. Contreras rubbed the aching knot on his head. He had a bad feeling.

Reaching behind him into his large saddlebag, he pulled out a heavy vest of chain mail. In spite of the heat, he put it on.

"You still have that?" Murieta asked him.

Contreras nodded. "The woven metal, it stops the little balls of lead."

"I know. I remember the Frenchman who made it," Murieta said.

"*Si,* the same one you made put it on to prove it worked," Contreras said, giving up on a clip to fasten the vest.

"You know you're going to burn up in that thing."

Contreras waved him off. "It'll be fine." He tried to fasten another clip but his big belly wouldn't allow it. "*Pendejo,*" he whispered.

"We shot that Frenchman ten times," Murieta said.

"You told him you wanted to make sure it did what he said it would do," Contreras said, fanning the vest. It really was hotter with it on.

"I remember. I also remember I lost it to you in a game of monte," Murieta said. "But I thought you sold it to Reyes."

"And now I wish I had," Contreras said and yanked off the vest with an oath.

Murieta laughed. "I told you it would be too hot, besides, you don't need the armor. Your hide is tough enough."

Grumbling, Contreras stuffed the heavy vest back in his saddlebag. He still had that bad feeling. Suddenly, he heard Murieta shout, "Here they come!"

Murieta was laughing. He took his hat off and waved it over his head. The great herd of horses off in the distance heading north looked magnificent from the top of the knoll where he sat. He guessed there must be two or three thousand head, and a dozen cowboys guiding them.

"Do you see them?" he asked.

"Oh, I see many horses," Contreras said. "Too many to try to steal. And too many *vaqueros* with them to fight today."

"No," Murieta said and pointed. "There, coming this way. Two riders. That's *Señor* Pico with the red sash around his middle, and his son, Romulo. Come on."

He rode down the knoll, Contreras following. Seeing Pico's face brighten as they got closer was truly a good sign.

"*¡Patrón!*" Murieta shouted.

"Joaquin!" Pico shouted back.

Murieta embraced Pico, neither one dismounting his horse, and then greeted Romulo, reminding him that some still said they looked like brothers.

"It's been too long," Pico said to Murieta. "And you bring all this heat with you."

"*Si,* and my *amigo,* Feliz Contreras, too," Murieta laughed. "Much has happened since I saw you last."

"Yes, I know," Pico said. "I read the papers."

"They lie," Murieta said, feeling his anger rising.

"So do I," Pico said. "But the difference is—"

"He knows when he's doing it," Romulo cut in.

As they all shared a laugh, Murieta saw the understanding on Pico's face.

"*Gracias, patrón,*" he said and clapped Pico on the shoulder. "Now, somehow you look different."

"My hair is grayer," he said and then patted his stomach, "my belly is bigger, but life goes on."

"And so do these horses," Romulo said and excused himself to get back to the herd.

"Come, we'll go to the house," Pico said to Murieta as they started toward the herd. "You will eat and rest. I have fresh horses. My wife will be pleased to see you. At least as much as I am."

"*Gracias,*" Murieta said and then noticed Pico looking over at Contreras who was watching behind them.

"Is someone after you two?" Pico asked.

"I think he's restless," Murieta said.

"Maybe," Contreras said, wiping the sweat from his face. "Or maybe those two we killed this morning have friends who are after us."

"What happened this morning?" Pico asked.

Murieta told him about the two robbers.

"Nothing is the way it used to be," Pico said.

Murieta heard the melancholy in Pico's voice but there was nothing he could do. The *gringos* weren't leaving and Pico was staying and Murieta knew he'd be gone soon enough. Everyone had made his choice.

Pico inquired about his plans and Murieta told him he would be back in Mexico by Christmas and of his vow never to return.

"I think it's the right decision for you," Pico said.

Murieta asked Pico if he would help him this one last time. Pico agreed, of course. Murieta opened his large saddlebag and showed him the canvas sack.

"Five thousand dollars," Murieta said. "It's all I have with me. I'd like you to see that the neediest get it, as you have done in the past for me."

"A lot of people around here know you have a good heart," Pico said.

"And others would say different," Murieta said. He remembered the letter he had stuck in his vest and pulled it out. "And would you see to posting this letter?"

When Pico took it, Murieta saw the puzzled look on his face.

"Mrs. Gilbert Opdyke?"

"Let's say I think she might like to have it," Murieta said.

"He was one of the *gringos* we killed today," Contreras said.

Murieta still didn't entirely know why he took the letter in the first place. He wasn't going soft, he just figured the stupid *gringo*'s wife should have her man's words, especially the last ones. He'd want Rosita to have his.

Looking at Pico, holding the letter in his hand and studying him, Murieta had the feeling his friend figured the same thing as he nodded and put the letter in his pocket.

As they reached the left flank of the drag of the herd, Murieta sensed something might be troubling his friend. He knew it would be impolite to ask outright, but how to ask without offending at all?

"My friend Eulogio de Celis has made a proposition to me," Pico said.

Murieta was startled, not only because Pico suddenly spoke, but by what he said.

"He asked if my brother and I would consider purchasing half interest in all this," Pico said, extending his arm out.

"All this what?" Murieta asked.

"His Rancho San Fernando. He says he would rather share it with my brother and me than have to give it over to pay a debt to El Boticario."

Murieta knew that meant pharmacist, and Ana had told him about El Boticario, a *gringo* named John G. Downey, who had married a woman from a poor *Californio* family a few years ago. He had opened a successful drugstore, the only one between San Francisco and San Diego, and became a moneylender as there were no banks. By virtue of the marriage, the local *Californios,* who assumed Downey would act in the local traditions allowing them all manner of hospitalities, had accepted him. But Murieta had not been surprised to hear that traditions and hospitalities meant nothing to a *gringo*.

"What did your friend do?" Murieta asked.

"Two Christmases ago he had guests," Pico began. "They'd never seen Los Angeles before and he thought it would make great entertainment for them. Eulogio goes to El Boticario and asks him for fifty dollars. He gladly signs the note El Boticario requested. He is one of us, a *Californio*. Eulogio never thinks of it again. He'll repay the loan eventually."

"Of course," Murieta says. "It's understood."

"Not any more," Pico said. "El Boticario demanded payment and the interest this past Christmas. Eulogio says he knew nothing of any interest but he could have the fifty for him the following day. El Boticario tells him no. He shows him the note bearing Euligio's signature and the terms he agreed to. The note has the interest at the rate of twelve and a half per cent a day, compounded daily. Fifty had grown to over five thousand dollars!"

"Pendejo," Contreras said.

Murieta seethed. "Go on."

Pico said that since de Celis didn't have this money, El Boticario allowed him to sign a new note for the five thousand dollars with interest at five per cent a month, compounded monthly and due in three months. El Boticario said it was only business, personal feelings weren't involved, but he required security. De Celis offered his cattle, all three thousand of them.

"And he didn't pay in time. *¿Si?*" Murieta asked.

Pico nodded. "But El Boticario didn't come back in three months. He waited a year."

"Puta madre," Contreras said.

"He took the cattle, which he said now only covered part of the note," Pico said and took a drink from his canteen, then offered it to Murieta. "Eulogio still owed nine thousand dollars. He signed another note, at five per cent a month, compounded monthly. He used his forty-thousand-acre *rancho* as security and now he's afraid he'll lose his home. This El Boticario is a black hand. And Eulogio's not the only one. I know of four others El Boticario has his hooks into."

"All the *gringo* understands is money," Murieta said, handing Pico back the canteen and nodding his thanks.

"Maybe it's our own fault," Pico said. "We're living too far in the past."

"No, you're honorable men," Murieta said.

"That used to be enough," Pico said. "The land still looks the same, but it's changed. Since we have chosen to stay, we have to change with it, become like it."

"Not you," Murieta said.

"The *Californios* are dying. I know it as well as I know how to handle a horse or use a *riata*."

"You'll never be like the Yankee *gringos*," Murieta said. He saw a sad smile on Pico's face, and an idea came to him.

"Allow us to rid you of this *pendejo*, El Boticario," Murieta said.

"That's a good idea," Contreras said, opening his water bag and taking a drink.

Pico looked stunned. "I cannot allow it."

"*Señor*," Contreras said, "it would give me great pleasure to flay his skin from his body, hang him, and shoot him."

The old man shook his head.

"It would be the end of him and your problem," Murieta said.

"I'm afraid the *gringos* will always be here," Pico said, pulling out a handkerchief and wiping his face. "Kill El Boticario and another like him will come. It's the way of things now."

Murieta saw the resignation on Pico's face, and realized the man wanted no trouble with the *Americanos*. It occurred to Murieta that his friend seemed beaten by the *gringos*, he was becoming like them. Things had changed too much, he thought sadly.

125

"Besides," Pico said, "you're giving up your *bandito* ways. And I wouldn't have wanted to see them catch you."

"If they had, you wouldn't have allowed them to hang me. *¿No?*"

He saw Pico hesitate just before Romulo came riding up fast, shouting that *gringo* riders were coming! Seven or eight of them. Coming hard.

"Lay low on your saddles," Pico said quickly. "Run like the wind."

Murieta started to speak but Pico let out with a wild scream, drew his pistol, and fired it into the air. Everything seemed to happen at once as he heard other shouts from Romulo and the *vaqueros*. He saw Contreras fire his revolver. He drew his own, raised it high and fired, and three thousand horses bolted at once.

Chapter Twelve:
The Pursuit

Murieta gave Diablo his head, hunkered low in his saddle, tucked his knees in, and pushed his toes into the stirrups. He could feel the thunder rolling through the ground as the great herd, frightened and furious, charged across the valley floor. With the swirling dust and dirt thrown into the air, he couldn't see Contreras or Pico, but he laughed. Blood pounded in his head. If his horse fell he'd be trampled to death. He felt alive, scared, and giddy.

Up ahead, Murieta thought he could make out the San Fernando Mission, Pico's house, and other buildings sitting on the open plain. Beyond them rose the rough foothills, then the mountains, and the V forming the pass. Using his spurs, he gained on the point of the breaking herd.

Regardless of how he thought Pico had changed, his friend had bought him and Contreras time and cover. And Murieta had never known Contreras to be wrong at sniffing out *gringos* and trouble. Contreras had been right again, but it was too late now. If these *gringos* want us, they can fight through Pico's horses, Murieta thought. And if they aren't chasing us, they'll have a sight to tell their children about.

Murieta flew past the old church, the herd in violent pursuit. Maybe the *gringos,* too. He couldn't tell. But he caught a glimpse of the gates of Pico's corrals standing open, and the hired hands there scrambling to turn and stop the wild herd, no doubt still being pushed by Pico and his *vaqueros.* This was the kind of confusion Murieta knew he needed.

Looking back over his shoulder he saw Contreras closing fast and hundreds of horses still running behind them, a massive cloud of dust swirling, engulfing the church, house, and corrals. As he started the climb into the foothills, Murieta could see no riders giving chase. A few minutes later he turned again and saw the herd had scattered, fanned out, dust trails rising in all directions.

He licked his dry lips and saw Contreras coming up through the rocks below.

"¡Muy bien, hombre!" Murieta shouted, and he saw Contreras raise his hand.

Halfway up the foothills Murieta stopped and waited for Contreras. Grinning and breathing hard, they marveled at the hazy chaos below. Murieta saw them first. They were like dark specters, galloping out of the lingering dust. Eight mounted riders.

"Those aren't Pico's men," he said.

He looked at Contreras. Their grins widened, like naughty schoolboys playing tricks on the teacher.

"You remember the meeting place?" Murieta asked.

"I'll see you there, *jefe.*"

As Contreras made for the pass, Murieta veered into the hills and canyons to the northeast.

Spurring his horse along a crest, he glanced back. The posse was maybe a mile away. He chuckled, then tried to spot Contreras but picked up no movement.

Looking back down at the *gringos,* Murieta saw the posse divide. Two were following his trail. The other six continued up after Contreras. Make your shots count, Feliz, Murieta thought, and see that they're all dead before you take your knife and start cutting. He took a swallow of water from his water bag knowing he had to conserve what little he had left. His clothes were soaked with sweat. Looking up, he saw an infinite and cloudless blue sky, and felt the heat hammering down mercilessly.

He wished he'd been able to get a fresh horse from Pico, but took comfort in knowing this posse had no advantage there, either. He patted the damp heated neck of Diablo.

"This is why I keep you well fed and don't allow you to get fat and lazy," he said to the horse. "Let's see how much the *gringos*' horses can take, eh? And let's hope they aren't riding your brothers or sisters."

It surprised Murieta how doggedly the two *gringos* remained on his trail over the long, heated miles of sagebrush-covered hills and through craggy canyons. Riding through a dry streambed he heard a bullet whistle past his ear. He looked back. The *gringos* were so close! A few hundred yards maybe. Closer than he thought! How did he lose so much ground and not know? The heat was playing tricks. And one of these *gringos* was a fair shot, or was it luck? Murieta bet on luck. Determined no bullet would find him this day, he spurred Diablo's flanks. Drawing his revolver, he twisted around and fired at the *gringos*. The shot went wild. He knew it would. This heat sapped his strength and energy. The excitement he'd felt before had drained out of him, carried in every drop of sweat. But he knew it could be no different for the *gringos*.

Exhausted and unsteady, Murieta fired a few more times, each shot wide of its mark. And when the *gringos* fired back, they did no better. Murieta figured they were too worn out to take careful aim, just like him. He even felt too weary to reload. Urging Diablo on, he widened the distance, wishing those damn *gringos* would go away.

Climbing up a rocky hillside, he walked his horse, keeping a watchful eye for his pursuers. Diablo was tired, he knew, and needed the break.

When he thought it was safe, Murieta stopped and poured some of his water into his cupped hand to let Diablo drink.

"Just a bit now," he said. "A ruined horse would be as bad as having no more water, eh, Diablo?"

Murieta took a swallow for himself. The water was hot, but wet. He had to conserve what he had left, maybe a few cupfuls. Corking the bag, he slung it over the saddle horn and checked for *gringos*. Pulling Diablo's reins behind him, he started walking and nearly stumbled over a stone. He forced himself to pick up his feet, to move forward, trudging past juniper trees and thorny yuccas.

Murieta blew out a breath and looked up at the sun, shielding his eyes with his hand. The sun hung there, huge, white, and burning. The afternoon had become an inferno. He wiped his face on his sleeve. He heard Diablo snort. A horse would run itself to death for a rider, Murieta knew well. Those *gringos*, he wondered, were they smart enough not to ride their horses into the ground?

"How you like the heat, *gringos*?" he chuckled weakly and glanced behind him. He saw the two *gringos*, mounted, coming around a hillside, still following his trail.

"Sons of a whore," Murieta muttered as he leapt on Diablo and slapped his rump.

He refused to give in and the *gringos* wouldn't give up. The heat bore down, relentless, blistering, and dry, and Murieta saw only his disadvantages. He could do nothing about the tracks he left, whether he was in sight or not. I have been chased, shot at, and escaped before, Murieta thought, but these two *gringos*, they don't stop. Persistent *pendejos*. I could wait and ambush them. Would they expect it? He decided they would.

Murieta knew of a small lake near the grand pointed rocks. He had to reach it for the water he needed and for Diablo whose neck, chest, belly, and flanks were soaked a frothy white.

"Stay with me, *mi amigo*," Murieta said in a parched whisper, patting the exhausted horse's lathered neck.

Drawing in a deep breath through his nostrils, all Murieta sensed was hot, heavy dryness. Then he noticed blood dripping onto his shirt. He sniffed and tasted blood. His blood. He had a nosebleed.

Glancing behind him he didn't see the *gringos*. He put his head back, the heel of his palm to his nose to stop the bleeding. He closed his eyes against the sun. His throat felt dry. He had to try to stop breathing through his mouth. Closing his mouth, he tasted more blood. Not much. He tried not to think of water. He'd been dry before, but not like this. Cool water. A taste. Enough to fill his mouth. To feel it on his tongue, down his dry, burning throat. He'd buy a swallow for a bag of gold. Two bags! Just a swallow of water . . .

Murieta jerked his head down and checked his hand. There was only a little blood.

Looking up ahead, he saw the ground shimmering in the heat. His lungs hurt from the hot air he breathed in. He closed his eyes and bent over and breathed in through his nose. When he straightened back up, something was up ahead. It was hazy and strange. He blinked and rubbed his eyes. A saloon. How could it be out here? And coming out the door was Contreras, calling to him and holding up a glass pitcher full of water. Murieta couldn't hear what he was saying. He started toward him.

"Feliz!" he cried. "*¡Mi amigo!*"

Murieta fell to his knees, got up, and saw Contreras tip the pitcher and pour out the water onto the floor.

"No! Stop! *¡Agua, por favor!*" Murieta cried.

Stumbling a few steps toward his friend and the saloon, Murieta fell again, his face into the dirt. He lifted his head and felt the scratches where stones had scraped his face. Contreras and the saloon were gone, replaced by boulders and yuccas.

Feeling the sun continuing to beat down on him, Murieta got to his feet. His nose was bleeding again. Walking back to Diablo, he took the reins in his hands and pulled himself up into the saddle.

"Just a little more," he said to the horse and gently kicked him.

Opening his water bag, Murieta made himself only take a swallow and then wet his hand enough to rub over his face. As he passed through the spot where the saloon had been, he cursed this miserable dusty heat that sapped a body dry.

Murieta didn't know how long he'd been on the run, but he was grateful to see the sun finally dipping toward the western horizon. At a rocky outcrop near the head of a canyon he stopped. He heard Diablo cough and saw his tongue hanging loosely from his lathered mouth. Murieta poured water from his water bag into his hand. Diablo lapped and drank. Murieta rubbed water on Diablo's legs, cooling him a little. The water bag was nearly empty now. He raised the bag to his mouth and took the last for himself, betting he'd get to the lake before long.

He climbed up into the rocks and listened. It was quiet, as though every living thing had come to an eerie stop in the heat. Had the *gringos* given up? Maybe they had gotten smart after all. Or maybe they had passed out. Fell off their horses. Broke their heads open. Dying slowly. The idea pleased him.

Peering over the rocks he saw them coming over a hill, ever on his trail. Who are these *pendejos*? he wondered. Looking more closely at the two, he saw the blue coat one had on. He'd seen it before, but where?

It was nearly twilight and the heat was still blistering when Murieta finally reached the shallow, sweet-water lake. He jumped in and drank, and then remembered Diablo. Looking around, he saw the horse, his nose down, sucking up the water. He pulled the horse's head up and told him he would have to wait a little bit, that drinking too much water right away was very bad for overheated horses.

"I wish I had *aguardiente*," Murieta said, patting Diablo's chest. "I would rub you down with it. Cool you more, make you feel clean." He scratched the horse's nose. "I could use some myself. Not for my outside, but my inside. My friend, *Señor* Pico, he has barrels of it. Did I tell you it's the local brandy here? We could both use some. *¿Si?*"

After a few minutes Murieta let Diablo drink while he filled his water bag. He saw the grand pointed rocks, maybe a quarter mile away, jutting up out of the ground, impossible to miss. He intended to hide among them and kill the *gringos pendejos,* if they had the *cojones* to follow him in there. Looking back across the rolling hills covered with patches of buckwheat and chamise in thickets, Murieta saw no riders. He put on his *serape.* Figuring he had climbed around two thousand feet, he knew it would get cold quickly once the sun went down.

Mounting Diablo, he started for the pointed rocks. He was feeling better now. And he was hungry. Even one of those hard biscuits that Contreras had would be good now. He checked over his shoulder for sign of the *gringos.* Maybe they had shot each other. Maybe they gave up. Or maybe Contreras had found them and was waiting for him at the rocks. This would be a story to tell the others at Arroyo Cantoova.

He chuckled at the thought and then felt the searing hot flash of a bullet enter his back. He slumped forward, then heard the report of the rifle crack in his ears.

Drawing himself up, Murieta wheeled his tired horse around and reached for his revolver. Fighting the pain, he raised the gun, but could find no target, his eyes refusing to focus. The barrel wobbled, his arm unsteady. Where are they? More shots.

Another bullet tore into his chest. It felt like fire racing through every part of his body.

Murieta tried to control Diablo as he reeled, whinnying and snorting in agony. Diablo was hit, too, blood running down his neck. Stay up! Murieta's mind screamed. We stay up and kill these *gringos* together!

But he realized Diablo was rearing up on his hind legs to fighting stance.

In that same instant Murieta saw the riders charging at him out of the yellow glow of the setting sun. He felt himself slipping from the saddle. It seemed that the earth and rocks were reaching for him.

CHAPTER THIRTEEN:
THE GRINGOS

Murieta felt like his senses were all twisted around. Voices in his head kept saying "Who are you?" and "Why'd you run?" but he couldn't see any faces. He tried to get his clouded eyes focused but shadows were playing some kind of trick on them. Nothing looked real. Blotches wavered. He wanted to rub his eyes, but he couldn't bring his hands up. Then, he saw his legs stretched out in front of him in the dirt. One of them was tied up in a splint of juniper, the *calzonares* pant leg torn up, many of the brass buttons missing, a few hanging from loose threads. He tried to swallow but realized his mouth was raw and dry. Maybe he'd been breathing through it instead of his nose. Then he heard the crackle of fire and saw the shifting shadows of a campfire burning a few feet from his boots. No, only one. The boot was missing from his splinted leg. And his ankle was badly swollen.

Raising his head, he saw beyond the fire a great reddish-yellow glow dancing on a massive rock face a hundred feet high. The rock slanted upward, layers on layers, great huge slabs, folded on itself, its jagged peaks pointing crazily, accusingly at the sky. But across that rock face two strange dark shapes seemed to shimmer, drift, disappear, and float back again. One was large and hulking, the other smaller and spidery. Specters? Shadows? Demons?

They moved near the campfire and Murieta could make them out more clearly. The *hombre grande* wore a shabby sombrero

135

and was drinking from a canteen while the little one, who wore a tall hat, was tagging after him. Murieta saw them squat near the fire, saw their mouths moving, and he heard voices, bickering voices.

"Hells bells, Needle, you want something to eat, check his saddlebag. Maybe something's in there."

"Only thing in it was a piece of newspaper and an old Mex Bible. No valuables. Besides, I'd sooner eat a month-old dead dog than a damn greaser's leavings."

"Well, since we got no dead dog, I guess you'll have to go hungry."

"Shit, Clegg, I'm just saying I'm hungry's all."

"And I'm tired of listening to your belly-aching all day long, so shut up."

Then the pain struck and Murieta sucked in a tense breath, feeling like he was skewered with thousands of heated vicious shards of glass through his back and chest and leg, tearing him to shreds and then seeming to ease off slowly.

"Hey, he's awake," he heard the one called Needle say followed by the sound of running footsteps.

Murieta saw this fiery-haired *gringo* with ugly teeth looking him in the face. It was strange. He recognized him . . . he'd seen him somewhere before, but didn't know why . . . couldn't tell from where. The *gringo* was talking at him fast.

"You're Joaquin, ain't that right? Just say it's so. You're him. Tell us. Come on now, Mex. Say it. Say it!"

Murieta didn't answer. He didn't want to. He closed his eyes and hoped he was not in hell.

Opening his eyes again, he knew it wasn't hell, but almost wished it was as he realized he was in the hands of the *gringos*.

He saw the face of the *hombre grande* called Clegg before him, clearly, keenly, and he was saying something, and it sounded kindly.

136

"How you feeling? You was rambling before, couldn't make much sense of it since I don't speak much Spanish. Being you're all busted up, I expect you're hurting pretty good."

"To hell with how he's feeling," he heard the other one say. "Find out who he is."

Murieta pulled his head away when Clegg brought a cloth up to his face, then realized Clegg was going to wipe his brow and cheeks. He heard Clegg's voice.

"Hold your horses. We'll find out, all right?"

"I just want to know before he up and dies on us is all," Needle said. "I already got his gun and two knives. I could sell those for a pretty price if they belonged to a Joaquin."

Murieta saw the *hombre grande* Clegg close his eyes and sigh. He smelled the alcohol on his breath. Then the *hombre grande* brought a canteen up for him to see and nodded at him. Murieta nodded back and Clegg put the lip of the canteen to his mouth.

"Careful now," Clegg said.

Murieta pulled his mouth away suddenly, sputtering and choking, realizing it was *aguardiente* Clegg had in his canteen.

"It'll keep the chill off tonight," Clegg said. "Have a little more. You'll need it."

Murieta took a drink, the hot sweetness warming his throat and chest.

"This brandy's all I got," Clegg said. "And that one," indicating Needle, "he won't let you have any of his water."

Murieta saw a sadness in Clegg's eyes.

"If your name's not Joaquin why not just say so?" the *hombre grande* asked quietly.

It was coming back to Murieta, the day, the flight on horseback, Feliz, the heat, the shots, the blackness. Where was Diablo? He glanced around and saw two horses tethered to a scrub tree off to his left. Diablo wasn't one of them. Then he remembered Diablo rearing, fighting, and bleeding. Suddenly, Murieta jerked, seized by burning pains in his chest and shooting through his leg and felt the ropes cutting into the flesh of his wrists. He realized the two *gringos* had bound his hands behind him and tied him to a juniper tree. There he sat, two holes in him and a broken left leg. Maybe a broken ankle, too. He looked down and saw they had used his *serape* to cover him, to keep him warm. The serape was bloody with two stains. The blood must have seeped through. He figured the *gringos* had also patched up the holes they put in him as he felt something wrapped around his chest. And then there was that splint holding his leg straight and only a little brandy to help the pain.

"No sabe," Murieta muttered through gritted teeth and watched Clegg shrug and walk away.

Why tell them anything? Murieta thought. The big one, he bandages my wounds and gives me drink but I still bleed like a pig . . . *No sabe.* I know nothing . . . except I have been in this California of theirs too long . . . and the bone in my leg is in pieces . . . Where do they think I'll run? He chuckled.

"Shut the hell up, you greaser son-of-a-bitch!" Needle shouted.

Murieta saw him, inches away.

"Ain't nothing funny here! You sabee just fine, I bet."

"There's no need for that," Clegg said.

"You know that's how guilty greasers do when they know they been caught," Needle said as he straightened up and tucked his thumbs into the dirty red uniform sash he wore over his gun belt. "They shut up, act like they don't understand. 'No sabee' he says. That your big joke, huh?"

Murieta watched him without expression and recognized the hate on Needle's face, watched him yank his hat off, and felt the agony as Needle kicked his good leg hard. Murieta screamed. He'd kill this *gringo pendejo* gladly given the chance.

Opening his eyes, hate clearing his vision, Murieta looked at the wild fiery hair and that crooked black-toothed grin. Where had he seen him?

"How you like that big joke, Mr. Joaquin?" Needle leaned in close. "I don't hear you laughing now."

The beefy hand of Clegg spun Needle around.

"That's enough," Clegg said. "You're a ranger, and the lieutenant won't take kindly to you beating on the prisoner."

Rangers! Murieta thought, the disgust rising like bile. So these are what the *estupido* governor has sent after me.

He watched Clegg move over to the fire and Needle turned back to him and leaned in.

"You better watch out, you damn greaser," he said low.

Those words! The fiery hair. It was coming back to Murieta. This was the *gringo* he saw dragging the body in San Gabriel, the one who fell on his ass.

"Get away from him, Needle!" Clegg roared.

Needle jerked straight up. Murieta could tell the *gringo pendejo* was scared of the *hombre grande*.

"Hell, Uriah, I was just trying to scare the greaser some," Needle said. "Maybe get him to fess up before Lieutenant Quick gets here."

"Get more wood for the fire. It's cold, and it's going to get colder," Clegg said and took a pull from his canteen.

Murieta heard Needle grumble as he walked away, but kept his eye on Clegg who was leaning against that giant wave-like rock and sucking on that canteen, the one with the *aguardiente* in it. He didn't let that canteen get far from his mouth.

Murieta watched as the burly giant pushed himself away from the rock wall, came over, and sat down by him. When he offered another drink to him, Murieta accepted. This fire felt good going down his throat.

"*Gracias,*" he said.

Clegg took a pull, then said, "I don't believe you're this Joaquin with the thousand-dollar price on his head. See, I've heard stories about all these Joaquins being protected by evil spirits. That's why they ain't been caught."

After taking another pull, he tipped the canteen to Murieta.

Grateful, Murieta took a drink and tried to figure out what evil spirits Clegg was talking about. He was beginning to feel light-headed from the brandy.

"I believe in them. Spirits, I mean," Clegg said. "I was in Georgia rounding up runaway Cherokees. You know, Indians? And some of them had powerful magic on their side. Reason they never did get caught. Some didn't have magic. Just bad superstition." Clegg upended the canteen to his mouth and then pulled it away.

"Empty already," he said and looked at Murieta. "You understand what I'm saying?"

Murieta said nothing. He knew Clegg was getting drunker, and so was he.

"If you was that Joaquin," Clegg said, "we wouldn't have caught you because of that magic you'd've had. That's why we didn't catch some of them Cherokee. But some we did."

Murieta saw a strange, distant look in Clegg's eyes. And as quick as it came, it was gone.

"Some we did," Clegg said again. Then he blinked, wiped his mouth, and grabbed onto the juniper branches to pull himself up. "I got to go get another canteen, try to chase away those demons that refuse to stay put off. They always come to me."

As Clegg lumbered away toward where he had his saddle propped up against a boulder, Murieta had to strain to hear him.

"Can't do nothing about them spirits," Clegg said. "They just won't stay away. Can't grow a new leg either, or undo what I done to those Indians long ago."

Murieta heard a hollow clunk when Clegg dropped his empty canteen. He hoped it was water Clegg was reaching for when he saw him take hold of the strap from around the horn of his saddle and yank up another canteen. Murieta counted two more canteens hanging off his saddle.

"Agua, señor," Murieta called out. He could feel his dry lips cracking and his head getting lighter. *"Agua, por favor."*

Clegg didn't appear to have heard him as Murieta watched Clegg open the canteen and take a long pull.

Murieta knew water could become as precious as gold. The fever to possess either of them had resulted in many a killing in the past few years as he and his *compadres* had murdered for both. He looked away in frustration and noticed his water bag hanging on his saddle. His vision was getting a little fuzzy but he could tell it was within arm's reach. He hadn't realized it had been there all this time. And he remembered that water bag was nearly half full.

"Agua. Aqui." Murieta said, his mouth too dry to shout. He jerked his head toward the saddle when he saw Clegg looking his way. *"Aqui."*

Murieta heard a sound like boots scraping on rocks and saw Needle returning, carrying an armload of chamise and manzanita branches. He stopped on the other side of the fire opposite Murieta and dropped the wood into a pile.

"You say something there, greaser?" Needle asked, crouching and tossing more wood on the fire, making it crackle and spark brightly.

Seeing the cinders jump like popping corn, Murieta imagined hundreds of them leaping onto this *gringo pendejo* and consuming his vitals.

"Did you say ah-goo-wah?" Needle asked, grinning. "I don't speak no Mex greaser lingo. You want something, you ask in American, sabee?"

¡Pendejo! Murieta thought. If El Bruto was here you'd be screaming for mercy! If I wasn't tied up . . . Give me my water! It was getting hard for him to hold his head up. He heard Clegg cough.

"Get the Mexican some water," Clegg said, wiping his mouth.

"Why do I have to do everything?" Needle whined, still hunched down and throwing a few more branches on the fire. "I build the fire, get the wood, lug the saddle off his dead horse, and now you want me to give this greaser bandit son-of-a-bitch some of *my* water."

"Give him his own water, right there on his saddle, you jackass!" Clegg roared.

Startled by Clegg's angry explosion, Needle jumped, lost his balance, and fell on his ass. Straightening up, he felt a shiver of anger and embarrassment race down his back, followed by drops of cold sweat. He glanced at the Mexican, searching for any sign he had witnessed this moment of mortification and awkward display. No sir, no greaser would live to tell a story like that about Ned Needle. Seeing the Mexican's chin resting on his chest, Needle was satisfied his honor was safe. Setting his jaw, Needle slowly and deliberately walked to the Mexican's saddle.

Murieta read the disgust on Needle's face as the *gringo* uncorked the spout on the water bag and held it to his mouth to drink. Though very warm, the water tasted sweet. He tried not to gulp but he wanted it, needed it so badly. It spilled over his mouth and ran down his cheeks onto his bloody *serape* covering his chest.

"Hurry up," Needle said impatiently and then pulled the water bag away.

"Mas," Murieta said weakly, but it was no use as he watched

Needle push the stopper back in the bag and toss it at the saddle where Murieta heard it land with a wet plunk.

Lowering his head, Murieta closed his eyes, trying to clear his head and gather his thoughts. He hoped Contreras had gotten away. Maybe he'd show up, and if he did, he wouldn't stop him from gutting this clumsy *gringo* fool this time. And that would be a grand story to tell his *amigos,* Valenzuela and Three-Fingered Jack and Enrique . . .

He saw their faces, drunk, laughing. Enrique's gold front tooth shined.

. . . I want to see you, he thought . . . laugh with you again . . . tell each other our adventures . . . go home . . . to Mexico . . .

He saw the people of his village greeting him with flowers. Where was Rosita?

. . . I must dig up the money, the gold I buried in Arroyo Cantoova . . . take everything from these greedy *Yanquis* . . . nothing sacred to them . . . live in peace . . . with Rosita . . . my beautiful Rosita . . .

He saw dark red blood on Rosita's torn white linen clothes.

. . . live happy . . .

Reaching down he took her soft, beautiful raven-colored hair from her bruised, bloodied face.

. . . Rosita? . . .

He held her long black hair in his bloody hands.

. . . Rosita, talk to me . . .

The hair slipped through his fingers.

. . . What have they done to you? Why did I bring you here . . .

"Hey Uriah," Needle hollered, "this greaser's crying."

Looking up, Murieta saw Needle walking toward him, snickering.

"Them slug holes we put in you hurt?" Needle asked, a taunt

in his voice. "You want your mama?"

Murieta turned his face away. He felt the tear tracks on his face and was angry this *gringo* saw them. He hadn't meant to cry. He had to be strong and not think of Rosita now. Show them no weakness.

"Go keep a watch for the others, Ned," Clegg said.

Looking up, Murieta saw Clegg coming toward the campfire, his walk unsteady. Needle went stiffly to his saddle a few yards away near where the rangers' horses were tied and snatched up his short blue cloak and water canteen from around the saddle horn.

As the two men passed each other, Murieta saw Needle raise his chin and sharply whip the blue cloak back over his shoulder, like he was daring Clegg, trying to call him out.

Murieta figured if the old drunk *hombre grande* were to kill that nasty little *pendejo,* he'd happily swear it was an accident. He was disappointed when Clegg paid Needle no mind.

After Needle walked off into the darkness, Clegg stood on the other side of the campfire and did something Murieta didn't expect. He went over to the horses, reached into the pocket of his soiled gray trousers, and came up with a few sugar cubes. He gave a couple to his chestnut mare and some to Needle's spotted horse.

He turned and Murieta saw him adjust the shiny Army Dragoon revolver he kept stuck in his wide black belt, pull off his shabby sombrero, and wipe his face with a yellow kerchief he took from inside his cloak.

"I better have a look at that tourniquet," Clegg said.

Murieta stiffened against the pain when Clegg checked the tourniquet and splint on his leg.

"You busted that leg in two places," Clegg said. "One's just above your ankle. Sorry I had to cut your boot off. Other one, your bone come through above your knee. I set it best I could and patched you up. Don't want you to end up like me." He patted his wooden peg. "Better have a drink."

Murieta felt the sweet hot burn again down his throat and into his empty belly. That brandy helped ease the pains shooting through his chest and leg.

"I shouldn't be using this for anything 'cept my horse," Clegg said as he held up the canteen and took a drink. "Helps cool the horse's back where the saddle lays, but I poured enough over his old heated hide so he wouldn't feel all galled after that ride you took us on today."

Murieta gritted his teeth and sucked in a sharp breath when Clegg gave the tourniquet a turn.

"Hell of a ride," Clegg said, admiration in his voice as he secured the tourniquet knot. "Spooking that herd, that was damn good thinking."

From out of the darkness came Needle's voice.

"Oh, man, something shit up here! Something big, too!"

"Probably a mountain lion," Clegg said.

He sounded unconcerned.

"Might be a bear," Clegg went on as he looked into the fire. "Whatever it is, if it eats Ned it'll have the runs for a week." He sniffed and rubbed his nose. "As I was saying, real smart running that herd. Of course, we were suspicious already, following your trail, but that stampede got us mighty curious."

Murieta had decided that Clegg didn't care if he understood what he was saying or not. The *hombre grande* wasn't trying to trick him. He was just talking.

"Here," Clegg said, offering the canteen, "you want more? *¿Mas?*"

Murieta nodded and tilted his head back. The brandy numbed the pain and warmed his blood.

"Didn't bring any food," Clegg said. "Kind of a hurry we got in this morning. Want another?"

Murieta took another drink, then Clegg had one.

"I prefer whiskey," Clegg said as he wiped his mouth on the back of his hand. "I'd be over to the El Dorado right now enjoying the company of my whiskey from a bottle. And my lady friend. Well, she's more a friendly acquaintance from back in Georgia. Dolly Akin. She come out here with me, oh, fifteen or so years ago. Good woman. Gotten old and tough. We hug on occasions when I feel like it."

Murieta thought of Rosita and did his best to push her from his mind. It felt like his head was full of cotton from all that brandy hitting his empty stomach.

"Nice place, the El Dorado," Clegg said, taking another drink. "I was John Hughes's first customer the day he opened. Sweeps that dirt floor at least twice a day. I call it home. Dolly, she doesn't like it I say that. Says I got a home." He rubbed his hand over his face. "Sometimes, if it's not busy, Mr. Hughes let's me sleep on his billiard table. Wish I's there now."

Murieta almost slipped speaking in *ingles* saying that he wished he was back in Mexico, but caught himself before Clegg took notice.

"*Señor*," Murieta said, nodding his head at Clegg's canteen, "*tiene mas . . . por favor.*"

"Oh, drink! Sure," Clegg said, tipping the canteen to him. "You know I'm surely sorry about perforating you, and especially your horse. I'd feel better if I knew I didn't, him being such a fine animal, but you took us on a damn helluva ride. I had to stop you."

Murieta wondered if those other *gringo* rangers had stopped Contreras the same way.

"But, let me tell you," Clegg said, "I don't know who you are but you're one tough *hombre* bastard." He raised his canteen as a toast and drank. "I've been to *fandangos,* couple rodeos, about twenty, thirty bull and bear fights. I even seen the elephant, but

I never seen anybody handle a horse like you. I don't know if you're Mex or *Californio,* but by God you're the finest I seen on horseback. Here's to you." Clegg took another long swallow.

It had to be the fault of the brandy that made Murieta think he was taking a liking to this *gringo.* Trickery wasn't the game of this *hombre grande.* Murieta accepted another pull from Clegg's canteen and closed his eyes to rest, maybe to sleep. This *gringo,* he thought hazily, this one could perhaps be trusted . . . like the one on the road to . . . to Mariposa . . .

A dreamy mist gave way to a rocky streambed and Murieta saw he was with his compadre, *Three-Fingered Jack, who was telling him he'd been suckled as a baby by the same whip-tailed scorpion as El Bruto. They laughed and saw a* gringo *miner scrubbing out a pot near his lean-to. In an instant, Jack had lassoed the* gringo *around his neck.*

"Now stand and deliver," Murieta told him.

And the gringo *miner asked if it was Joaquin Murieta who was robbing him because if it was the famous Joaquin, he was welcome to all he had if he'd allow him to live so he could later tell his grandchildren about this day.*

Murieta laughed and asked the gringo *how much gold he had.*

The gringo *showed him fifty dollars in gold coin. "That's all."*

When Jack said the gringo *was lying, Murieta told him to have a look. Finding nothing in his belongings, Jack turned the* gringo *miner upside down and shook him. The* gringo *hadn't been lying.*

Murieta congratulated the gringo *for being an honest man and left him alive.*

Darkness enveloped him. He sensed time passing from weeks to months until he emerged from a dark forest onto the sandy banks of the Mokelumne River and saw a gringo *digging for gold. Drawing his Colt, Murieta took aim and the* gringo's *eyes and his met.*

147

The gringo *shouted, "My grandchildren haven't heard my story yet!"*

Raising his hand, Murieta left him to his diggings and returned into the darkness, leaving not a gringo, *but an honorable man behind him.*

"No, I got no idea who you are," Murieta heard a gruff voice say.

Murieta's eyes snapped open. Confused. Disoriented. He saw fire, heard it crackling. The pain in his chest and leg surged and then ebbed. Calming down, he recognized the *hombre grande*.

"No idea at all," Clegg said, his canteen resting on his belly, "but you ain't no Joaquin Murieta."

Ugly suspicion suddenly flared in Murieta's mind. Had the *hombre grande* really been trying after all to get him drunk, to fool him into speaking English, or maybe revealing his name? And then a calm settled over him, as though a fever had broken, and Murieta wondered, for the first time, if it mattered any longer.

"But from the look of you," Clegg said, "and the fact you're still alive, means you're somebody all right. A smart somebody."

Murieta stared into the fire and wished he'd left California sooner. He wondered if he'd see Rosita and Mexico again. He heard Clegg cough and sniff. Looking over at him, he saw Clegg was staring into the fire. Brandy had dribbled over his white mottled whiskers and down his sagging jowls and mixed with other stains on the dingy shirt he wore beneath his open cloak.

"Damn I wish I wasn't here," Clegg said.

Holding his Colt revolver in his lap, his finger on the trigger, Ned Needle sat perched on a large gray rock. It jutted up like a lone crooked tooth on the other side of the rise above camp. He didn't like being out here alone in all this dark, but since he had to be here, he congratulated himself on choosing a spot that was smooth and not too uncomfortable. That made him chuckle as it got him thinking about Clarissa being smooth and not too uncomfortable those times in Screaming Addie's wagon. She also had that little wiggle that had caught his eye right off. Of course, when he heard that Mex-loving Deputy Tyner say that wiggle of Clarissa's could ignite lust in pagan and prophet alike, he knew it was time to teach that son-of-a-bitch a lesson. And he sure as hell had done that.

Sitting up and craning his neck toward the glow of the campfire below, Needle wanted to be certain Clegg wasn't coming this way. Satisfied, he reached into the pocket of his cloak where he'd stuck the pieces of jerked beef he'd stolen earlier that morning from the jar in the Headquarters Saloon. Oh, hell, all that was left was a piece about the size of a silver dollar. Of course, he'd been sneaking bites of it all day. He shoved it into his mouth and sucked on it to loosen it up. At least he had something since that worthless Clegg had packed no food or coffee. Damn fool made sure he had plenty of that brandy he likes, though. No way Ned Needle was going to share what little food he'd been smart enough to bring with that undependable idiot Clegg. And forget giving the greaser anything, even if he'd had something to give him, which he wouldn't have done anyway.

Feeling the night desert chill coming on, Needle raised the collar on his cloak and tucked his arms around himself, still keeping his finger on the trigger of his revolver.

"July was bad enough. August days bake a man's soul and freeze it again at night," he mumbled.

And that greaser refusing to talk particularly vexed him. He'd see to taking care of that big son-of-a-bitch Clegg, too. Though he disliked Wheat more, Clegg's treatment of him this night, like hollering at him in front of that Mex, was downright insulting.

Needle set his revolver down and rubbed his hands together to warm them up. He was cold, tired, sore, and hungry. Hell, everything happened to him.

He heard something snap close by. He stopped sucking on the jerky, held his breath, and listened. Nothing. Damn, he hated it out here. That sliver of moon hanging in the inky sky was no help. The shadows hereabouts were darker than that sticky black muck Injuns and greasers called *brea* bubbling up from pits a few miles outside town. No, he didn't like these shadows. They gave him the willies. Fierce willies.

But Needle never let on about that to anyone. He knew if the truth were known, the consequences to his well-being would be grave indeed. That was why the shadows and the stillness of the night put real fear in his heart. It was coming back to him. Racing up from a dark place, that fear of finding himself fifteen years old again on a cold December morning in '46, riding with Captain Archibald Gillespie and his volunteers into the San Pasqual Valley northeast of San Diego where reports had claimed rebellious *Californio* lancers were encamped. It was his first battle.

He had been given orders to deliver an urgent message to Captain Johnston who would lead the attack. Leaping on his horse, he had felt like his bladder was about to burst. He knew the black truth of the humiliating defeat for the Americans at San Pasqual. He was well aware why the attack had been critically delayed in starting. He had stopped behind a bush to pee.

After the retreat, when he was asked about delivering the message, Needle recalled that Mother Needle hadn't raised any dawdling boy. She had beaten the gospels of crafty and capable into him. So he'd done what he knew would make her proud and allow him to keep his hide. He lied. But that night, and like so many nights since, he got sweaty, his heart thumped hard in his chest, and his breathing almost stopped because he could hear dead men coming through the darkness for him. Like this night.

He felt a cold shiver run up his sweating, sticky back. Push that fear away now. Nobody was there. Think of something else! That greaser son-of-a-bitch they had tied to the tree had to be guilty of *something*. That's it! Maybe that Mex wasn't a Joaquin and not worth a thousand-dollar reward, but he'd committed some crime, otherwise why'd he and his friend run? Hell, at the very least he needed to be taken back to Los Angeles and strung up. Folks would pack picnic baskets and come in from all over the county to see a hanging in the plaza. Fire the cannons, too. Make it a real celebration, like the Fourth of July or Washington's Birthday. The Bella Union Hotel would fill up, all six rooms. There'd be brisk business in every saloon in town, too.

Feeling the jerky loosening up some in his mouth, Needle began chewing on it slowly, warming to his reverie about hangings. Regardless of where the hanging took place, a hanging was necessary. Maybe he'd convince Quick to take action.

"We got a whole county full of greaser lawbreakers, and justice waiting," Needle said out loud, rehearsing his argument. "No. A whole *state* full of greasers—that's better—and so far, us rangers haven't brought in a single one committed for hanging. Seems to me that's leaving the local citizens feeling kind of ugly and gloomy." That sounded pretty good!

Looking back down at the campsite, he saw the fire burning higher, and Clegg sharing his canteen with the Mex. He shook his head in disgust.

He heard a noise. Louder. Clearer. Out in front of him. He sat straight up and spit out pieces of jerky. He wiped his clammy hands on his coat and grabbed his revolver. A lot of shadows loomed out there. He clamped his jaw tight to keep his teeth from chattering. He was getting scared, the kind of scared when he was fifteen. He felt like he needed to pee. And right now.

Frozen to the spot, Needle cocked the revolver. He'd seen this place before in the light of day. Huge rocks, hundreds of them, jutting up out of the ground like giant rowels on a spur. Evil-looking things. Everywhere. A chaos of crags. Monstrous things, like the devil clawing his way out of hell.

Sharp shadows could cut a man clean if he crossed them, of that Needle felt certain, as certain as the tiny beads of sweat forming on his face. Shadows moved, rocks moved, was that another sound? The fire was supposed to keep animals away! But the fire was down there and he was up here. The revolver kept shaking in his sweaty grip. A couple of minutes could pass like hours to a frightened boy, and Needle was trying hard to stay a man. His mind raced. A damn bear can outrun a man and mountain lions could get me before I was off this rock and Captain Johnston, is that you out there? It wasn't my fault! I swear it wasn't! But I had to pee!

Needle's eyes were wide open. There was no movement, no sound. Something evil lived here. Where is everybody? Hold on! What's that? The shadows on that rock face looked like a skull— and it was grinning, wicked like! He glanced up at the black sky. Was that slice of moon laughing at him or giving him the evil eye? His hand hurt he was holding the revolver so tight. What's that noise? It was near the grinning skull. His breath caught in his throat. His whole body tensed. Oh, Lord! No skull was leering at him. It was Captain Johnston's bloodied, torn face!

Needle's mouth opened in a silent scream and he pulled the trigger, the roar of the Colt making him jump.

"Needle!" came Clegg's shout from below.

"I—It—was a bear," Needle weakly shouted back. "Or something."

"What?"

"It's gone!" Needle hollered down. He licked his dry lips, wiped his face on his sleeve, and tried to calm himself.

"Be careful you don't shoot somebody you shouldn't," Clegg said.

Needle thought he also heard him say, "dumb kid."

"You just go to hell," he whispered, feeling stupid and sorry for himself. "I'm the one out here risking his life. Everything happens to me."

That was true all right. And the more Needle thought about it, the truer it got. While Clegg was down there warm by the fire, guzzling his brandy and coddling that Mex, he was out here in the cold, keeping watch, fending off bandit and beast alike. Hell, Clegg ought to be thanking him! That's right, damn it, because he deserved it! Then Needle started wondering why he wasn't back in town right now enjoying all the accolades and free whiskey he'd be getting for bringing in *the* most wanted criminal in the whole country. They might even roast up a steer and a hog. That was the fare at the Fourth of July shebang. Good eating and plenty of it.

Thinking about a big Fourth of July kind of celebration had taken his mind off his troubles. And he did like the song so he started singing it to keep himself company.

"Oh, say can you see, by the dawn's early light, what so proudly we hailed, at the twilight's last gleaming? Whose broad stripes and bright stars . . . through the . . . through the perilous night . . . hmmmmmmmm, hmmmmmmmm were so—"

"Ranger Needle!" came a shout from the shadows. "Stop that caterwauling! You'd be a dead man right now if I was a bandit! And what was that shooting?"

Damn it! For the second time that night Needle was caught unaware and fitfully embarrassed.

"Lieutenant Quick, that you?" Needle knew he sounded

ridiculous, but he had to say something.

"Of course it's me and the rest of us," Quick said.

Needle saw them coming out of the shadows looking worn and bone-tired.

"We got wounded men here, too," Quick said as he rode by Needle. "And what were you shooting at?"

"Scaring off a mountain lion," Needle said, scrambling off his rock. "Did you get him, the other bandit that run off?"

Following them into camp he saw they had no extra horse with a body draped over it. And he couldn't tell if anybody was carrying a sack that might, just might, be holding the head of any Joaquin.

Needle sorely wanted to brag he had captured the notorious bandit. That would give him a barrelful of prestige. And Clarissa would probably give it to him for free from then on. And, he hoped more than anything, it would send the specter of Captain Johnston away for good.

Though feeling drunk from the brandy, Murieta heard the riders coming in and Needle's question about the other bandit. He concentrated, straining to listen for the answer.

His heart sank when he heard someone say, "Oh, we got him all right. He's lying at the bottom of a canyon a few miles back that way. But Sam Prizer's in bad shape."

Murieta saw the other *gringo* rangers ride into the camp, their shadows long and ghostly against the giant wave rock. He also saw that Clegg looked unsteady, shaking his head, like he was trying to clear it.

"Let's get him down," Clegg said as he took the reins and held onto Prizer's horse. It seemed to Murieta the *hombre grande* was doing it to hold the horse steady as much as it was to keep himself on his feet.

Murieta had seen Clegg drink half his canteen down after

Needle had fired that shot. Clegg was taking another swig now, and Murieta saw a Negro boy jump off his horse to help Prizer to the ground on the opposite side of the fire from him.

"Set him . . . set him down easy, Charley," Clegg said and wiped his hand over his mouth, which was hanging slack.

"What happened to Prizer, Lieutenant?" Needle asked.

"Got shot," the blond-haired *gringo* leading the men in said.

That gladdened Murieta considerably, knowing Contreras hadn't gone down without a fight. And when he saw the blood-soaked front of Sam Prizer he knew he'd been belly-shot. That *gringo*'s pudgy face was pale and ashen, like a dead man. He heard Prizer moan.

"I don't know how he managed to ride this far," a bald *gringo* said.

"Get his blanket roll, Wheat," the lieutenant told the bald *gringo*. "And then let's get those horses bedded down."

"Good thing I picked that hill to come over. Could have missed seeing your fire in all this rocky country." Charley said to Clegg. "I'm no good tracking at night."

"You did fine, Charley," the one called Wheat said as he unrolled Prizer's blanket and covered him.

"You rest easy, Sam," Clegg said.

"Water," Prizer said weakly.

"Have a little of this," Clegg said and got down next to Prizer. Holding Prizer's head up, Clegg tipped the canteen to his mouth. "Might help more."

Murieta knew there was no harm in giving that *gringo* something to drink. He wouldn't make it to morning anyway. He noticed Clegg take a good pull from his canteen.

"How come you boys don't have any coffee on?" the ranger with his arm in a sling asked as he came over and squatted next to the woodpile Needle had left by the fire.

Whatever happened to that ranger's arm, Murieta hoped

Contreras was responsible.

"On account of you didn't bring any, Doyle," Needle said. "So did anybody bring any coffee? Or maybe—"

"I got coffee."

It sounded like a woman's voice. Murieta looked about wondering if he was hearing things. Had all that *aguardiente* made him *loco*? While the rangers went about pulling saddles off their horses and making camp, he counted six wearing the blue coats. No! Only five had the blue ranger coats. A sixth one was tying the reins of a small round-bellied mustang to the horse line someone had strung. This *gringo* wore different clothes. A big floppy hat obscured his face. Did he really hear a woman's voice? And what would a woman be doing with these men?

"Doyle, how's your shoulder?" the lieutenant asked as he came over to the fire.

"I'll be all right," Doyle said.

"I know a couple of saloon gals who'll be fussing all over you," Wheat said.

The *gringo* wearing the floppy hat squatted down by the fire and started making coffee, but Murieta still couldn't see his face. He stopped trying to see it when he heard Needle ask the lieutenant about the bandit he'd been chasing.

"He was a big man," the lieutenant said. "And he put up a nasty fight."

"Guess you didn't bring him with you," Needle said.

"You figure that one out by yourself?" Wheat said as he dropped his saddle near a manzanita bush.

It sounded to Murieta like this *gringo* Wheat didn't like Needle much. And he noticed Needle didn't say anything to him. He just stood there. Then Murieta heard terrible words.

"But the lieutenant fired the shot that dropped him," Doyle said, looking up from the fire.

Murieta hoped the lieutenant would be killed the same way someday.

"We probably all got a piece of him on the way," Quick said. "We found a lot of blood on the trail."

"He was on foot," Wheat said, tossing a wet saddle blanket over a bush. "Pushed that horse of his right into the ground. Dead when we found it."

"That man pushed himself, too," Charley said as he uncinched his saddle.

"Got up in some rocks," Doyle said. "After awhile, his head came up just right. That's when the lieutenant took a bead and pulled the trigger. Next thing, he was rolling down into the canyon."

"If the lieutenant didn't kill him, that fall sure as hell did," Wheat said.

"He was big, and real shiny, too," Charley said and began rubbing down his horse with a damp cloth.

"Shiny? How?" Clegg asked, shaking his head.

"Like he was wearing something like a coat of iron," Wheat said and began rubbing *aguardiente* over his horse's wet back.

"Iron!" Needle shouted.

"I know for a fact I hit him," Doyle said, tossing a piece of wood on the fire, "but the slug bounced off."

"It was a good thing the lieutenant plugged him," Wheat said. "Otherwise I do believe we'd still be hugging that slope we were fighting him on."

"Hell, boys, an iron coat!" Needle said. "They say Three-Fingered Jack has one! That he won it off of Joaquin Murieta in a bet to see who could kill the most miners in a week. Ain't that right?"

Murieta knew Needle was looking right at him, but he ignored him and stared into the fire, thinking about his *amigo* and hoping he was at peace. But he had the sobering suspicion

157

he was looking into a burning example of where Contreras had likely gone. He wished for silence and another drink of brandy to forget the pain he felt deep in his soul. But the *gringo* making the coffee spilled grounds into the fire, making a lot of smoke, and the other *gringos* kept talking.

"It wasn't Three-Fingered Jack," the lieutenant said.

"No disrespect, Lieutenant, but how do you know?" Needle asked. "Did you count his fingers?"

"There weren't any trophies," Doyle said.

"What do you mean 'trophies'?" Charley asked.

"Jack always carries strings of ears and scalps hanging on his saddle." Doyle said. "This saddle had nothing."

Hearing that made Murieta happy. He knew ears and scalps was just a story Jack started to scare the *gringos*.

"He was an unfriendly cuss, whoever he was," Wheat said.

"Tomorrow we'll see if we can't drag him out of that canyon," the lieutenant said. "He slid down pretty far. It was too dark to try today."

"Maybe it was the Animal," Needle said. "He's supposed to be a big son-of-a-bitch."

"The Animal hasn't been seen down this way in more than a year," Wheat said.

Murieta smiled.

"Well, our prisoner over here can sure as hell tell us who it was," Needle said. "Of course, he ain't much for talking. But he says 'no sabee' real good."

Tired, Quick wiped his face with the red bandana he pulled from around his neck and ran his thumbs over his moustache. He squatted down to examine the prisoner.

"You know, Lieutenant," Needle said, leaning down close to Quick's ear, "if the one you nailed was the Animal, this one here could well be the Joaquin Murieta."

Quick ignored Needle. Pulling the *serape* covering the prisoner aside, he looked at his wounds, then his leg. Glancing back up, he saw the hard look on the prisoner's face.

"Uriah," Quick said, half-turning to Clegg who was still sitting next to Prizer, "looks like you did a good job patching him up."

Clegg nodded.

"Two shots to bring him down," Quick said.

Clegg grunted.

"I shot his horse," Needle said.

"But what I don't understand," Quick said, ignoring Needle and walking over to Clegg, "is why you tied the prisoner to a tree. Look at him. He can't run away."

When Clegg blinked back at him blankly, Quick wondered if the man had heard him. He leaned in toward him, about to repeat the question. Clegg's eyes were red and filmy, and Quick smelled the brandy on his breath. Glancing at the campfire, Quick saw the coffee starting to bubble.

"Get coffee into him as soon as it's ready," Needle said to Addie, who nodded.

Clegg lowered his head, looking ashamed.

Turning to Wheat, Quick said, "Cut the prisoner loose. Charley, get his saddle and prop him up. Try to make him comfortable."

He looked back at Clegg. "What did you tie him to a tree for?"

Clegg blinked as though he didn't understand the question. But he did understand it. A hole was opening inside his gut.

. . . Why did you tie him to a tree? . . .

The hole grew. Widened. Deepened. In spite of all the liquor he'd consumed this night, that chasm needed filling.

. . . Why did you tie him to a tree? . . .

He thought he'd burst into tears. The firelight was hurting his eyes. He moved sluggishly away to the boulder where his saddle was and sat down heavily, his canteen falling out of his hand.

They would come, he knew. The demons, like snakes. Screaming! Swirling around him.

. . . Why did you tie him to a tree? . . .

He covered his face with his large sweating hands. It was no use. They didn't block out the sight of hundreds of weeping Cherokees moving, stumbling, crawling, dressed in rags many of them, old men, women, children. Beyond them he saw the great rounded mountains of Georgia in the distance. His vision raced back toward those mountains, through thick dense forest to caves cut into the earth.

. . . Why did you tie him to a tree? . . .

He saw the barely clothed Cherokees he and his fellow soldiers had lashed together in groups to trees.

"It's what we did with the prisoners," Clegg mumbled to himself. "What we had to do."

He picked up the canteen. It was empty. He reached for one of the other two he still had on his saddle.

After Clegg had walked away, Quick snapped at Needle, "What's been going on here?"

"Well, ah," he stammered, "we, we been trying to find out who this greaser is but he won't talk nothing except Mex."

"I mean with Clegg."

"I don't know what's wrong with him," Needle said. "He's like he always is, you know." He made a motion with his arm, as though tipping a bottle back to drink.

Quick shook his head. He'd deal with Clegg later.

"All right then," Quick said. "You say this one only speaks Spanish?"

"Not one word of American."

Prizer moaned loudly, and Charley, who had just helped Wheat prop the prisoner up against his saddle, went over to him.

"He's feverish," Charley said, feeling Prizer's forehead, and asked for a wet cloth. "It'll help cool him down."

Wheat wetted a cloth and Quick passed it to Charley. Quick went back over to the prisoner. Wheat had just covered him with the *serape*. The prisoner was leaning back against his saddle and taking a long drink from a canteen.

"I gave him my *aguardiente*," Wheat said to Quick, indicating the canteen. "He'll need it for the pain."

Quick bent down again to face the prisoner who was looking over at where Clegg had gone.

"Hey, *hombre*," Quick said.

When the Mexican met his eyes, Quick studied him, and wondered if this could really be the notorious bandit Joaquin.

"My name's Quick. Lieutenant Ambrose Quick. *¿Comprende? ¿Como se llama? ¿Murieta? ¿Valenzuela? Digame. ¿Se llama Joaquin?*"

As the corners of the Mexican's mouth slowly curled into a smile, Quick thought he looked like he was enjoying this.

"*No se*," the Mexican said and, holding the canteen in both hands, took a drink.

Quick's expression hardened. "You don't know?"

"What don't he know?" Needle asked.

Quick kept looking at the Mexican. "He says he doesn't know what his name is."

"This is the kind of horseshit he's been pulling ever since we got him," Needle said. "I say we got us a Joaquin. Maybe Murieta."

Quick stood and faced Needle. "What makes you so sure of that?"

"Because he won't say."

"And what does that prove?"

"It proves all of nothing," Wheat said, squatting by the fire drinking coffee.

"It's greaser ways, Wheat," Needle said, "playing like he don't understand what we're saying."

"Not good enough," Wheat said.

Needle cocked his head to one side and counted on his fingers. "He's a greaser, he ran when we chased him and his friend, he damn near tried to kill us with a stampede, he shot at us, and now he's trying to save his greaser hide with his little games. I say we haul him up to the governor, collect the reward, and be done with it."

"That's enough," Quick said. "We're rangers, not a mob."

"Right," Wheat said. "We don't know who he is. And you don't hang somebody without a trial. That's the law."

"And who the hell are you, his lawyer?" Needle asked, his voice rising.

"He's just saying is all," Doyle said, cradling his wounded shoulder and sounding irritated.

"Did all of you go crazy in the hot sun?" Needle yelled. "Lieutenant, this morning you was cock-sure we was after the Joaquin Murieta."

Quick was sick of listening to Needle and was about to tell him so when Addie Moody spoke.

"All I know is, I want the Joaquin son-of-a-bitch who cut up my sister."

Quick saw she was sitting on her haunches by the fire, pouring herself a cup of the coffee she had made. The raspiness in her voice was like the dry hot wind that blew off the desert, but there was something steely in it, too. She stood up and adjusted the pistol sticking out of the belt tied around her sagging pants. Nobody moved.

Murieta knew he was getting drunk. He also knew he hadn't been imagining things earlier because there was a woman with them, and she was standing there facing him, but her figure looked like a boy's dressed in the loose clothes she wore. When she raised her head, he saw the dirt smudges on her cheeks and her dark hair pushed up under her hat. Even so, there was something familiar about her. But her face had been dusted with powder, her hair hanging in loose curls. And she had worn a dress that exposed the whiteness of her long neck, the small bony shoulders, the swell of her bosom. Two other girls with powder and paint on their faces were there, too. In San Gabriel. At the Headquarters. *Putas,* whores.

Maybe if he got drunker it would all go away. He closed his eyes, put the canteen to his lips, took a swallow, and felt the warm, sweet burn. When he opened his eyes, he was still in the hands of the *gringo* rangers, he couldn't walk, and that cursing whore was still there.

She was blowing the steam away from her coffee. She took a sip and put her other hand on the butt of her Dragoon revolver. Then he heard her say, "Are you that son-of-a-bitch?"

CHAPTER FOURTEEN: THE CONTRARY MAN

Murieta knew the woman was wrong. The words just came out. "My mother was a saint, little *gringa puta,* not a bitch," he said.

Then he heard Needle clapping his hands and saying, "Damn it, I told you that greaser pepper belly talked American!"

But Murieta was looking at the woman. Her eyes flashed, her jaw jutted forward. She threw down her cup and pulled out the Dragoon. He sensed confusion around him and somebody hollered, "Look out! She's going to ventilate the Mexican!"

Though he didn't know how much brandy he'd consumed, Murieta still recognized the business end of an Army Dragoon pointing at him from only a few yards away. That little black hole suddenly loomed large and menacing to him. He cursed the brandy, though it felt like he was sobering up by the moment. It was too late to play dumb now. He raised his hands.

Then the woman pulled the hammer back and that unmistakable click as the cylinder turned and the hammer locked into place sounded deafening to his ears. Everything—fire, rocks, shadows, faces, the sound of his heart beating, the breath he pulled into his lungs and held—seemed razor-sharp to him.

"*Madre de Dios,*" he whispered.

He saw Quick snatch the Dragoon by the barrel, forcing it up.

"Give it here, Addie!" he shouted.

"I'm going to kill that Mex peckerwood!" she yelled, refusing to let go of the weapon.

Wheat grabbed her arms from behind.

"Addie, it's me," Wheat said. "Turn that hog leg loose!"

"No!" she shouted and struggled. "I want to kill him for Claire."

Quick twisted the pistol from her hands, but she broke free of Wheat's grip, turned and slapped and kicked at him. He took hold of her and shook her hard.

"Addie! Enough, now!" Wheat said.

"All right!" she said, teeth bared, her breathing hard. "All right."

Wheat held her a moment more before turning her loose.

Murieta felt a shudder in his chest as he breathed again.

The others looked as relieved as him, like Charley who had his head back and mouth open. Clegg was sitting propped up against his saddle, sucking on his canteen. Murieta couldn't be certain, though, if Clegg was aware of what had happened or not. Needle, though, seemed giddy.

And this woman Addie was angry and agitated. She'd take a few steps, her hands on her hips, turn and go back again, shaking her head. She sat down by the fire, pulled her knees up to her chest and held her arms tight around her legs. Wheat came and sat next to her, offering her a canteen, telling her it was brandy. She put her head back and took a drink. Murieta recognized the evil look she shot him.

Quick stood next to him. Looking up, he saw him shove the Dragoon inside his belt.

"It'd be best if you answered my question now," Quick said. "What's your name?"

Murieta felt like a bucket of icy water had been dumped on his head. Pulling his hand from under his *serape*, he saw fresh blood on his palm glistening black in the firelight. In all the excitement he'd somehow opened his wounds. Blood was seeping into the bandages around his leg where the bones had broken through. It was swelling. He realized he might have to lose it. The whole leg. Too long, he thought, I stayed too long. The *gringos'* work was done. They wouldn't need to shoot him again.

He nodded at Quick and was about to take a sip from the canteen but paused. If I'm buried here, he thought, I'll be in a land of strangers. Will they mark it? Would Rosita be able to find me? My pride speaks loud. *¿No?* It shouldn't have happened this way. Now it's too late. Can I trust this *gringo* Quick? He heaved a sigh.

"*Si, señor,*" Murieta said, "I am going to give it to you. But, I'm a little bit drunk and very hungry. If you could give me coffee and maybe something to eat first—"

"We got nothing!" Needle said. "Now, talk!"

"Shut your mouth!" Quick shouted.

"Just trying to help," Needle said, raising his hands.

"Go do it somewhere else," Quick said. "Check the horses."

After Needle walked away, Quick asked Charley to fix a couple of tins of coffee. "And did somebody bring food?"

A canvas sack landed near Murieta's feet. Looking across the fire, he saw Addie giving him that evil look again.

"Corn dodgers," she said.

Quick pulled one out of the sack and handed it to him.

Needle walked over to the horse line, shooting a nasty glance over his shoulder at Quick. He kicked a rock out of his way. The horses were fine, but he knew this greaser was a Joaquin, damn it. And that big damn pepper-eating friend of his was either Three-Fingered Jack or the Animal, sure as hell. Needle recalled the two Mexes on horseback in San Gabriel the previous night, the ones who tried to mess with him while he was dragging Abel Tyner's body. One of them was a big man, too. And come to think of it now, he thought he'd caught this Mex here staring at him a couple of times tonight, like he knew him or recognized him or something. But that couldn't be. Needle knew he'd kept his head down. He didn't give them a chance to look at his face. Of that he was certain, as certain that he had jumped Abel Tyner from the shadows, beat him senseless for being a greaser-lover who was after his girl, then hauled him behind a pile of adobe bricks and left him there. Come to think of it, how did Tyner get himself under that sycamore tree?

Oh shit! Needle thought. Maybe this greaser and his friend did it! Let's see. Tyner comes to, heads for home, meets up with them two greasers, and that was it! They cut him open. So what if the greaser recognizes me? If he says he does, that's proof he was in town! It's their tracks going by Tyner's body, not mine! Oh, this is fitting together real fine. Mother Needle would be proud of her boy.

"Muchas gracias," Murieta said, accepting another corn dodger from Quick. They were as hard as Contreras' biscuits from that morning, but these corn dodgers were like sweet bread to Murieta this night. And the coffee was good because it was hot.

"Tell me something," Quick said and took a sip of coffee from his tin. "Were you in San Gabriel last night?"

Murieta tried the coffee and wondered if maybe this ranger was playing a different game now. Alright, he'd play along. He nodded.

"Maybe have a run-in with anybody?" Quick asked.

Looking past Quick, past the fire, Murieta saw Needle by the horses.

"Maybe him," he said, nodding at Needle.

"I see," Quick said.

The way he said it, Murieta could tell Quick didn't believe him.

"Anybody else?" Quick asked.

Murieta thought of Ana Benitez, and suddenly he felt very tired. Last night with her seemed a million miles away. He shook his head.

"So you didn't kill anybody last night?"

"No."

"What about your friend? Your *amigo*?"

"He's dead."

Quick snorted. "You're a contrary one, aren't you?"

"You *gringos*," Murieta said, "you always think Mexicans are guilty of something."

"You have to admit you gave us plenty of cause today."

"And *gringos* are never wrong?"

Sam Prizer lay on his back close to the fire. He thought he heard Clegg snoring somewhere nearby. He turned his head and saw Quick and the Mexican talking. They were on the other side of the fire, about ten or twelve feet away. Prizer lifted his head and saw Charley, Doyle, Wheat, and Addie huddled together a little ways from his feet, closer to the fire. They were drinking coffee and looked like they were trying to listen to the lieutenant. Laying his head back down, he saw Needle coming from the direction of the horses. He was about to ask him for some water when he felt that gnawing pain in his belly increase. He rolled over on his side and held back a cry. He couldn't hear what Quick or the Mexican were saying, but he had a clear view of them. Particularly the Mexican.

Murieta asked Quick to check the tourniquet around his leg. He grimaced as Quick first loosened then retied it. He also saw that his leg had turned purple and was still swollen.

"That doesn't look good," Quick said.

Murieta nodded.

"And there's nothing else we can do right now," Quick said.

"Maybe it's time you tell me who you are."

Murieta sighed, told himself again it didn't matter anymore, gave Quick a lop-sided grin, and said, "*Me llamo* . . . Joaquin Murieta."

Murieta saw the disgusted look on Quick's face and then caught sight of Addie trying to get to her feet, nearly knocking the coffee tin out of Doyle's hand, but Wheat kept her sitting down. Wheat said something to her but Murieta couldn't hear it. At that same moment, though, he heard Needle and saw him come out of the shadows into the campfire light.

"What'd he say?" Needle asked. "He say Joaquin?"

"Murieta," Addie said and spat.

"Hell, I knew it!" Needle shouted. "Joaquin Murieta! One thousand dollars!"

"Needle!" Quick snapped.

"One thousand dollars sitting right here and I got him!" Needle said, and did a little dance. "I own the catbird seat! Oh, say can you see!"

"There's no proof!" Quick said. "He can say any damn name!"

"But he said that one! Lucky day!"

"Shut your trap, you idiot!" Wheat shouted at him.

"Go to hell or make me shut up!" Needle shouted back.

It looked to Murieta like they were going to fight.

Prizer didn't like it that Murieta was giggling, like he was enjoying a show. He fought the pain and drew his Colt. It shook in his unsteady hands. He gasped for breath. His eyes wouldn't focus. Lying on his side like this, the pain in his gut was unbearable. He tried to pull the hammer back.

Lord, he prayed, let me do this one thing.

★ ★ ★ ★ ★

Quick stood up and took a step toward the fire and Needle.

"Enough! Back off," Quick said. "That's an order."

"This is a personal matter," Needle said, "between me and Wheat."

Quick saw Wheat jump to his feet, fists balled.

"You're due this, you little shit," he said and started toward Needle.

"Horace, don't!" Addie said.

Quick saw a flash and Needle had his Bowie knife in his hand.

"Oh, shit," Doyle said, getting up and backing away from the fire, coffee tin in hand.

"Come on, you," Needle said, waving the knife at Wheat. "Wet your horns. You been asking for it."

When he saw Wheat's hand go to his knife, Quick pulled Addie's Dragoon from his belt.

"Stop it!" Quick shouted. "Needle, not another word! Drop that knife. Now!"

When Needle didn't budge, Quick raised the Dragoon, pointed it at him, and cocked the hammer. Everything seemed to stop suddenly, and the only sound was the crackling of the fire. Quick saw Needle's eyes dart over to look at him, and he could tell the insolent little bastard knew he was serious.

"You're right, Lieutenant," Needle said, lowering his knife. "Got a little carried away. I'd appreciate it if you'd put down that cannon, though."

"Drop the knife," Quick said, keeping the Dragoon leveled at Needle.

Quick saw Needle hesitate, and he heard the Mexican who claimed to be Murieta call out.

"No! Let them fight. I'd like to see this *pendejo* killed and—"

A shot roared out. Quick flinched. There was a metal clang, a

170

hiss, and then smoke and dying cinders wafted into the air. The coffee pot skittered along the ground. He heard Doyle shout, "Damn it!"

Quick turned. Doyle had spilled his coffee on himself, apparently startled by the shot. Quick saw Prizer roll forward, moaning, and the barrel of his revolver gouging the earth. He'd fired his shot and hit the coffee pot.

"Sam!" Charley shouted. He jumped up and got Prizer rolled onto his back.

Quick and the others gathered around them. Doyle was wiping coffee off his coat. Quick saw Clegg coming over. The shot must've brought him out of his stupor. Quick dropped to his knees next to Prizer, his belly oozing blood through the bubbly wound. He weakly clutched at Quick's cloak, trying to pull him close.

"I'm . . . I'm sorry I . . . missed," Prizer said, his voice weak and rattling. "I . . . I jus' wanted my name . . . in the paper. Folks'd . . . know who I was. Mean somethin' to my wife. I never . . . give her much. Tell her I tried. Tried . . . to . . ." His eyes fluttered. "Lieute'nt?"

Quick leaned in closer. "Yes, Sam."

"I never . . . expected this."

Murieta watched the campfire crackle and burn as fiery cinders climbed into the air, then disappeared, burned out. But that spilled coffee had doused a portion of the fire. From deep in his chest his breathing shuddered. His shoulders convulsed. The shiver ran down his back, out to his hands and through his legs. He took a drink of brandy and pulled his serape closer.

A moment later, he saw Charley come up on the other side of the fire and add more wood. Cinders sparked brighter and popped. Other movement, something beyond the fire, caught his eye. Wheat was covering the dead ranger with a blanket. The other *gringos* stood close by, huddled together, except Needle who was standing a few feet away, a hand on one hip, looking off and shaking his head. Their shadows shimmered against the giant slabs of pointed rocks.

Murieta heard Quick call this Sam Prizer a decent man and wished he'd known him better. Then the lieutenant asked the others if they had anything they wanted to say.

Well, Joaquin Murieta had something to say! He wanted to tell them this Prizer was fortunate El Bruto had only shot him. It could've been much worse. He also wanted to tell them his *amigo* was lying at the bottom of a canyon. Alone. No blanket to cover him, and that mountain lions would catch the scent of blood and death and find him.

Murieta lifted the canteen to his lips and sudden pain like white-hot irons seared through his chest and back. He had only moved his head! He kept his eyes closed and took slow sips of the brandy, letting the soothing warmth circulate. Thankfully, the pain started to lessen and he heard Charley talking. He was saying he once asked Prizer what brought him to California.

"Sam told me he tried selling shoes in New York, running a ferry crossing in Tennessee, farming in Arkansas, and panning for gold here in California," Charley said. "He failed at all of them. But Sam said becoming a ranger seemed like a pretty good idea, seeing's how he'd run out of country."

A cinder popped and flew out of the fire, landing near Murieta's boot. He watched it burn, fade, and die in that fleeting moment. It occurred to him that the *gringo* ranger wasn't the only one who had run out of country.

Chapter Fifteen: The Truth

"Go on," Quick said to Clegg, "empty it."

With a look Quick could only describe as sorrowful, Clegg upended his canteen and turned his face away while the last contents of it poured out on the ground.

"You're no good to me drunk," Quick said.

"I know I let you down some, Ambrose, and I'm real sorry," Clegg said as his arm dropped to his side.

They were standing near the horses where Clegg had his saddle and bedroll laid out.

"That's the last, right?" Quick asked.

Clegg nodded.

Looking at Clegg's ruddy face, Quick saw the broken purple veins crisscrossing his nose and cheeks and hoped he was telling him the truth. He turned to go but Clegg took hold of his sleeve.

"Ambrose," Clegg said, "I want to tell you about this prisoner."

"What about him?"

"Well, all that's happened has got me more clear-headed and I'm thinking it can't be he's Joaquin Murieta."

Quick shifted his head around Clegg to look back across the clearing at the Mexican. Sitting up against his saddle, all bloodied and stove up, this fellow who claimed to be the most-wanted bandit in the state was staring into a tin of coffee he held in his hands. Quick didn't know what to believe. That always made him uncomfortable, particularly now since he perceived it as a weakness, and weakness was something one hoping to achieve elected office could ill afford. His head ached, and his stomach hurt from lack of food.

"I've got my suspicions," Quick said, turning back to Clegg, "but tell me why you think he isn't who he says."

"It goes back to when I was tracking them Cherokees," Clegg said as he leaned in close to Quick and kept his voice low. "Andy Jackson said they had to be moved, you know, to the Indian Nations. Some of them I caught told me a story, a powerful superstition."

Quick saw Clegg's hands starting to tremble, and sweat was evident on his forehead.

"You want to sit down?" Quick asked.

"No! I got to tell you this. The Cherokees, they didn't want to leave their homelands. And they was talking about one of their own they hated, this fellow by the name of Watie who, they said, was responsible for their miseries. Watie sold all the Cherokee land to the government."

Quick was losing patience. What did all this have to do with the Mexican? "I don't have time for this."

"They said Watie couldn't be killed," Clegg said, clenching his fists and squeezing his eyes shut. "Twenty men tried to kill him and he got away clean. Twenty men, Ambrose! The Cherokees said Watie was charmed, protected like, and nothing man could make could kill him."

"Uriah, I can't—"

"That's Murieta, too, don't you see? Bullets been flying around him for years and he's never been scratched. But this one's hit twice and busted his leg all up. He's just not who he claims. Can't be."

Quick saw the desperation in Clegg's eyes, heard the pleading in his voice. Quick felt sick at heart. Clegg was a sad case.

"You got to believe me, don't you?" Clegg asked.

Quick was grateful that Charley came over at that moment with a tin of coffee in each hand.

"Boiled up what we could salvage like you asked, Lieutenant," Charley said.

Quick saw Charley sneak a worried glance at his friend.

Taking the tin, Quick thanked Charley and asked him to sit with Clegg for a while and make sure he got the coffee into him.

"Thanks for what you said," Quick said to Clegg. "You rest easy for a bit."

Snapping open his gold watch, Quick saw it was a quarter to one. Twenty-four hours ago he was marching through *Calle de los Negros* feeling humiliated. Twelve hours later he was excited about proving his worth chasing the likely murderers of Abel Tyner. Now he was raw-boned tired and thinking there were but two kinds of luck, and his was leaning precariously toward bad. He took a sip of coffee. He'd deal with the Mexican all right, but before that, he'd deal with Needle.

Needle was sitting by the fire, clutching his blanket around his shoulders, and keeping his eye on Quick, the big drunk Clegg, and the nigger kid over by the horses. He knew he was going to have to do some fast-talking to Quick pretty soon and started rehearsing what he'd say in his head. We caught this bandit, the Joaquin Muricta. That'll be real good for you running for mayor. There's a thousand votes waiting for you in Los Angeles. Needle liked that, but it wouldn't hurt to have some of the others agree with him about this greaser. It'd help bolster his argument.

There was Addie sitting away from everyone, huddled in her blanket, looking into the fire, and chewing on a corn dodger. Needle figured she showed her colors when she tried to ventilate the Mex. Good thing she was prevented because he wasn't about to share the glory of plugging the infamous Joaquin

Murieta with any woman. And Wheat running his mouth off about proof only proved he was a damn greaser lover, so his vote was cast. Needle didn't see Wheat anywhere anyway and figured he was off taking a piss. And Needle knew Clegg didn't see it his way and that the little darky would go along with whatever Clegg said. That left Ezra Doyle. Doyle was sitting up against his saddle on the opposite side of the fire from him. He had his blanket covering his legs, the blue jacket around his shoulders, and his hat over his face. Needle got up and moseyed over to him.

"Hey, Doyle, you awake?" Needle whispered.

Doyle pulled his hat off and looked at Needle, his eyes squinting from the firelight.

"Good," Needle said, hunkering down beside him. "I was wondering about something." He jerked his head toward the Mex. "You thinking maybe this one's who he says he is?"

"Don't know," Doyle said. "They say Joaquin Murieta's gone up north, back to the gold fields."

"First I heard of that," Needle said, irritated.

"After he killed Joshua Bean some months back, he went *vamos*. He wants gold. All we got around here are horses and cattle."

"How're you so sure about that, him running back up north?" Needle asked.

"Just what I heard."

This conversation was no help to Needle, who didn't care much for Doyle anyway. In Needle's mind, Doyle was the product of the unnatural copulation of an Irishman, who was pretty close to being a white man, and an Italian, who was no better than a greaser. And if that wasn't enough, Needle figured Doyle's loyalties were suspect since he worked for that Mex landowner Lugo who claimed to be a good American now. It then occurred to Needle he might be able to trick Doyle into revealing his loyalties.

"You hear that about Murieta heading north from your friends at Lugo's, did you?" Needle asked.

"No," Doyle said, rubbing his eyes. "Clegg told me he heard it."

So much for tricking Doyle, Needle thought.

"Well, he say who he heard it from?"

"From Abel Tyner."

Needle wondered why in the hell he bothered talking to Doyle in the first place.

"But," Doyle said, "if you want to know if I think this one we have here had something to do with Abel's killing, I say yes."

That perked Needle right up.

"His friend put a slug in me and killed old Sam," Doyle said. "He's got some talking to do. And maybe some hanging to do, too."

"You know, I like you, Ezra," Needle said. "Always have."

Then he noticed Quick's rawhide boots standing next to him.

Needle looked up at Quick and grinned.

"I'll take your Colt and your knife," Quick said.

Needle's grin disappeared. He sprang up, dropping the blanket and squaring his shoulders, but then he thought better of it. Challenging Quick would look bad with all these witnesses, like that damn Wheat he saw coming toward the campfire out of the darkness. Addie and Doyle were just a few feet away. Clegg and the nigger kid could see everything plain enough from where they were, too. So, drawing in his lips, Needle pulled his weapons and handed them over.

Snatching his blanket off the ground and setting himself back down by the fire, Needle started thinking. He knew how much Lieutenant Quick wanted to be Mayor Quick. He'd just stay here and ponder some more what to say and wait for the right time to say it. Mother Needle didn't raise any muddleheaded child.

"Afraid we don't have anymore to eat," Quick said and sat down by the Mexican.

"I don't feel much like eating," the Mexican said.

Quick took in a deep breath. "All right, let's try it again then," he said. "Why should we believe you're the bandit, Joaquin Murieta?"

"Why not?" the Mexican asked with a little laugh, mixing brandy with the coffee in his tin.

Quick studied him, trying to get a read from his face. Either he was telling the truth, or what people like Ned Needle said about Mexicans was true, that they were liars, pure and simple.

"Because maybe it's just too easy," Quick finally said. "And maybe I don't see us being that lucky. No lawman's gotten this close to a Joaquin before, unless they were dead, like that deputy from San Luis Obispo. I hear he got his brains splattered all over the plaza."

He hoped for a reaction from the Mexican. None came.

"Some here think you're fooling us, trying to throw us off," Quick said. "Others want to collect the reward the governor put on Joaquin's head, if that's who you are."

"And what do you think?"

Quick picked up a twig at his feet and tried drawing in the dirt with it, but the ground was too hard.

"I don't quite know what to think," Quick said, dropping the twig. "Maybe you can tell me something that'll convince me."

It appeared to Quick that for a moment the Mexican was holding back a smile.

"You think I'd lie to give Joaquin Murieta time to run, eh?" the Mexican said. "You think I lie to protect him?"

"You tell me," Quick said, crossing his arms.

"The truth," the Mexican said. "When you and your men attacked me, I was on my way north, to my *compadres*. You've heard of them. Three-Fingered Jack, Joaquin Valenzuela, Joaquin Carrillo. I won't see El Bruto, or as you *gringos* call him, the Animal, because you killed him yesterday." He pointed his finger at Quick. "And if I had the chance, I would kill you for that."

"Now that's the first thing you've said that sounds true."

The Mexican looked tired.

"I'm the leader of the Joaquins. We have over a hundred men with us."

That's far-fetched, Quick thought.

"I have gold buried in the north for myself," the Mexican continued. "When you and your men came after us, *mi amigo* and me, we were riding to meet my men."

"Where's that?" Quick asked, feeling skeptical.

"I told you, the gold fields."

"That's too thin. 'Gold fields' covers a lot of territory."

"Near Tulare Lakes," the Mexican sighed. "Arroyo Cantoova. You know it?"

Quick nodded. "Heard of it."

"I decided to take my gold and go home. I've had enough. I was going to tell my men."

"Just like that?"

"It's the truth."

"You say," Quick said and shrugged.

"I robbed and killed many men," the Mexican said, his voice loud. "I stole horses and cattle. I don't know the names of the men I killed, but one was your General Bean last autumn. I shot him five times in the chest, near his house. He insulted the honor of a Mexican woman. And I shot the deputy because he wanted to kill me. I dared any *gringo* to catch me if he was man enough. I offered ten thousand dollars on the poster in San Gabriel." He made a writing motion with his hand.

"What the hell kind of confession do you want?" Needle suddenly shouted from across the other side of the campfire.

"Damn, he's telling you everything!"

Quick paid Needle no mind and looked at the Mexican. "You admit you shot Abel Tyner, then?"

"If that was his name," the Mexican said.

"I'm talking about last night," Quick snapped. "The man you shot."

The Mexican shook his head. "I shot no one last night."

"Right!" Needle shouted and jumped up. "You slit his throat instead."

There goes my chance, Quick thought. He had hoped to trip up the Mexican about how Abel had been killed, but now Needle had given it away. Damn fool idiot!

"I told you the truth," the Mexican said to Quick. "I killed no one last night."

"We got us the mother lode of bandits here, Lieutenant," Needle said.

Before Quick could tell Needle to stay out of this, Wheat spoke up.

"Excuse me, Lieutenant," he said. "The reason we chased these two was because of Abel. This fellow's admitting to a hell of a lot, and maybe there's truth in it, but Abel's not part of it."

"Well maybe his friend cut Abel when this one was taking a crap or wasn't looking or something," Needle said. "What the hell, Wheat! Why's everything got to be perfect with you?"

"Because we don't hang innocent men."

"But he's dying. Don't you see he wants to make it right before he meets his Maker?"

"You're the one always going on about how you can't trust the Mexicans."

"Well, if you're so damn sure he ain't the Joaquin Murieta, prove it."

"You prove he is Joaquin Murieta."

"Enough!" Quick said. "His claiming to be Murieta is like

him saying he's the governor. Half his story we all know. And the other half sounds preposterous. A hundred men?"

Quick and the others were startled as Addie started banging her coffee tin on a rock and kept banging it.

"I got something to say," she said and stopped banging the tin. "I know about men. All kinds. They'll say lots of things to get a ride, and after the ride, too. Sweet things. Each of you knows what I'm talking about."

Quick thought it was like she was daring any of them to disagree.

"You'll promise love, money, marriage. Respectability. Am I right? So, if there's one thing I'm certain of, it's when a lie passes a man's lips." Looking at Quick, she indicated the Mexican. "He's been doing a lot of talking, Ambrose, but you aren't listening."

"Are you saying you believe him?" Quick asked.

Murieta didn't like this. The *gringos* had been arguing and now everything turned quiet. Quick was talking to Addie alone, away from the others. He couldn't hear what they were saying and decided the others couldn't either. Charley had left Clegg and he and Doyle were adding more wood to the fire, and that warmth felt good. Wheat and Needle stood at opposite sides of the fire. Wheat was rubbing his hands together and watching Quick and Addie. Needle moved from one foot to the other, glaring at Wheat, then over at the lieutenant and the *gringa,* and back at Wheat. Murieta really hoped someone would shoot Needle.

Feeling cold seeping into his bones, Murieta pulled his *serape* tighter and took a drink from his coffee tin. Less than a swallow remained. He stared into the fire and his gold came to mind, the gold he'd dreamed of, the gold he'd killed for. Some eighty thousand dollars' worth he had buried in Arroyo Cantoova. It waited there for him in canvas bags inside a small cave where three dead pine trees, overgrown with long, yellow moss, stood silent guard above it. He expected soon enough he'd be as dead as those trees. He couldn't die here and no one know it. Someone had to believe him. Someone had to help him with what he needed to do.

Then he heard footsteps and saw Addie coming toward him. Alone.

"I don't have a gun," Addie said, "and no knife, neither."

She sat down facing Murieta, held her blanket close, crossed her legs Indian-style, and looked him in the eye, hard, like she was searching for something. She thought she'd be able to tell right away just by looking at him if this was the man she'd been wanting to find for so long. His eyes were black, but he didn't look evil.

Addie glanced over her shoulder. She saw Quick telling the others to move away. Looking back at Murieta, she said, "Ambrose asked me to talk to you. I said I didn't want everybody listening."

"So you didn't come to kill me."

"I told you I don't have a gun."

She waited, still considering him. Several moments passed.

"You still think I killed your sister," he said.

She drew out her breath. "I don't know yet. I'm not even sure of your name."

"Is that why you told the ranger he wasn't listening? Why you gave me food?"

She nodded. "Didn't want you dying before I knew for certain."

"Whatever happened to your sister, I'm sorry."

Thinking of Claire's tortured body, Addie hardened her heart. "Why shouldn't I believe it was you who killed her?"

"I never killed women and children."

"But you rape them."

"No. That's a lie the paper told." He coughed, leaning forward.

Addie saw blood dripping from his mouth and handed him his tin. He waved it away and pointed at his water bag lying nearby. She handed it to him and watched him take a sip then lay his head back.

"Would you tell me what happened to her?" he asked.

"Somebody cut her up."

"I mean, did you see her?"

Addie nodded slowly. "After she was brought back. We were working a tent city together. She'd gone off with a man."

"Did you see the man?"

"No."

"Where was it? The tent city."

"Near Big Rock. You been there?"

She helped him bring the water bag to his mouth.

"I know it," he said and licked his lips. "But I was never there."

"You could just be saying that to save your hide."

"*Si*, but I haven't been there. *Sobre la vida de mi madre, es verdad.*"

"Don't speak that Mex at me."

He nodded once. "If I could help you find the man who did it, I would. I think I understand."

Suddenly, Addie felt her anger shoot through her. Heart pounding, she leaned in at him and spoke low and hard. "What do mean, you understand?"

"*Gringos*. They attacked my wife. They raped her. Cut her hair off. Beat her."

Addie leaned in closer, holding in her hate. This smelled like a lie and if she thought he was playing her, she'd break her promise to Quick and kill this man with her own hands on the spot.

"Why didn't you protect her?" she asked, menace in her whisper. "What were you doing? Off killing some prospector? Or just being a lazy Mex?"

When he raised his head and met her eyes, she backed off but kept her eyes locked on his. She saw him slowly bring his hand up and point at his back.

"Pull my shirt and coat away," he said.

She hesitated, then reached over and saw the whip scars crisscrossing his skin.

"I couldn't protect her," he said.

"Those don't lie," Addie said, sitting back down. "You can't fake them." She saw it in his face, the truth of it, and started steeling herself to the possibility that maybe Murieta really didn't kill her sister.

"You've thought it was me all this time," Murieta said. "Tell me why. Please."

"There was a witness, sort of," Addie said. "He was the man who brought Claire's body back to town. He said he was on his way to his diggings and heard a woman. Sounded like a woman anyway, he said. Thought she was laughing but then he heard her cry out 'No.' He followed the sounds and then heard her say 'Don't, Joaquin' and then no more. When he brought her body in she'd been raped." Addie raised her head, sniffed, holding back tears. "Whoever did it opened her stomach with a knife. And more. Son-of-a-bitch."

"I'm sorry."

"The man who brought back her body. I'll never forget his face. He scared me."

"What do you mean?"

"The way he looked," Addie said. "Hard, like nothing good ever happened to him. And, when he said what happened, he just said it. Cold like." She shrugged. "Maybe it was the blood, too."

"The blood?"

"He was covered in her blood. His clothes, his boots, gun belt. His whip. Everything."

"His whip?"

She nodded. "Coiled. Hanging off his belt."

"Tell me what he looked like," he said, and coughed again. It sounded deep and rough.

"Almost bald. And blue eyes, I'm pretty sure."

"Did he have a red moustache?"

"It was dark, but I don't remember if it was red," she said. "But he had one. It drooped down. Like this." She motioned with her hand on her own face.

"If it helps," he said, "if it's who I think the man was, he's dead."

"What are you saying? You knew him?"

"It might be the same man who whipped me, one of the ones who raped my wife. I killed them all. The one with the moustache I killed in Los Angeles three years ago."

Addie felt her heart racing in her chest, anger and relief swelling around it. She wanted to believe him. She felt that no lies were coming out of Murieta's mouth. He was another soul battered and beaten by circumstance. Maybe the man who murdered Claire was dead, Addie thought, and now maybe I can find a little peace. She wiped her eyes, blinking back tears.

Murieta bent forward, coughing and hacking. She saw more blood on his sleeve.

Addie eased him back against his saddle. Her hand brushed his *serape*. There was fresh blood there.

"Maybe you believe me," he said. "And maybe what I've told you helps."

"Just know my saying you didn't murder my sister isn't going to count for much with some of these rangers," Addie said and looked back at the others. Wheat was talking to Quick, the two of them glancing over at her. Needle had squatted by Doyle and was adding wood to the fire, keeping a watch on her with the narrow-eyed look of a critter that was waiting for something to die. They were waiting for her to come tell them everything, that was certain.

Addie set her jaw and turned to Murieta. "I have to ask you something. I can see why you hate us, but why kill so many who didn't do anything to you?"

"I didn't kill them all," he said quietly.

"Well, that won't get you much in the way of leniency from the governor," Addie said, an edge creeping into her voice. "And folks aren't much on forgiving robbery and murder."

She was finding this Mexican tolerable somehow, something she didn't expect, and it was starting to cause her considerable discomfort and agitation. Mexicans weren't to be trusted as far as she was concerned. She didn't like them, didn't associate with them, and yet here she was swapping intimacies with one, one she had expected to empty her revolver into. But she also knew that when she'd had the chance earlier, she'd hesitated for that split second. Thirst for vengeance had eaten away at her, but she knew she couldn't commit cold-blooded murder. And that's what it would've been without his admitting he killed Claire. Would she have killed him had he admitted it? Right now, she couldn't say for certain.

Suddenly, Murieta was coughing again. He'd dropped his coffee tin.

"It hurts to breathe," he said.

She handed him his water bag and he took a cautious sip, his eyes closed.

"I have a favor to ask, if you would help me," he said.

"I got no pull with the governor, if that's what you're after," Addie said.

She saw a little smile on his lips.

"I don't want to spend eternity in an unmarked piece of ground," he said. "This is a land of strangers. Would you have a proper marker placed on my grave? Rosita will come looking. Maybe she'll find you. She'll want to take me home."

Addie pulled her blanket closer. She was feeling the cold.

"You are Murieta, aren't you?" she asked.

He nodded. "Maybe she's looking up at the same stars I'm seeing right now."

Addie turned her head away and rubbed her arms. She felt herself trembling. It wasn't just the cold. This man had touched feelings she had buried long ago. It was beginning to overwhelm her and she didn't like it. Then she felt him touch her arm.

"There's something else," he said.

Needle didn't notice Doyle had moved back a bit from the growing campfire because it was getting too hot for him. Adding wood to the fire was Needle's answer to staying warm as well as keeping the haunting, menacing dark at bay. And trying to keep his mind off of that, he kept a watchful eye on Addie and the greaser whispering across the way. But he was getting antsy waiting.

When he saw Wheat leave Quick and walk over by the horses with Clegg and the nigger, he decided it was time to lay out his plan to Quick, the plan he'd been formulating and rehearsing in his mind. He quietly got up and went around to where Quick was spreading his bedroll. Mother Needle's advice came to mind. "Life and horseshit got a lot in common, boy, so you say whatever you got to to get what you want, 'cause it ain't lyin'— unless it's me you're lyin' to."

"Lieutenant?" Needle said carefully, hat in hand.

"Not now," Quick said, not looking up at him.

"I just wanted to apologize. For, you know, pulling on Wheat and all."

"Fine."

"I guess the excitement at having caught this bandit here got me," Needle said, hanging his head. "I mean the better of me."

Quick faced him. "Is that all?"

"Well, I guess. Actually, Lieutenant, I'd like—"

Quick cut him off. "I won't return your weapons. And you should consider yourself lucky I've decided not to report that sorry incident to Captain Hope when he returns."

"That's right decent and obliging of you," Needle said, still hanging his head. "And I thank you for it."

He glanced at Quick, dropped his eyes, and began his gamble. "But that wasn't what I came to see you about. This Mex here, he's a sly one, wouldn't you say?"

When Quick turned to look at Murieta, Needle also glanced over and could see Addie holding the water bag up to the Mex's mouth. They were a few yards away.

"I don't think I would say," Quick said.

"I mean the chase and all. You got your suspicions for figuring he's not the Joaquin he says he is. But I was thinking, let's say you're right. Let's say he ain't the Joaquin Murieta. But let's say he's one of those other Joaquins."

"I see no more proof of that than his being Murieta."

"Yeah, I can see that," Needle said, feeling pleased he had managed to keep Quick engaged. "It's just this one running like he did and playing he didn't know how to talk American when he did."

"Get to your point," Quick said.

Needle let it out, talking faster as he went on. "Well, this Mex claims to be the Joaquin Murieta and the way I see it, whether he is or isn't, he's wanting to make a name for himself. And folks back in town'd like to see this banditry disposed of. And you done that already when you dropped that big Mex, and folks'll remember that and remember you. So if you was to bring in this one, seeing how he's real adamant he's who he says, whether it's him or one of them other Joaquins, the fact is, he and his dead friend are responsible for killing Sam and shooting Ezra. And likely the murder of Abel Tyner. So as I see it, it appears to look bad for him and good for you, politically speaking, I mean."

Needle didn't like what he saw in Quick's eyes.

"Are you suggesting I use this man's life for my own gain?" Quick asked.

Needle realized immediately things were not going the way he had hoped. What would Mother Needle do?

"No, no," Needle said. "I'm saying we take him back to town, see what a judge says. What I'd do."

Quick was ready to punch Needle. That little bastard's suggestion was exactly the kind of despicable, self-promoting, shameless thinking he would expect of Don Antonio! And he might well have hit Needle in the nose except Wheat came over at that moment.

"Lieutenant?" Wheat asked.

"This is private talk," Needle said, sounding peevish.

Quick had no more desire to talk to Needle. "What do you want, Horace?"

"Addie says you need to come see the prisoner," Wheat said.

Without a word, Quick turned along with Wheat and left Needle standing there. He heard Needle say, almost under his breath, "God damn asshole Wheat." Quick caught sight of Wheat's sudden movement and heard the sound of flesh hitting flesh, hard and fast, followed by a distinct thud, like the sound of a large sack of wet flour hitting the ground.

He turned and saw Needle lying sprawled in the dirt. It didn't appear that anyone else had noticed. Clegg and Charley were still over by the horses. Doyle had his hat over his face, maybe sleeping. Addie and the Mexican were talking.

Quick saw Wheat straightening his coat.

"He called me a dirty name," Wheat said. "I'll tolerate that from no man."

Quick patted him on the back. "I'll see Addie and the Mexican directly." He squatted down next to Needle to help him up.

"You better be more careful where you're walking here in the dark, Ned."

"He hid me," Needle slurred, sitting up and holding his jaw.

"Who did?"

"Thad basdard, Whead."

"I didn't see anything," Quick said, taking Needle's arm, "and I was right here."

Quick stood up straight after Needle yanked his arm away from him. He held back a grin as he watched Needle get up, spitting blood and reaching into his mouth to check for loose teeth.

"It occurs to me, maybe you should think about keeping your mouth shut if Wheat's anywhere in earshot," Quick said, walking away, then chuckled, "Might as well try teaching a jackass to dance."

If the rangers weren't to be disbanded in a few weeks, Quick figured he'd've made two strong recommendations to Captain Hope: promote Wheat to the rank of sergeant and boot Needle out of the unit. Of course, Quick would have liked to have kicked him out weeks ago but Captain Hope had guaranteed every volunteer would serve until Joaquin was taken or the rangers were disbanded.

"Wheat said you wanted to see me," Quick said as he came

up to Addie and the prisoner.

"*Señor,*" the Mexican said, his voice sounding tired and hoarse, "I want to ask you, *por favor,* allow me to make my confession."

"I'm glad you've finally seen fit to do so," Quick said and sat down. "Let's start with your real name."

The Mexican coughed.

"That isn't what he meant," Addie said. "He wants a priest."

The way she said it made it sound like it was real distasteful to her.

"We're a little short on them out here," Quick said, looking at the Mexican.

"Are there any Catholics with you?" he asked. "Maybe the *grande* ranger. Or that one Wheat."

"They aren't papes," Quick said. "Doyle might be but I doubt he's in any mood to do you a favor." Then he looked at Addie.

"Oh no," she said, shaking her head. "I already told him I don't go near them bastards."

"You only need to tell him what I say," the Mexican said. "Nothing more."

"Me and holy rollers don't see eye to eye," she said.

"If I have any soul left," the Mexican said, "it might not be damned forever. *Por favor.* For my wife's sake."

Addie avoided Murieta's eyes. She knew he was looking at her.

Damn it! She didn't like Mexicans, clergymen, Indians, and a whole passel of others. Being married to a Moravian minister who was trying to convert Comanches down in Texas a few years ago had left her bitter and hateful. When she couldn't get pregnant, her husband decided to ride her every night until she did. And when that failed he got angry, a righteous, fear-the-wrath-of-God angry and declared, "There is something unclean about you!" Then he struck her. She packed a bag and stole away that night, never looking back, hoping the whole lot of them would burn in hell.

"I can't," she said. "It's too much to ask. Can't you just leave it be?"

Angry and frustrated with herself, she stomped over to the other side of the fire and sat, her back to the two men.

Murieta was scared. A priest had to hear his confession. He knew Rosita would go to heaven and he wanted to be with her. So, even though he was still angry with God, he knew he had to try to do what he could, for Rosita's sake.

"I'll do it," Quick said.

Murieta hadn't expected that.

"I'm no pape but my folks saw to it I was baptized," Quick said. "Just tell me what I have to do. That is, if you've got no objection."

"None," Murieta said. He saw no other choice. He was losing the feeling in his leg. That numbness was inching up toward his vitals. Time was running short. "It's a sacred trust I'm giving you. I must ask you to swear you will go to Padre Anacleto."

"I know him."

"You understand you must tell the padre everything I say. Only him. No one else can know. Your word *hombre, ¿por favor?*" He took hold of Quick's arm.

"I've heard how important this confessing is to you people," Quick said. "And I know you have to tell the truth or it won't count. None of this playing around anymore. *¿Comprende?*"

Feeling weaker, Murieta motioned him closer.

Addie clutched her blanket around her shoulders. She shivered. Not against the chilly night air, but the coldness she felt in her soul. Glancing around, she noticed Needle sitting close by curled up in a ball, rocking slightly, and staring intently into the flames. Something ugly was going on behind those eyes.

Needle's mind was a jumble. He had to find some way to get Quick to see good reason. He wanted to fix Wheat. And his bladder was screaming for relief! He had to think of something else! Lord, he wished he didn't have to pee. This night was blacker than black out here. And he didn't like the dark.

Watch the damn fire, he told himself. The burning branches reminded him of blackened, charred bones. Hell, stop thinking of dead things. Unless it was Wheat! That would do it! Maybe he'd catch Wheat alone back in town, like he did Abel Tyner. But instead of just beating on him like he'd done Tyner, he'd drag him off somewhere, gag him, string him up over a fire, and let him cook. Mother Needle would approve, no doubt. A little planning was all.

But this damn Quick was a different problem requiring a different approach. And nothing had worked so far.

Suddenly that urge hit him real bad. He couldn't wait any longer or he'd piss a puddle sitting right there! Dark or no dark, gun or no gun, he had to go! Scrambling up, he moved fast to a thicket of junipers outside the clearing growing out of the base of some rocks. He tried not to notice the big black shadows dancing around him and closing in. And those rocks reaching out of hell! Don't look at them! Just undo your buttons, do your business, keep your eyes on that fire, and why did you wait so *damn* long to do this? It'll be noon and you'll still be standing here!

Then he heard it! Out in the dark. A noise. A rustling. A whoosh-sounding thing. He felt cold and clammy. What the hell's out there? he thought, feeling scared like a little boy. Something was coming! Something bad! It was coming for him! Captain Johnston and his dead men had found him!

★ ★ ★ ★ ★

Murieta blessed himself with the sign of the cross. His throat felt dry. He took a swallow from his water bag and said, "Tell the priest I ask for his blessing and it has been a long time since my last confession. You will remember to see Padre Anacleto?"

"I said I would," Quick said, sounding irritated.

"*Si, gracias,*" Murieta said, then bowed his head. "You must know it is more than my confession I'm giving you. You have my eternal soul to put into Padre Anacleto's hands. I do this for my wife so I may see her in heaven." He fought back the pain in his chest. "Here are my sins. Three commandments I have broken. I have killed many men. Much gold and money I have stolen. Tell the padre, none of these things I am sorry for, but I ask for forgiveness and his prayers to God. He'll know I'll need them."

Quick waited, then said, "You said there were three commandments you broke. You only mentioned two by my count."

Murieta groaned against the sudden bolt of pain in his leg. Once it passed, he took a deep breath.

"*Si,*" he said, his voice dry. "You know it's very important I tell the truth in my confession. It's no good for me if I tell you a lie to take to the padre. My third sin is the lie. I told many lies to *gringos,* but only to protect *mis amigos.* And *señor,* I did not lie to you about who I am. Please, help the woman to mark my grave when I'm gone."

"Good Lord above," Quick whispered and sat back. "I'll be damned."

"I am not the monster you expected. *¿Si?*"

CHAPTER SIXTEEN:
THE PROOF

Before Quick could answer, Clegg's screams nearly jumped him out of his skin.

"Snakes!" Clegg was shouting. "Snakes! Get 'em off me! Help! Get 'em off!"

Quick ran over to him, the camp in commotion. The horses had spooked and were fighting against their ties, trying to break loose, whinnying fiercely. Doyle had bolted upright, eyes wide and mouth agape. Needle ran back into the clearing, the front of his trousers wet. Charley looked disoriented, like he'd woken up suddenly.

"Uriah!" Quick shouted, grabbing Clegg by his coat.

A look of horror was on Clegg's face.

Wheat and Addie were at Quick's side.

"Slap him!" Wheat said.

Quick jerked his head at him.

"That's what the barkeep at the El Dorado does when he's like this," Wheat said.

Quick shook him again. "Clegg!"

Clegg's eyes focused and he looked like he would burst into tears. Quick saw a canteen lying at Clegg's side. He picked it up and shook it. There was liquid inside. Putting it to his mouth, he took a taste and spit it out. Brandy!

"You told me you didn't have any more," Quick said.

"I'm sorry, I'm sorry," Clegg said. "I lied but I paid. It was snakes, slithering out that hole I seen. I tried calling for help but they had me, crawling up my pant legs, all over me. And next I knew, I heard screaming."

"That was you," Addie said.

Quick turned to Charley who looked scared. "I thought you were keeping an eye on him."

"I fell asleep," Charley said.

"I'm right sorry everybody," Clegg said. "Drink and me—I just couldn't help myself. But Ambrose, it wasn't Charley's fault. It wasn't."

Quick's patience was sorely frayed. "Uriah, no more. You understand?"

"I do."

"Good," Quick said and took the canteen, uncorked it, and poured out the remaining contents at Clegg's feet.

Clegg reached out, his body jerking as though seized with spasms, but his big shoulders slumped. Then he put his face in his hands.

"That's the second time I've had to do this," Quick said, tossing the empty canteen down. "There better not be any more foolishness." He turned to Wheat. "Stay with him."

He walked back to the Mexican.

"Lieutenant?" Charley asked, catching up to Quick. "You told me to watch him and I let him down. I let you down. I'm real sorry."

"We all make mistakes," Quick said. "Just learn from it."

Charley felt some relief and followed Quick to the fire. He stopped to warm himself while Quick went over to the Mexican. A moment later, Charley saw Needle come over and start talking to Addie. He couldn't help overhearing them.

"Did that Mex tell you anything," Needle said, "like maybe how he killed Abel?"

"Go to hell," Addie said.

When she walked away, Charley threw a branch on the fire and noticed Needle looking at him.

"Hey," Needle said, "this was your fault for not watching that drunk."

"Yeah," Charley said, feeling bad. "Won't happen again."

Needle stepped in close, surprising Charley. Ned had hardly spoken to him directly since becoming a ranger, and never before that.

"Next time somebody tells you to do something, do it," Needle said, his voice low and hard. "Going sleeping like that you could get us all killed." Needle turned to leave. "Stupid nigger."

Charley didn't move. He was feeling so low already. No one else appeared to have heard what Needle said. Or they paid it no mind. He crossed his arms and stared into the fire. No, he'd never make a mistake like that again. And he wasn't going to let Needle call him that name again, ever.

When Murieta heard from Quick what had happened, he was genuinely concerned about the welfare of the *grande* ranger, but Quick told him it would all be fine.

"And I want you to know," Quick said, "I'll see to it your grave gets a proper marker."

Murieta's worry vanished, the weight was lifted, the tightness in his chest evaporated. He could only nod his thanks. He believed and trusted this *gringo*. This one was an honorable man, and therefore, better than a *gringo pendejo*. Murieta felt better now for the first time since the night before when he had been with Ana Benitez. It would be all right. He could rest and dream of better things, of Rosita, and drift away. Easily. Finally.

Needle was still riled up about being scared, and that his trousers were still damp and stinking. But more importantly, he wanted answers about what they were going to do with the Mex, and he was determined to get them. A decision needed to be made! As far as he was concerned, it was time to get it.

Sitting down close by Doyle, Needle told him his plan, wanting to make sure Doyle was with him. When he agreed, Needle stood up.

"Listen here everybody," Needle said. "I say this prisoner of ours is who he says, the Joaquin Murieta. I say he and his friend killed Abel Tyner. I say we take him in and collect the reward."

"I say yes," Doyle said.

"Anybody say different?" Needle asked.

"I do!" Wheat hollered.

"You just back off," Needle said, stabbing his finger in Wheat's direction as he was still sitting with Clegg. I'll fix you later, he thought.

"Needle, you're wasting your time," Quick said, coming over to the fire.

"That Mex shot at us!" Needle said. "Me and Clegg."

"And his friend shot me," Doyle said, pointing at his shoulder. "And it hurts."

"We fired at him and his friend first!" Wheat said. "Somebody takes a shot at me, I'd shoot back, too."

"I say he's Murieta," Doyle said.

"We got no proof of that yet," Wheat said.

"Tell that to Abel," Needle said.

Next thing Needle knew Quick was facing him.

"I don't want to hear any more of your jabbering," Quick said. "I'll decide what we do with him."

"Well, Lieutenant," Needle said, "seeing this is a democracy we're living in, I say we take a vote on it."

"We're rangers doing our job," Quick said. "There's nothing to vote."

"But—" Needle said and got no further when Addie cut him off.

"Well, there's something I want to know," Addie said to Needle, her hands on her hips, "and that's why are you so fired up about this man being Joaquin Murieta? And how come you're throwing around Abel's name? You act like you and him were friends when everybody knows you hated him because he was married to that Mex woman."

"Yeah," he said, "but I didn't cut his throat over it."

"But you were in San Gabriel last night," Addie said, walking around the campfire to him. "Did you see this man over here?" She pointed to Murieta. "And what about Abel? Did you see him after you left Clarissa?"

"No!" Needle lied with emphasis, and told himself he'd have to have a talk with Clarissa when he got back about keeping her fat mouth shut. "Now what about the vote?"

"Let's ask the Mexican if he saw you," Addie said.

"It don't matter if he saw the governor himself!" Needle said. "What matters is that Sam Prizer is dead and Ezra here is wounded bad. I say he's the Joaquin Murieta. And I think Sam would agree. Ezra, you still with me?"

"Yeah," Doyle said and rested back against his saddle.

"So that's three," Needle said.

"I say no," Wheat said. "And Uriah says the same."

"And I say no, too," Addie said, her mouth a thin line. "I say all you want is the reward from the governor, Ned Needle, and I won't make it that easy for you. And I'll tell you something else. That man lying over there shot up and dying that you want to take back so bad is more man at this minute than you'll ever be in your whole miserable life!"

Needle ran his tongue over his front teeth. He guessed Addie and the greaser had gotten right cozy during their little talk earlier. He jerked his head at Charley. "You. What do you say?"

Charley looked surprised.

"Come on," Needle said. "Is he the Joaquin Murieta or not?"

Charley looked over at Murieta, then to Quick and back at Needle. "I don't know, exactly."

"Great," Needle said, throwing his hands up. "The darky gets his one and only chance to vote in this state and he doesn't know."

Needle saw Charley move toward him and took a step back, but then Addie got hold of Charley's shoulder.

"He's a horse's ass," Addie said loudly. "Don't give him any mind. There's nothing to besting a fool."

And there's nothing to be gained from a nigger and a whore, Needle thought.

"Lieutenant?" Needle said, snapping his head in Quick's direction.

Quick was standing alone on the far side of the campfire, hands tucked snug under his arms, and staring at the flames, orange, hot, and leaping. The very man he had been sworn to apprehend by the power of the State Legislature and Governor Bigler himself was here, in his hands. And it gnawed at him because that same man's soul was in his hands, too. There was also a reward of one thousand dollars waiting. But so was his word, his trusted word, to deliver Murieta's last confession to Father Anacleto. Quick realized he had made a grave decision, the kind that could destine the rest of his life. And he couldn't forget his matrimonial intentions toward Lucy Barton, and showing her father he wasn't a full-time nobody. "Sure you got ambition," he recalled Sheriff Barton saying, "but you're wastin' it and makin' the wrong kinda name for yourself."

"Lieutenant?" Quick heard Needle say again.

The wrong kinda name for yourself. The words kept rolling around in Quick's head.

He glanced over at Murieta who appeared to have fallen asleep.

It was quiet. The *gringo* rangers had finally gone to bed. Murieta heard only the sound of his heart beating. Nothing more. Peaceful. Serene. An idyll. Like the evenings he lay under the stars with Rosita in his arms. Nothing could hurt him then. No harm would befall them. The world spun as surely as the bee spun honey. Both had held the promise of sweetness.

The cold was lifting. He could feel it. The pain in his leg had gone. His breathing was steady. The fire of the bullet wounds cooled. His chest relaxed with each new breath. Pangs of hunger and thirst had vanished.

He had made his peace. Lieutenant Quick had given his solemn word. He would take his confession to the padre. And if the padre's prayers could offer salvation and repose for his soul in the sight of God, then maybe he would see his beloved Rosita in heaven. Some day.

A *gringo* approached. He looked familiar. It was the man with stories to tell his grandchildren. His *amigo*! And who was that with him? Feliz Contreras! They were both on horseback, looking much like the last time he saw them, and smiling at him.

"My children and their children will know the generosity of Joaquin Murieta," his *gringo* friend said.

"And I already know it," Contreras said.

Before he could thank them and tell Contreras to get away before the rangers saw him, they turned their horses and rode silently away into blackness that gave way to the sun's orange glow, the light of the new day. The darkness was gone.

Somehow, Murieta had managed to make it through the long night to the dawn. Maybe the rangers would get him back to Los Angeles after all. He could give Padre Anacleto his confession. Maybe they could bring Ana Benitez to see him. And

Rosita would come.

Then he heard her voice, Rosita's lovely, honeyed voice. "It's a new country, *mi amor.* A new life. Have no fear anymore."

Murieta opened his eyes. A brilliant white glow rose behind the rocks. But they looked different now! No longer a jagged chaos, but smooth and graceful, like waves on the ocean, yet stilled in place, as though they had been halted in their majesty. And above them, stretching back beyond the horizon, were clouds thick and white, like a field of blooming dandelions, but these were set against a sky of radiant blue, and the underside of each cloud was dappled in shining gold.

Then he saw an even more heavenly sight! Brighter than the sun. But he didn't flinch, close his eyes, or look away. The brightness moved toward him. Enveloped him. He smiled. It was Rosita, with her long, flowing black hair, and her dark eyes round, laughing and filled with love. Her soft arms reached for him and took him in close embrace. He could feel her warmth, and then her soft full lips kissing his mouth.

"You're more beautiful than my memory of you," he said.

He could feel her holding him close, so close he felt her heart beating against his chest. He heaved a gentle sigh. All was light around him. And then it flickered. Everything was still. He couldn't feel the heart beating. He was afraid and began to tremble.

Then he saw Rosita smile at him.

"Don't be afraid, my love," she said.

And he was not.

"Lieutenant!" Needle said again, irritated.

When he didn't answer, Needle figured Quick was ignoring him on purpose.

Impatient, Needle curled his lower lip in, and then he saw Charley out of the corner of his eye taking a drink of water from his canteen.

"Well," Needle said to him, "made up your mind yet?"

"Let him alone," Doyle said.

"That's alright, Ezra," Charley said and then capped his canteen and looked at Needle. "No, I haven't."

"Oh, good," Needle said sarcastically, turning away from him. "The nigger's going to think on it awhile more. Dumb as dirt."

Needle heard a growl behind him and felt a hard shove and he was on the ground, face first, his arms splayed out in front of him. Somebody grabbed his coat, spun him onto his back, and sat on top of him. He saw Charley, his mouth open, heard a fierce shout, like a war cry, and two hard blows hit him in the face. Needle tried to get his hands around Charley's neck and a dark fist hurtled into his face again. He let out a loud, piercing yelp and suddenly the weight was off his chest and he sat up, his hand to his nose.

"He busted my damn nose!" Needle shrieked, looking at the blood on his palm. "I'm bleeding!"

He saw Wheat holding Charley back and then Addie's face close to his, looking at him.

"It isn't busted," she said and then chuckled. "But your face is going to look like raw beefsteak."

"Damn it to hell! Why's everything happen to me?" Needle said, pulling a yellow bandana from his trouser pocket.

That suited Quick fine. Maybe nursing his face would keep Needle quiet for a while.

Quick told Charley to go with Wheat to keep an eye on Clegg and to also keep his distance from Needle. Then he went over to Murieta, not at all sure what he wanted to say to him, or even why. He realized Murieta was dead as Addie came over and knelt down beside him. Before he could say anything to

203

her, Quick heard her gasp as she stiffened and crossed her arms, pulling her blanket tightly over her chest. She knew now, too.

"I spent years cursing his name," Addie said quietly after a moment. "Then he's dying and he asks me for help. It's . . . I just don't know."

Quick knew one thing. The man he had made a solemn promise to was also the man who could give him everything he wanted. Now he was dead. And he hated himself for thinking what he was thinking, but he couldn't help it. He saw Needle stomping over to him, holding his bandana to his swelling nose.

"I demand charges be brought against that little bastard," Needle said. "He snuck up on me from behind and knocked me down and proceeded to beat on me. All unprovoked."

Quick didn't look up at him. He just shook his head.

"Wait one minute now," Needle said. "That greaser dead?"

"He is," Quick said.

"That's good for us," Needle said.

"And what's that supposed to mean?" Addie asked, sounding angry.

"It means one thousand dollars, is what it means," Needle said and shoved his bandana into his pocket. "All we need is to take in the proof."

"Well, he told me he lied," Addie said. "He's not Murieta. So go away."

"Stop it, Addie," Quick said quietly.

He saw the disbelief on her face.

"He's Murieta," Quick said. "We both know it."

"Damn! The answer to everything you want is lying right there in front of you, Lieutenant," Needle said.

"Just be quiet," Quick said sharply.

"This is your chance," Needle said. "You can write your own ticket. The man who got the Joaquin Murieta. Tell the governor what he said." He pointed at Murieta's body. "Take him the proof."

"We're burying this man here come light," Addie said and turned to Quick. "You promised him you'd bury him."

"We don't need a whole body," Needle said.

Quick frowned at Needle. "What did you say?"

"We try taking him as is, the governor'll smell him three days before we get there. The reward is on Joaquin's head, so to speak."

"You can't allow this savagery!" Addie said, grabbing Quick's arm.

"Got to put your biscuit in the gravy while it's hot," Needle said.

"Ambrose, please!" Addie said.

Quick knew this was his chance, what he'd been waiting for. There was Lucy and fame, and there was his promise that he'd given to this man. But there was also the oath he'd given as a ranger, too.

"This is about courage, not worrying about making a mistake," Needle said.

Quick could hear the bands playing, the cheers of the crowd. He'd wave to them, Lucy at his side. All that reward money, even after splitting it with the others, would still leave him more than he'd ever had before, enough to get him started. The man who got Joaquin Murieta, Ambrose Quick! A known man! Most famous man in the state. No laurel too great. No request refused. No man alive would dare call him a full-time nobody then. Folks would want to vote for him! They couldn't stop themselves! He'd win by a landslide!

"You gave him your word!" Addie shouted.

"Everybody all right? What's going on there?" Wheat hollered and headed over to the fire.

Quick saw Charley helping Clegg stand up.

205

"Don't do this," Quick said to Addie, his voice low but urgent.

"You've left me no choice," Addie said.

"You're leaving me no choice!" Quick said.

Addie turned to the other rangers. "This prisoner of yours is dead. The lieutenant here said he'd see to his burial. And now he's talking like he won't."

"The man's dead, let's bury him and be done with it," Wheat said with a shrug. "Can't prove anything by what he said."

"Sounded like wild talk to me," Charley said.

"It wasn't wild talk," Quick said.

"What're you saying?" Wheat asked.

"This man here is Joaquin Murieta," Quick said. "He confessed, in no uncertain terms."

"You Judas!" Addie cried at Quick and slapped him.

Quick gritted his teeth at the hard sting of it, and his face flushed red with anger, but he was sure he'd done the right thing.

"Damn," Doyle said.

"What did he tell you?" Wheat asked.

"It was more than enough to convince me," Quick said.

"Why don't you tell them everything, you sorry son-of-a-bitch," Addie said, and stormed off.

"If she's that mad, it must be true," Wheat said.

"That man sure had me fooled," Clegg said sadly, leaning on Charley for support. "This changes everything."

"It does," Quick said. "We did the job we signed on for. Now I intend to keep my word and bury this man as he asked, but we need to take proof, tangible proof, of our capture to the governor. I see no other choice."

"What's that mean, that proof?" Charley asked.

"The reward's on his head," Needle said.

The others looked at each other or down at the ground. Quick heard Clegg mumble something.

"Speak up," Quick said.

"I was saying I wished there's some other way," Clegg said.

"There isn't," Needle said and chuckled.

Quick wanted to smack Needle, but he knew the obnoxious little shit was right.

"You know, Ned," Wheat said, "you're daddy didn't beat you enough."

"Oh that bastard son-of-a-bitch did," Needle said. "Used his bullwhip on me when I turned ten. My mama got me out of there and we never looked back."

"Hey!" Addie called out. "You say bullwhip?"

"Yeah."

"What did he look like?"

"Who?"

"Your father."

"What the hell you want to know for?"

"He have a moustache?"

"Yeah," Needle said, "and that's why I don't. And if I ever saw him again, I'd kill him."

Quick wondered why she was asking Needle about his father, but then he saw the dawn breaking, a hot, white glow in the east and he knew it would be another blistering day.

After using a rock to sharpen his Bowie knife and taking a drink of brandy to steady his hand, Quick got to it. He wished it wasn't Needle holding on to Murieta's head to keep it from moving but nobody else would do it. Quick didn't blame Charley and Clegg for not watching. He did hear Charley puking. But Wheat and Doyle watched.

"I never seen anything like that before," Doyle said and put his hand over his nose and mouth.

"God help us," Wheat said.

Quick stopped, took a couple of deep breaths, and wiped his forehead.

"Why don't you carve bandit in his belly while you're at it?" Addie shouted. "He's dead and still got more grit than you!"

Quick started cutting again and struck bone. He felt his stomach turn but kept going, reminding himself that the man who brought in the head of Joaquin Murieta could write his own ticket.

CHAPTER SEVENTEEN: THE LIE

When Quick found the ground in the clearing proved too hard to dig into, especially since they had no pick or shovel, he had Needle and Wheat tie Murieta's headless corpse over the back of one of the horses. With Murieta's head rolled up in his blanket and tied to the back of his saddle, Quick led them to the nearby lake where he hoped the soil would be softer. They saw Murieta's horse when they got there. Mountain lions had gotten to it during the night. Ants were at it now.

Though the soil was softer, Quick said a shallow grave would have to do for the time being.

"And cover it over with dirt and rocks so the animals won't vex him," he said.

While Needle and Wheat saw to the burying, Quick fashioned a cross from manzanita branches and said he would put a proper marker with Murieta's name on it when he returned from seeing the governor. Then he dunked his nearly empty canteen in the lake to fill it and told the others to do the same.

"It's a long ride back to town," Quick said.

When they returned to the clearing, Quick was glad the others had nearly finished breaking camp. Though Clegg was suffering from the sweats and shakes, Quick saw he had lashed Prizer's blanket-wrapped and tied body over the saddle of his horse. He told Quick he'd see to taking the body to Prizer's wife.

Quick returned Addie's Dragoon to her. He had thought of

unloading it, but then he didn't.

"You think you buried your sins, but you just buried yourself," she said and finished saddling her horse.

Handing Needle his pistol and knife back, Quick made him promise he wouldn't use them on Wheat or Charley.

"Hell, with all our good fortune, I clean forgot about all that," Needle said, grinning, his nose still swollen and his eye turning red and puffy.

Quick didn't believe him.

"One other thing," Needle said. "Since nobody else has put a claim on it, I want the Joaquin's saddle."

"Fine," Quick said. "If nobody else says they want it, it's yours."

Needle grinned like a kid on Christmas morning.

Quick called out to the others. "Anybody want Joaquin's saddle?"

Addie didn't look his way. Doyle shook his head. Wheat, Clegg, and Charley busied themselves with their gear. No one was interested.

"Now you tell me something," Quick said, turning back to Needle. "How do you plan to get it back to town?"

Needle's grin disappeared.

"That's right," Quick said. "We got no extra horse, and that Mexican saddle is heavy. And we're pulling out very shortly."

"Damn!" Needle said. "Looks like I'll have to come back for it."

A few minutes later, Quick gave the order to mount up and saw Needle hastily covering Murieta's saddle with chamise and manzanita branches.

Sending Charley on ahead to find the body of the Animal, Quick led the others south. He noted the long shadows they cast against the craggy rocks, and the fact that no one spoke.

About an hour later, when Charley rode up saying he'd found

the Animal's remains in the wash at the bottom of the canyon where he fell, Quick said they'd stop and bury him. When they got there, he fired a couple of shots at vultures that were feeding on the body. He hit one and the other flew off. Quick watched him circle overhead. No one said a word when Needle announced he was taking the Animal's bloody chain mail coat as a souvenir.

Quick hoped to avoid seeing Andres Pico, or anyone else for that matter, who might consider Murieta a friend or hero and therefore make trouble. He also wanted to avoid any confrontation because they were all exhausted, and this heat didn't help matters as it sapped the strength. About mid-morning he cursed his luck. Coming back over the pass and peering down into the San Fernando Valley, he made out a figure on horseback leaving the shade of an oak tree and heading off in the direction of the old Mission at a fast clip. Whoever it was had likely seen them and was on his way to tell Pico.

It wasn't long before Quick saw Pico, his son Romulo, and five of his hired men riding toward them from across the valley.

"Might be trouble," Quick said, reining in his horse. "Just be ready."

He checked to see that Murieta's head was secure, and then drew his revolver out of the holster a bit, making sure it would slide out easily in case he needed it. The other rangers did the same, though Doyle, his arm still in a sling, stuck his revolver inside his belt for an easier pull. Quick noted that Addie was keeping her face turned away from him.

"*¡Amigos!*" Pico shouted as he rode up to Quick.

"*Señor* Pico," Quick said, and then nodded at Romulo who nodded back.

"I'm glad to see you're safe," Pico said, not taking his eyes from Quick.

"My father was very worried about you after that scare with

the herd yesterday," Romulo said. "Something frightened them. A terrible thing."

"Yes, we're fine," Quick said. He knew damn good and well several shots had been fired to stampede the horses. Hell, he'd heard them! But he didn't know who fired them, and he'd never get Pico or anybody who was with him to admit it.

"We sure as hell are," Needle said, walking his horse up to them and patting the blanket roll on the back of Quick's horse. "Everything's going to be right as right can be."

Quick wanted to shoot Needle right out of his saddle. He saw several of Pico's men stiffen. He also noticed Pico's eyes turn down, becoming sad. Then the old man looked back up at him.

"And what is that you have that's so special, *señor*?" Pico asked.

"Just the head of—" Needle began.

"Ranger Needle!" Quick barked. He hoped his glare would be enough and Needle would know to keep his mouth shut.

Needle sniffed and sat back in his saddle, looking sullen. The other rangers appeared calm, but ready. Addie was looking off, shaking her head.

Quick turned back to face Pico and said, "We're on our way back to town. With evidence. We were chasing a suspected murderer."

"Evidence?" Pico asked.

"There was a crime," Addie said low.

Quick paid her no attention. He did remind himself that Murieta had admitted his crimes. And that severing his head from his body was not a crime.

"That's right, *señor*," Quick said, adjusting his hat. "Criminal evidence. It's my sworn duty as a ranger to deliver it."

For a moment no one spoke. Or moved. Then Quick saw Pico's hand move back toward his pistol. Quick tensed. Pico's hand came to rest on his thigh. Relaxing some, Quick's mind suddenly cleared. Nobody wanted to die out here today. It was too damn hot! Come to think of it, why was Pico so curious about them anyhow? Quick was not about to be buffaloed.

"Yesterday, did you see two men headed north?" Quick asked. "They'd've been headed for the pass."

"No," Pico said.

"Are you certain?" Quick asked. "Maybe some of your men saw them. Romulo?"

Romulo shook his head slowly.

"Could be those two were responsible for the stampede," Quick said. "I could've sworn I heard shots fired."

Pico's face betrayed nothing.

"We were following a trail that led right into your herd," Quick said. "Could've killed somebody, all those horses. Any of your men hurt?"

"No, thank God," Pico said. "And I believe you must be mistaken about a shot. My men know better."

"Maybe not your men," Quick said. "Maybe a couple others. Like I said, their trail was leading right into your herd."

Quick watched the old man's eyes. They remained steady and unrevealing.

"You know there was a murder in San Gabriel early yesterday morning," Quick said. "Have you heard about it? A deputy got his throat cut. We were after the men we believed might have done it." Quick damned the infernal heat and his own exhaustion, blaming them for his not having thought out a strategy sooner with Pico. The stampede had more than likely been Pico's idea to help his Mexican bandit friends escape. Again, he knew he'd never prove it.

"I've heard nothing," Pico said.

"Ugly thing," Quick said. "A man murdered."

"Did you find the men? The ones responsible?" Pico asked.

Quick was hoping Pico would say something about Murieta, mention his name, anything to acknowledge Murieta's presence. But the old man kept silent on that score. Quick decided it was time to get to it.

"The name of Joaquin Murieta came up back in San Gabriel," Quick said. "You're acquainted with him, aren't you?"

Pico nodded.

"And when was the last time you saw him?"

"No se."

Behind him, Quick heard Needle snicker.

"So you didn't see him yesterday?" Quick asked.

Pico looked down for just a moment.

"Señor," Quick said, "did you see Joaquin Murieta yesterday? Or maybe the big man who rode with him?"

Pico was looking him in the eye now.

Quick fought to keep the edge out of his voice. "Did you?"

Shaking his head, Pico denied having seen his friends yesterday. He said he couldn't recall the last time he did see them. Maybe two years before. Maybe longer. Pico felt his heart torn in two. Silently he begged his *amigo* Joaquin to forgive his lies, and his weakness before these *gringos*. And Pico knew, pitifully, that he had put his desires to be a good *Americano*, a friend to the *Yanquis*, above his loyalty to his friend. There was a time Pico could recall that he would have killed, without hesitation, any man who had committed the barbarism he knew these rangers had done to his friend. *Compadres* never turn, he could hear Murieta say. It tore at him.

Pico shut his eyes. He only wanted the *gringos* to leave.

He heard Quick say they were going. Pico opened his eyes and, as the rangers turned their horses, he saw Romulo easing his hand toward his pistol. He reached out and gently covered his son's hand.

★　★　★　★　★

That evening, Quick and the rangers arrived in Los Angeles, except for Addie and Wheat who had decided to go back to San Gabriel. Quick hadn't heard Addie say a word since the encounter with Pico. Wheat had surprised him, though, telling him, "You take my share of the reward. I don't believe I want it. I'm done with rangering, too."

Exhausted as he was, Quick was pleased that word of the capture and death of Joaquin Murieta blew through town faster than those hot desert winds. He even heard somebody clanging a dinner bell racing through the town streets announcing the news. The sound of gunfire seemed to echo everywhere. It was like the Fourth of July.

Quick's immediate concern was to procure a large clay jar filled with brandy and arsenic from Doc Osborn to preserve Murieta's head for the journey to the governor. Doc Osborn was only too glad to help.

Shortly after Quick returned to the barracks with the jar, Needle and Doyle came in and told him folks were whooping and hollering and that free beer flowed up and down the alleyways of *Calle de los Negros*.

"All the Mexes are upset and crying and lighting little candles everywhere," Needle said. "And there's folks wanting to buy us all drinks and calling us heroes. Some are even calling you the next mayor!"

Stepping outside, Quick saw the gun smoke hanging lacy in the air from the gunshots, but he hadn't expected to see Sheriff Barton and Lucy coming his way. He was caught even more unaware when Barton shook his hand and, with a big grin, told him that the murder of Abel Tyner and the other unsolved murders, along with cattle rustlings and horse thievings of the past twelve months, were considered solved!

Quick was about to tell him that Murieta hadn't killed Abel

Tyner when Lucy suddenly announced that she would gladly marry him once he returned from seeing the governor.

"You showed daddy, didn't you?" she whispered, throwing her arms around his neck and kissing him.

That kiss came as the biggest surprise of the night. In all the time he'd spent courting Lucy, she had never stuck her tongue down his throat.

Quick looked for Father Anacleto but the padre was away at Ygnacio Del Valle's *rancho* administering the Last Rites to a sickly infant. Murieta's confession would have to wait. Quick thought of writing it down but didn't feel like lifting the pen to do it. He wanted to see Orrin Appleyard, too, to give him the story of the capture but was told the reporter had been dispatched to the port of San Pedro to investigate the details of a suspicious wharf fire.

On his way back to the barracks, he wondered what he'd tell Guadalupe Tyner. Maybe it was best to go along with Barton. Why upset her more? Let her think it was done. Well, he'd sleep on it. And he had to pay his respects to Sam Prizer's wife. That would have to wait, too, though. He'd settle everything, after he saw the governor.

Getting a few hours' sleep proved futile. He was too exhausted and too excited at the same time.

Before sunrise, Quick and Needle rode out on fresh horses for the state capitol in Benicia, a small town northeast of San Francisco situated on the shore of the Carquinez Strait. He had asked Clegg and Charley to come with him, but they had declined. Doyle said he wasn't up for it, due to his shoulder wound. The thought of listening to Needle's jabbering for close to four hundred miles set his teeth on edge. But he knew he shouldn't go alone, not with what he was carrying, in case someone tried to jump him. So, with Murieta's head sloshing in the bulbous clay jar he had in a sling tied to his saddle horn, Quick pushed the ride. Hard. It took five days.

Quick saw the Bear Flag fluttering from the rooftop flagpole before he caught sight of the building itself at the corner of First and G Streets. He was awestruck.

"It's like a temple the ancient Greeks or Romans built," he said, marveling at the cornices sticking out from the base of the steepled roof and the four tall white columns standing dignified at the entrance, giving the brick two-story structure a formidable, austere presence.

"Uh-huh," Needle said, scratching his cheek. "Romans. Sure."

"It's the grandest thing I've ever seen," Quick went on as they rode up to the hitching posts in front. "Nothing like this in Los Angeles."

Needle sniffed.

"This is where political decisions get made," Quick said as they tied their horses to a post. "Not some damn hotel room Don Antonio calls an office."

"Let's go stand the governor on his ear," Needle said.

Quick untied the sling holding the clay jar containing Murieta's head from his saddle horn. He held it close, like he was protecting it from any harm, as they mounted the stairs, passed between the majestic columns, and entered through the open door.

It was midday and they could hear a lot of angry hollering and accusations from the rooms near the end of the long hallway. A thin-faced man dressed in a frock coat much too large for him hurried by carrying a pile of papers in his hands. Quick tried to ask him where they could find the governor and the man jerked his head but neither Quick nor Needle were sure just where he was pointing.

Then Quick saw another man with short bandy-legs wearing

a fur cap. He had no teeth but he did have a determined look on his face and was holding a dead chicken in his hand. Considering the lack of feathers, gray pallor, and stiffness of the bird, Quick guessed it had been dead a few days.

"Mister," Quick said, "do you know where we can find the governor?"

"Foller me," the man said with a wave of the chicken.

Quick and Needle were right behind him as he bounced past two doorways and turned into a third. Inside the cramped office, Quick saw a man standing on a ladder sorting through a number of scrolls neatly arranged on several shelves.

"Say, mister secretary," the man with the dead chicken said.

"What now, Mordecai?" the man sighed and stepped down from the ladder, brushing off his coat sleeves with his freckle-covered hands.

"These two gents want to see the governor," Mordecai said and then looked back at Quick and Needle. "This here's Ben Ryland, the governor's secretary." He turned to Ryland. "But as I'm here first, I need to see him first."

"Well, the governor is with Mr. Marlette, the Surveyor General," Ryland said. "And as I've told you before, the governor can't intercede in this matter on your behalf."

"That's all I been hearing," Mordecai said. "The sheriff can't help. The mayor won't help and my elected representative I can't find."

"This is a local matter between you, the sheriff, and the neighbor you claim shot your chicken," Ryland said.

Quick and Needle exchanged looks.

"Ain't no claim I'm makin'!" Mordecai said, brandishing the chicken. "That skunk bastard Yancey kilt my chicken an' I seen him do it! I know my rights of petition, Ben, and I intend to do them rights and get satisfaction!"

"He has no time for this," Ryland said to Mordecai and then

addressed Quick. "And as for you gentlemen, making an appointment would be the proper thing to do."

"Guess I'm going to make camp here until he does have time to see me," Mordecai said.

Needle pushed Mordecai out of the way and said, "We got to see the governor right now."

"Back off, youngster," Mordecai said.

Quick could take no more. What was happening to the head in the jar? Was it swelling up? Had the eyes popped out? Would the governor or anybody else be able to recognize it? And five days of listening to Ned Needle talking a streak about what he was going to do with his share of the reward and going back to Los Angeles and tying the Mexican flag to the tail of every donkey he could find was all too damn much!

"I am Ambrose Quick," he said in a loud voice, stepping up to Ryland, "a lieutenant in the California Rangers, and I've got something here the governor needs to see."

"I don't care who you boys are," Mordecai said. "I was here first."

Fed up, Quick was about to pull his revolver to make his point, but he saw Ryland had reached into his desk, pulled out an Army Colt, pointed it at Mordecai, and cocked it.

"Sit down and be quiet," he said.

Quick was glad to see Mordecai comply and next thing he knew, Ryland was coming from around his desk, hand extended.

"Welcome, sir," Ryland said and put down the Colt to shake Quick's hand. "It is a pleasure. The governor is proud of you rangers and all you've done for the citizens of this state."

"That's more like it," Needle said.

"Would you tell me the nature of your business and I'll gladly let Governor Bigler know," Ryland said.

Quick adjusted the jar in his arm. "What I've got is proof—"

Suddenly, Quick felt himself pushed into Ryland. He caught

himself and turned in time to see Mordecai dash to the large door of the governor's office. Needle lunged after him but missed. The door opened wide and Quick charged in after Mordecai and Needle, with Ryland fast behind him, all of them calling out the Governor's name.

Quick saw two men huddled over rolls of maps at a wooden desk situated in front of a tall open window. One was a pudgy man and the other had a sallow face.

"Quiet down!" the pudgy man shouted. "What is all this, Mr. Ryland?"

Quick figured the pudgy one for the governor and everyone spoke at once.

"I'm sorry, sir," Ryland said.

"I been a-tryin' to see you fer two days!" Mordecai said, waving the chicken in front of him.

"I'm a lieutenant of rangers, and I have urgent state business!" Quick said.

"The public demand for roads is the current urgent state business, sir," the sallow man said, pointing at the map scrolls on the desk.

Quick decided there was no more urgent state business than what he had in that jar, and everything he'd done to get it this far. He wasn't thinking. It was like something snapped inside him. He slammed the jar down on the governor's desk, yanked off the lid, reached inside, grabbed a handful of Murieta's floating hair, and lifted the head up out of the jar. Everyone froze. Even Needle looked stunned. The only sound Quick heard was the dripping of brandy from Murieta's head back into the jar.

Marlette excused himself and nearly bolted from the office, his hand to his mouth. Bigler asked Ryland to escort an ill-looking Mordecai outside for the time being.

"I didn't get your name, sir," Bigler said to Quick.

Quick lowered the head back into the jar and wiped his hand

on his pant leg as he introduced himself and then Needle. Taking a deep breath, Quick spoke out loud the statement he had rehearsed for the last five days.

"Governor," he said, "we have brought you the head of the wanted bandit, Joaquin Murieta."

It struck Quick as odd that Bigler's face appeared so grim. He wondered why the governor wasn't pumping his hand and offering drinks and sending for a newspaper reporter.

Bigler came around to the front of his desk, leaned back against it, hooked his forefinger over the end of his nose, and stared at the jar for what seemed to Quick to be a very long while. Quick was feeling more confused and concerned by the moment. This isn't what he expected. It wasn't supposed to happen like this.

"Please sit down, Lieutenant," Bigler finally said, "and tell me how it is you came into possession of . . . this."

Quick sat on the edge of the nearest chair and related the story of the chase and capture. He told him of the admission, but not the "confession," that Murieta had made, and that he believed the man was indeed who he claimed to be.

Needle piped up that he was in personal possession of the chain mail coat that had belonged to Murieta but that he had taken off the Animal, also dead.

Quick watched intently as Bigler stepped over to a wooden cabinet with a fancy-looking lock sitting in a corner. Bigler took a key from inside the pocket of his black vest, inserted it into the lock, and opened the door, revealing a large clay jar about the same size as the one Quick had brought, and a smaller one next to it on a shelf. After rolling up his shirtsleeve, he took the lid from the large jar. The room filled with the sweet odor of formaldehyde.

"Lieutenant, Mr. Needle, I received this from Captain Harry Love three days ago," Bigler said. He reached down and lifted the severed head of what appeared to be a dark-haired young Mexican man out of the jar. "He assured me that this is Joaquin Murieta."

"It—it can't be," Needle said.

Quick sat silent and stunned. No, it couldn't be true. Had the Mexican lied about being Murieta? About his confession? About everything? The man was dying! That confession business is sacred to those people!

He heard Bigler talking after he replaced the head in the jar, but what he was saying sounded impossible.

Captain Love and his men had come upon a party of Mexicans with a herd of mustangs near Arroyo Cantoova, Bigler was saying. Love couldn't get a straight answer about a bill of sale or how they got them. A young Mexican rode out of the woods and told Love he could address all questions to him because he was the *jefe*, Joaquin.

"But he couldn't have been," Quick said, leaning forward in his seat.

"That's when everybody ran, according to Captain Love," Bigler said. "Love said he chased that Mexican for miles before he managed to shoot him down. And when he got to him, the Mexican was bleeding badly, raised his hand, and said, 'No more. Your work is done.' "

"Governor," Quick said, trying to think past what had turned into some kind of horrid nightmare. "Governor, I'm absolutely certain this," he pointed to the jar he had brought in, "is Joaquin Murieta. He—he confessed!"

"He's telling you the truth," Needle said. "I was there. I heard him. He swore he spent most of his life splitting skulls and severing neck veins. Stealing everything in sight, too!"

Quick shot Needle a look.

"He did swear that he was Murieta," Quick said.

Bigler grunted, then took the smaller jar from the shelf and handed it to Quick.

"What do you see inside there, Lieutenant?"

Quick opened it, his heart thumping hard and fast like it wanted to pound its way right out of his chest. He grimaced at the maimed appendage he saw floating in the jar.

"That's the hand of Three-Fingered Jack," Bigler said. "He was there, too, and tried to kill Captain Love. And Love would've brought his head, except one of his men shot off a good part of the bandit's face. Three-Fingered Jack was a well-known accomplice of Joaquin Murieta."

"And so was the Animal," Quick said.

"Be that as it may," Bigler said, "we're planning to exhibit this hand and the head of Joaquin around the state, starting in Stockton. Leaflets are being printed now. Everybody will get a good look at this scoundrel. It'll discourage other bandits and would-be desperadoes."

"But," Needle said, "we come all the way from Los Angeles for the reward."

"I already presented Captain Love with the reward money," Bigler said, spreading his hands.

Needle slumped, his mouth slipping open.

Quick was desperate, time was fleeting, and he couldn't see any other choice. He knew what he had to do and despised himself for it. But he couldn't, he wouldn't allow himself to be cheated out of his future! Not now, not after what he had done and, more importantly, what he had plans to do. He was the man who captured Joaquin Murieta! He would be the next mayor of Los Angeles! Lucy was going to marry him! He had the ambition, the makings, everything. He proved that!

He heard his blood pounding in his ears. He stared at Bigler. The sound of his blood stopped. Everything seemed to have come to a standstill. There was a terrible, frightening silence.

"Is there something else?" Bigler asked.

"Yes," Quick said. "There is. This man of ours, he knew he was dying and confessed, confessed on his oath, that he committed crimes of murder and robbery and that he was Joaquin Murieta. He asked me to take that confession to a priest! He told me his sins. Every one of them."

Instantly, Quick felt something cold burst from within him and spread through his skin. He thought his soul had escaped his body and a shiver shot through him. He didn't take his eyes off of Bigler. He was afraid to look away, afraid he might disappear if he did.

"You strike me as a decent man, Lieutenant," Bigler said after a bit. "Conscientious. Captain Hope wouldn't have entrusted you with such high responsibilities if you didn't possess the proper fortitude and fiber."

Yes, Quick thought, relieved. Thank God he believes me.

"That's the reason I'm certain what you're telling me is true as gospel," Bigler continued. "However, and it's important you hear what I'm about to say to you, I believe that perhaps in your zeal, you succumbed to a weakness. An understandable one to be sure, but a flaw, nonetheless."

Quick tried to swallow. What was Bigler talking about?

"As much as I believe you," Bigler said, "I don't believe you would go to such . . . grisly lengths," he indicated Quick's jar, "for a concocted story. But consider for a moment that this poor devil you have here is not Joaquin Murieta. Rather, he's one of his loyal lieutenants, one of the other Joaquins."

Quick was about to protest but then Bigler brought up his hand.

"My point, Lieutenant," Bigler said, "is how can we be sure of the story your man told? Those people are known to lie."

EPILOGUE

Ambrose Quick

Word of Captain Love's capture of the man believed to be Joaquin Murieta had preceded Quick's arrival by several days back in Los Angeles. Some folks shook Quick's hand, telling him he had still done all right. "You just got suckered by a Mex is all," they said. Others thought he had indeed captured the real Murieta, but only because they chose to believe it. And there were those, mostly Don Antonio and his supporters, who thought him a fool.

Orrin Appleyard stated that Quick had performed a commendable service in apprehending what he called "an obvious bandit and brigand in our community," and insisted that the paper publicly congratulate him. However, Orrin's editor, McMeans, refused, saying it wasn't newsworthy or appropriate. When Orrin told Quick of the decision, he wasn't surprised since McMeans and the mayor were both friends.

Quick's superior, Captain Hope, sent the former ranger lieutenant a letter, telling him his father would have been proud of his son. "You captured a Joaquin," he wrote. "You did this country a favor."

While Quick received no formal acknowledgment of his "accomplishment," the head and three-fingered hand Captain Love had presented to Governor Bigler were exhibited in Stockton, various mining camps in northern California, and San Francisco. That head, the barkers said, belonged to the "true"

Joaquin Murieta.

Of course there were naysayers, like the editor of the San Francisco newspaper, the *Daily Alta California,* who wrote in the August 23, 1853, edition: "It is too well known that Joaquin Murieta was not the person killed by Captain Love's party near the Panoche Pass. The head on display in Stockton bears no resemblance to that individual, and this is positively asserted by those who have seen the real Murieta and the spurious head." The debate over whose head was exhibited raged on. There were as many people who claimed the head was absolutely that of Murieta as those who declared it was not. Practically all agreed on one thing: they had known Murieta.

While Sam Prizer's wife thanked Quick for bringing her husband's body back, Lucy refused to marry him, claiming he had made promises to her and broken them.

He managed a few odd jobs through the winter: assistant auctioneer, calico bed comforter maker, and a stevedore at the port of San Pedro.

In the spring, the candidates for mayor of Los Angeles were to be announced. Quick had every intention of running. No one expected him to win. In the early hours of the day he was to announce his formal candidacy, he stepped into an outhouse to relieve himself and was shot in the back of the head. The murder was never solved. Some speculated it was a Mexican who did it in retaliation for the killing of a Joaquin. Others believed it was a hired killing by Don Antonio Coronel. Neither could be proved. Don Antonio did not serve a second term as mayor.

When Quick had been on his way back from Benicia with Joaquin Murieta's head still in the jar, his intention was to return it to its rightful place. At the lake near the pointed rocks, he discovered that the body of Murieta had been dug up and taken away. Murieta's saddle that Needle had so hastily and clumsily hidden was also gone. Greatly unsettled, he decided to bury the head and jar until he could figure out what do. Keeping the head in his possession was out of the question. He hoped to discover who took the body, or even its whereabouts. He never did. Nor did he divulge to a soul where he had buried the head of Joaquin, saying instead he had lost it while crossing the Sacramento River.

As for Murieta's confession, Quick delivered it to Father Anacleto some weeks following his return to Los Angeles. And he admitted to the priest his own "confession" to Governor Bigler, calling it "a repellant act of cowardice and betrayal" for which he felt there was no forgiveness.

Quick didn't speak to Guadalupe Tyner before departing Los Angeles to see the governor. When he returned, he discovered to his terrible surprise that he couldn't speak to her.

Ned Needle

Chose not to return to Los Angeles "looking like a damn fool." He headed for the gold fields that had already begun to show signs of petering out. About two weeks later, he came upon a Chinese prospector and decided to claim he was a tax collector. The Occidental spoke no English, but he knew what Needle was demanding. While digging through his belongings for the gold payment, he noticed Needle squat down by his fire. His mule was tied close by. For reasons unknown, that mule suddenly kicked up his hind legs and caught the side of Needle's head, sending him sprawling. The Occidental panicked, believing Needle had been killed. Certain he would be hanged for murdering a white man, he snatched up his belongings, climbed on the mule, and headed south. Several hours later, Needle came to, woozy, his head throbbing mightily. He managed to prop himself up against a large rock, disturbing a rattlesnake in the process. It sprang and bit him in the neck. Ned Needle was found dead the next morning.

Uriah Clegg

His heart sank a few weeks after the pursuit and capture of Murieta when John Hughes sold the El Dorado Saloon to the Reverend Adam Bland. The Reverend tore down the gilt-edged sign and announced that all would be welcome the following Sunday to join him inside the old saloon for services at the First Methodist Church of Los Angeles. This profane news shattered Clegg's spirit. He never recovered. Dolly Akin, his common-law wife, left him not long after. Clegg remained a drunk.

Two years later, his friend John Hughes convinced him to come north with him and join the state militia to fight Indians on the warpath in the northern counties. "They don't like living on the reservation and Governor Bigler doesn't like having Injuns on good land settlers could use better," Hughes said.

Clegg died of two arrows in his chest in a skirmish. He had no weapon drawn when the militia attacked the Indians. Hughes said, "He just kicked his horse and spread his arms wide."

Horace Wheat

Acted as a pallbearer, with Charley Biggs and Uriah Clegg, at Ambrose Quick's funeral. He tried to convince Addie Moody to attend the services but she refused, saying, "They ought to just leave him for the buzzards, if they'd even have him. I hope that son-of-a-bitch rots in hell."

Wheat accepted a job as deputy with Sheriff Barton but quit after less than a year. When offered a partnership in a saloon on *Calle de los Negros*, Wheat declined as he didn't care for the owner being that he was foul-mouthed, smelled nasty, and lived in illicit intercourse with a lewd Indian woman.

Following the Great Drought of 1864 that decimated the huge cattle herds in the county, Wheat signed on with a party to drive 10,000 sheep purchased from Navajo Indians near Santa Fe, New Mexico Territory, to Los Angeles. While in Santa Fe, he met and fell in love with a local widow. They married.

Before coming to Los Angeles in the '40s, Wheat had practiced law in Illinois. It was his misfortune that while arguing a case, he threw an inkwell at the opposing attorney when he refused to stop badgering Wheat's witness. The inkwell hit the lawyer in the head, killing him. Wheat had been forced to flee. Now, more than twenty years had passed. With his new life in Santa Fe, he ran for and was elected to a judge's seat.

Ezra Doyle

With the outbreak of the Civil War, Los Angeles proclaimed its Secessionist stand. Caught up in that furor, Doyle, with about two hundred and fifty other mounted volunteers outfitted by the city, set out over the desert for Confederate Texas. A surveyor named Pearson, later promoted to the rank of General, led them. Doyle never saw any action against the Union soldiers, though. He fell off his horse while attempting a Mexican rope dance, standing on the animal's back while it was running. Doyle broke his neck.

Charley Biggs

Shortly after he returned to Los Angeles, Charley went to the port of San Pedro where he convinced a ship's captain to take him onboard as an apprentice. Charley found the adventure he'd been seeking.

Addie Moody

As Los Angeles continued to grow, Addie foresaw more opportunity. She purchased a two-story building on Sanchez Street near the *Calle de los Negros* and soon had established "Screaming Addie's" as one of the finest houses of ill repute in the city. Local barons of commerce, city councilmen, and some state officials were known to patronize her business. She grudgingly allowed Mexicans after a time, but only in the first-floor rooms.

When the Chinese arrived and established their community

south of the Plaza in 1869, Addie employed two of the women as housekeeper and cook. She became a heroine to the Chinese community during the infamous Chinese Massacre of 1871. When a feud between two Chinese tongs erupted in gunfire resulting in the deaths of Chinese and white citizens, mobs of armed and mostly unemployed townsmen, already hateful of the Chinese who worked for extremely low wages, turned riotous. The mobs drove many Chinese from their shops and buildings, shooting some as they ran, while others they hanged from awnings, balconies, and corral gates. Addie hid her two Chinese workers in her brothel, going so far as to threaten several rioters away from her door with a double-barreled shotgun.

From that time on, Addie found gifts of beautiful silks, delicate porcelain, and special foods left at her doorstep on every Chinese New Year.

Clarissa

Sweet-talked any number of young men, none of whom, she felt, had the potential of Ned Needle. She took up with a gambler in Los Angeles who threw her out after three months. Arrested repeatedly for drunkenness and vagrancy, Clarissa was found dead one Sunday morning. She had passed out face down in the *zanja madre* along Alameda Street, having drowned in two inches of water.

Roy Bean

Ran the Headquarters Saloon for another ten years. He complained bitterly about the leniency he believed criminals were receiving in the Los Angeles County courts. Though he had no formal legal background, he put his name on the ballot for the position of district judge seven different times. In his seventh and final campaign, Bean addressed a rowdy, drunken Saturday night crowd in the Headquarters, saying, "I'll see to it justice gets done around here or by damn I'll go someplace where they can appreciate real justice!" The crowd cheered but he lost the election. Disgusted, Bean sold the Headquarters and left California for good. It was after the end of the Civil War that Bean, having taken up residence in Texas, appointed himself a judge and the "Law West of the Pecos."

Ana Benitez

When asked by Orrin Appleyard about the conflicting stories over who had captured the real Joaquin Murieta, she replied, "My friend is dead. That's all that matters to me. And saddens me."

Later, she confided to a friend that Murieta visited her in the night. "I heard his crying. I knew that sound. I sat up in my bed and said to him to please come and sit. I was so happy to have him with me! But he would not stay. He turned to leave and I got out of my bed calling his name. I tried to follow him but I fell. See, my knees are still swollen. I felt his hands on me, placing me back into bed. I said, please, don't cry. Then I saw his body was headless! The crying stopped and he said so sadly, 'They cut off my head, Ana. No rest can come to me until I get it back. No rest.' He kept on saying that. It made me cry. I couldn't stop. And his voice got weaker and weaker and then he was gone."

She died quietly in her home on Christmas Eve, 1853.

Orrin Appleyard

Reported diligently for the *Los Angeles Star* until December 1861. Southern sentiment was vociferous in Los Angeles, and Appleyard had let it slip that he was pro-Union. Not long after, while sitting in the newspaper office one night composing a story, Appleyard was shot in the back. No arrests were made.

Andres Pico

In 1859, Pico, representing a Southern California constituency, introduced a resolution to the State Assembly to divide California in half, with all land south of San Louis Obispo declared part of the Territory of Colorado. Though approved by both houses and ratified by the southern counties desiring the division, the resolution did not pass the United States Congress. Shortly thereafter, with the outbreak of the Civil War, Pico was asked by the Military Commissioner of California to command a mounted battalion of *Californios* for service against the Confederacy. Tired and in failing health, Pico declined.

Mayor Antonio Coronel

Spent the next twelve years awash in politics. After serving one term as mayor, he served nine terms on the City Council, was twice appointed to the Board of Education, was elected to the county Board of Supervisors, and served a four-year term as State Treasurer. But he may be best remembered as a friend and mentor to Helen Hunt Jackson, who, with Coronel's help, wrote her famous novel, *Ramona*. Wedding bells chimed for Coronel in 1873 when he married Mariana Williamson. He was 56 and she was 22. It was the first marriage for both.

Sheriff James Barton

Rounded up four suspects—all Mexicans—in the murder of Ambrose Quick. They were released within twelve hours.

Barton became the first sheriff of Los Angeles County to die in the line of duty. He and three deputies were in pursuit of Juan Flores, an escaped prisoner, when Flores and his men ambushed them on January 23, 1857. Barton and his deputies were killed. Flores was soon captured and jailed, then lynched by a mob. On the day of Barton's funeral, all business in town was suspended as many citizens paid their respects.

Lucy Barton

Was engaged to be married, twice. Both times she was left at the altar, her father having found fault with her fiancés and running them out of town the night before the wedding days. Then in the spring of 1856, she fell madly, impetuously in love with an actor in a traveling company. Her father didn't approve of this infatuation either. The acting troupe departed Los Angeles under cover of darkness. Lucy stole away with them.

Marshal A. S. Beard

Was suspected of skimming money from the taxes he collected and removed from office for malfeasance in October. He departed Los Angeles in the dark of night and drifted into obscurity.

"El Boticario" (John G. Downey)

On September 7, 1859, Downey was elected lieutenant governor of California. Less than four months later, he was sworn in as governor when Governor Latham resigned. Downey served only that term.

Later, he was instrumental, along with Phineas Banning, in convincing the Southern Pacific Railroad to enter Los Angeles. He opened the Farmers and Merchants Bank in Los Angeles, was a founder of the Board of Trade, donated 308 acres of land for the establishment of the University of Southern California, and was active in the Pioneer Oil Company and the Los Angeles Water Company. He also saw to the subdivision of Rancho Santa Gertrudis into fifty-acre parcels. Thus was the town of Downey born.

Governor John Bigler

Was the only governor of California elected to two terms in the nineteenth century. An active Democrat, Bigler supported James Buchanan for President. In gratitude, and to pay his political debt, Buchanan appointed Bigler Minister to Chile. The editor of the *Daily Alta California,* a savage opponent of Bigler, wrote on the eve of Bigler's departure, "May swift winds waft him to the place of his destination and may they always blow him away from these shores. California could spare a great many better men than John Bigler."

The mountain lake situated in the Sierra Nevadas on the California–Nevada border was proclaimed Lake Bigler in 1854. In 1870, the Legislature proposed a new name, Lake Tahoe.

Assemblyman Jose Covarrubias

Served as Commissioner of Military Affairs in the California Assembly, pressed for a road to be built through the formidable Sierra Nevada Mountains for freight and emigrant purposes, and favored a transcontinental railroad.

He never did run for governor of California.

Fray Blas Ordaz

Had indeed devoted much of his life attaining solace and salvation by helping others. However, he was weak in maintaining his vow to abstain from worldly pleasures having fathered three children, the youngest of which, at the time of his death, was eight years old. In a report to church authorities dated May 1, 1848, Colonel Jonathan D. Stevenson stated that Ordaz's "character is so notoriously profligate that his influence and respect is entirely gone." Ordaz died and was buried at Mission San Gabriel on November 11, 1850. Four other priests were present at his funeral, as well as his daughter and son-in-law.

Rosita Murieta

Spent the rest of her life in the home of her elderly parents. She never returned to California, or knew what happened to the body of her husband. Offers were made to steal the head of Joaquin and return it to her, but she refused them. When asked about the gold her husband was said to have hidden, she said, "He gave everything to the people."

Guadalupe Tyner

Within the hour of Quick and Needle's departure for Benicia, when word of the capture and beheading of Joaquin Murieta reached her, Guadalupe tore out her hair in despair and tearfully admitted to killing her husband, Abel. She believed he had been engaged on more than one occasion in sexual congress with the whore, Clarissa. Guadalupe was correct in that belief but District Judge Dryden explained to her at her trial two days later that "cutting your husband's throat was not the proper punishment under the law for such actions. But the sentence of this court is proper and will be carried out tomorrow at noon."

Guadalupe became the second woman hanged in the state, the first being another Mexican woman found guilty of murdering a miner in Downieville on July 5, 1851.

Orrin Appleyard reported the execution of Guadalupe Tyner for the *Los Angeles Star:* "More than a thousand people crowded into the plaza, many with picnic baskets in hand, to witness the hanging. Hundreds of others secured a view of the event from nearby rooftops. It required the services of several deputies to pull the pitiful sobbing woman onto the scaffold. Asked if she had any last words, she tried to speak, but no words were uttered. The rope was placed around her neck. Her arms were then pinioned and her feet tied. A black hood was placed over her face. After a moment, the scaffold door opened and she hung suspended between the heavens and the earth."

Six days after the hanging, when Quick arrived back in Los Angeles, Orrin Appleyard told him of Guadalupe's confession and fate. Quick hung his head and said bitterly, "Nothing's gone right."

AUTHOR'S NOTE

The bandit, Joaquin Murieta, lives both as fact and myth. I have taken the liberty of incorporating bits of both into this telling. The California Rangers and their captains, Harry Love and Alexander Hope, are not inventions. Neither are Governor John Bigler, Assemblyman Jose Covarrubias, Mayor Antonio Coronel, Sheriff James Barton, Marshal A. S. Beard, Andres Pico, Romulo Pico, Roy Bean, Fray Blas Ordaz, Eulogio de Celis, and John G. Downey "El Boticario." However, their words are mine.

Many thanks to John E. Fantz, Museum Guardian at the San Gabriel Mission in San Gabriel, California; Michael Dolgushkin at the California State Library; and the staff at the Vasquez Rocks Natural Area, Agua Dulce, California. Their assistance was invaluable.

Other sources include *Los Angeles: Epic of a City* by Lynn Bowman (Howell-North Books, 1974); *Gold Dust* by Donald Dale Jackson (George Allen & Unwin, 1980); *Glimpses of California and the Missions* by Helen Hunt Jackson (Little, Brown, 1914); *In Camp and Cabin* by John Steele (Lakeside Press, 1928); *The Los Angeles Star, 1851–1864* by William Broadhead Rice (Greenwood Press, 1969); *Reminiscences of a Ranger* by Horace Bell (Anderson, Ritchie & Simon, 1965); *On the Old West Coast* by Horace Bell (William Morrow & Company, 1930); *The Governors of California* (California State Library); *California's Missions* by Hildegarde Hawthorne (Appleton-

Century, 1942); *Lances at San Pascual* by Arthur Woodward (California Historical Society, 1948); *Franciscan Missionaries in Hispanic California, 1769–1848: A Biographical Dictionary* by Maynard J. Geiger (Huntington Library, 1969). And thank you to my parents for instilling in me an appreciation for and a love of California history.

Thomas D. Clagett
Santa Fe, New Mexico

ABOUT THE AUTHOR

Thomas D. Clagett graduated from the University of Southern California with a degree in Journalism, and then spent nearly twenty years working as an assistant film editor in Hollywood.

He is the author of *William Friedkin: Films of Aberration, Obsession and Reality,* about the Academy Award–winning director of *The French Connection* and *The Exorcist. Daily Variety* called it "Exhaustive and perceptive . . . more than that, it's a fun read." *Classic Images* said it's "the definitive work on the subject."

Clagett has contributed to several New Mexico magazines. He is a member of the Western Writers of America. *The Pursuit of Murieta* is his first novel.

A native Californian, Clagett lives with his wife Marilyn and their cat Cody in Santa Fe, New Mexico. His website is www.thomasdclagett.com.